GALACTAR

SAVAGE STARS BOOK 3

ANTHONY JAMES

© 2020 Anthony James
All rights reserved

The right of Anthony James to be identified as the author of this work has been asserted by him in accordance with the Copyright, Designs and Patents Act, 1988

The characters and events portrayed in this book are fictitious. Any similarity to real persons, living or dead, is coincidental and not intended by the author

This book is sold subject to the condition that it shall not, by way of trade or otherwise, be lent, resold, hired out, or otherwise circulated without the publisher's prior consent in any form of binding or cover other than that in which it is published and without a similar condition including this condition being imposed upon the subsequent purchaser

Illustration © Tom Edwards
TomEdwardsDesign.com

CHAPTER ONE

HIGH ABOVE THE muddy reds and sandy yellows of the gas giant Lapus-1, the Topaz space station followed its orbital track. At eight thousand metres in length, the station was a collection of differently shaped alloy modules, joined seemingly without an overall plan. Every few years, a new module would be transported from a shipyard on Earth or Lustre and attached wherever it would fit, ensuring that with the passing of time, the Topaz station became ever more haphazard in appearance.

Captain Carl Recker was one of the twelve thousand personnel currently onboard the station. He'd been assigned quarters that were hardly any larger than the interior of a gravity car, with space for a bed and a communicator. From the sleeping area, a narrow doorway gave access to a cubicle fitted with an all-in-one shower and toilet, a facility which Recker had never experienced before, had never even thought existed, and which he hoped never to encounter again.

And Recker was lucky his rank gained him this amount of space – most personnel had to make do with a sleeping pod and shared facilities.

He sat on the edge of his bed, with his short-cropped hair brushing against the ceiling and stared at the communicator's single screen.

Position in FTL vid-comm queue: 32.

His place in the queue hadn't changed in the last ten minutes and he was beginning to wonder if another technical problem had materialised somewhere in the comm system. The text on the screen updated.

Position in FTL vid-comm queue: 35.

Recker closed his eyes briefly. Higher-priority requests could push personal calls down the list indefinitely.

Position in FTL vid-comm queue: 47.

He was due back on duty soon and it didn't seem like he was going to get his channel to Earth in time. Feeling like a shit for missing his promised call, Recker typed out a message.

Mam, Dad, FTL comms choked with high priority traffic. Sorry. Not much I'm allowed to tell you. Everyone's trying so hard to make things right. Try not to worry. I'll give the comms another go once my shift is over. Love, Carl.

He put the message into the queue. Tiny data packets like this were usually sent in a few seconds and he waited for the confirmation to appear on the screen.

Message sent.

With nothing keeping him, Recker left his quarters and entered a long, narrow, low-ceilinged passage which led towards the command and control areas. It was cold, though the insulating properties of his spacesuit allowed him to ignore the near-freezing temperatures.

The corridor was – surprisingly – deserted. He set off towards the operation area of the station, his boots producing a rattle from the grating underfoot. Beneath the grating, pipes and cables ran, as a reminder of how long it had been since this accommodation module was signed off for use. Anything built within the last fifty years would have such visible aberrations hidden from sight.

Recker passed numerous doors leading to rooms as tiny as his own, and, every fifty meters, an airlift led to the levels above and below. This accommodation module was almost full and Recker had learned that the military planned to attach additional modules just as soon as they could be constructed. The space station already seemed full to bursting and Recker couldn't imagine what it would be like with another ten thousand personnel added to the pile. He hoped to be a long way away when they arrived.

The corridor ended at a wall. To the left was an airlift, currently three levels below this one. A screen on the facing wall showed a feed of darkness and stars from one of the Topaz station's external sensor arrays. Whoever designed this module evidently thought they were doing the occupants a favour by adding these *windows*. In Recker's experience, most people avoided them, like the view outside drove home how close they were to the void.

Recker paused and swept his fingertip along a touch-sensitive area at the bottom of the display and the feed jumped between the hundreds of arrays. One view of Lapus-1 held his attention for a few seconds. On the planet's surface, two huge storms which appeared like deep red swirls of incomprehensible violence were gradually drifting together and Recker was interested to witness the outcome.

Unfortunately, the collision wasn't likely to happen for a few days, so he spent a moment studying a different feed, this one of his current destination. Then, he turned away and called the airlift.

With a swish, the lift arrived. The car had room for one person in comfort, though Recker had once seen as many as six fit inside. This one was empty and he entered, then selected a level three below.

A few seconds later, he exited the lift into another corridor like the one above. Again, the passage was empty and Recker assumed this was because the next shift change wasn't due for an hour.

A door to his right provided an exit into the command and control areas. Recker pressed his hand onto the access panel and the door opened. Immediately, he heard voices and footsteps, while the brighter light made him squint.

The passage outside went left and right. Personnel, all wearing spacesuits and most of them carrying tablet computers or bundles of paper, hurried in both directions, talking rapidly into handheld communicators or taking jerky swigs from disposable cups filled with over-strong coffee.

A double-width door opposite opened, revealing a room filled with banks of screen-laden hardware, attended by a team of agitated-looking technicians. The door slid shut again, just as Recker entered the flow of human traffic in the corridor.

He strode amongst the people, unwilling to match

their pace. This module of the Topaz station was as old as the joined accommodation block, but it had been extensively modernised. Cables, pipes and maintenance panels were hidden behind panels and the floor was solid, rather than fitted with loose grating.

This area of the space station was reminiscent of underground facilities back on Earth, Lustre and other planets in the HPA. Recker sensed the differences. The faraway, muted rumble of propulsion and the slightest of vibrations, only felt in the quietest of moments, never let him forget where he was.

At another lift, Recker descended two more levels. His impatience was already building even though he wasn't late. The journey from his quarters to the docking station took twenty minutes on average and while he was aware many civilians had far longer commutes, he didn't enjoy this dead time – time which was neither his own, nor in any way productive.

From the lift, Recker proceeded into the next module, which was separated by a permanently open blast door. Signs he no longer noticed hung from above, offering directions to newcomers. This next module was home to the primary statistical analysis teams, as well as a few of the senior officers most involved with these teams. Right now, just about everyone in stats was tasked with the impossible job of predicting the future based on numbers derived from present data. Recker knew they were amongst the finest minds in the Human Planetary Alliance, yet they'd failed to predict the Daklan attack on Lustre and now they were having to completely re-think their models. What warning they'd given about the possible destruction of planet Fortune, he had no idea.

On balance, Recker was far happier to be on the frontline than having that kind of weight pressing down on him.

Topaz station had three separate docking areas, the largest of which could accommodate a riot class warship - not that facilities existed to perform anything other than the most routine of maintenance. Recker was heading to the tertiary docking area, which was a dedicated module that served no purpose other than as a launching place for sixteen identical shuttles.

Having traversed the square entrance tunnel leading to the module, Recker entered a rectangular space about three hundred metres by two hundred, with a twenty-metre ceiling. Eight access tunnels on each of the longest walls provided means to enter the shuttles, with status lights and information screens to advise which shuttles were available.

Recker spotted the closest green light, third on the left and he strode towards it. This hub room was busy with personnel, and the maintenance teams had taken one shuttle out of its access tunnel in order to work on it. Cut-down versions of shipyard tools, including a compact crane and a gravity loader were near the shuttle and a brace of ceiling-mounted robotic laser welders directed shielded beams into the transport's upper plating.

Whispers on the grapevine hinted that an officer had got drunk on illicitly obtained alcohol and decided to take a sightseeing tour on that shuttle. How this officer – rumoured to be a male comms lieutenant - had managed to circumvent security protocols was a matter of some conjecture. Of even more conjecture was how he'd managed to crash the transport into the heavy lifter *Maximus* which was parked outside the space station.

The unknown man's career was certainly in tatters and fortunately for Recker, that comms officer's name was not Adam Burner.

At the end of the third tunnel, another, shorter tunnel connected to the shuttle's side airlock. A pair of stony-faced soldiers stood guard, carrying their gauss rifles in a way which suggested they believed everyone was harbouring guilty intentions of one kind or another.

Recker greeted them cordially, waited for the shorter of the two men to scan his biometrics, and then entered the airlock. Less than a minute later, he was at the controls. Thirty seconds after that, clearance came through for his departure.

The docking clamps thudded as they disengaged and Recker piloted the shuttle along the red-lit launch channel, keeping his eye on the forward sensor feed. A door ahead opened, permitting him access to the second half of the launch tunnel. Finally, the outer door opened and he flew the shuttle outside.

As soon as he banked towards the position of the *Maximus*, Recker was presented by the wondrous sight of the Lapus-1 gas giant, near enough that the transport's limited sensor capabilities were able to provide an image of breath-taking clarity. Viewing the planet from the window inside the space station was one thing, from out here it seemed far more real. A few billion kilometres further away, the Gygor star was a bright dot, its warmth and heat hardly more than a whispered promise out here by the sixth planet in the solar system.

Eight weeks of seeing the same thing twice daily hadn't spoiled the sense of awe and Recker struggled to tear his eyes away. He located the *Maximus* heavy lifter on the shuttle's ten-inch tactical screen. The lifter was three hundred kilometres away, at the same altitude as Topaz station and following a similar orbital track.

Recker oriented the shuttle and took it towards the lifter. At the same time, he obtained a sensor lock and zoomed in to observe the progress the construction teams were making in converting the enormous vessel into a deep space construction and repair facility. The *Maximus* was greater in overall size and mass than the Topaz station and every time he saw the lifter, Recker was struck anew by the incredible feats of engineering required to put something like this into space.

Around the vessel, swarms of lifter shuttles carried the components required to fit the *Maximus* with not only additional missile clusters and Railer countermeasures, but also an additional layer of armour plating. A deep space fit out of this magnitude was something the HPA had never attempted before and Recker hoped the work would be completed without too many problems.

As he came closer, he saw that the lifter's underside main bay doors were sealed – as they had been ever since the spaceship arrived here in the Gygor system. The secondary, forward bay doors were open and it was from here the shuttles obtained their cargoes of gun barrels, half-built turrets and magazines required to equip the heavy lifter with the extra armaments everyone hoped it would never need.

Recker guided the shuttle towards one of the universal shuttle docking ports on the upper midsection of the *Maximus*. Matching speed and position required a few seconds and then he piloted the shuttle into the docking tunnel. The docking clamps engaged, a light turned green and Recker climbed from his seat and exited the transport.

Leaving the bay, Recker entered one of the huge main passages which connected the lifter's forward and aft sections. Walking ten kilometres wasn't a practical proposition, and the *Maximus* was equipped with its own internal gravity tram system, which could carry people to any of several dozen places.

Having chosen the closest shuttle bay to his destination, Recker didn't need to take the tram. Instead, he entered an airlift, this one already filled with a team of fifteen or twenty maintenance technicians. They laughed and joked, but it was obvious they were only going through the motions.

Recker got out at the same floor as the technicians and, not for the first time, asked himself if he should push more forcefully to be quartered over here on the lifter. The *Maximus* had no spare capacity and, though Recker wasn't too proud to share, some of his work was best done using the dedicated equipment on Topaz. He guessed he didn't mind too much one way or the other.

From the lift, Recker followed the technicians along another oversized corridor, which had stacks of square metal crates against each wall. A doorway in the right-hand wall opened into a cavernous warehouse of a size that wouldn't have looked out of place on the Adamantine base. Inside was enough equipment and components to build almost anything and it was here the technicians went.

Recker kept going until he reached a flight of steps which led down to a blast door. The door was left permanently open during normal operations and he passed through it into a vast space that filled the upper third of the *Maximus* and extended for a total of six thousand metres forward to aft.

As he always did, Recker stopped a few paces inside in order that he could take in the sights. This place was almost beyond comprehension – the kind of unbelievable accomplishment that even to this day, many people in the HPA didn't understand their military was capable of. Recker came to the *Maximus* every day and even he struggled to grasp the scale.

Although this bay might have just about accommodated the hull of a fleet battleship, if perhaps not its mass, at the moment it contained only a single craft. Five hundred metres from where Recker was standing, the alien spaceship *Vengeance* waited like a betrayed old friend. The bay floor wasn't nearly strong enough to support 2.7 billion tons, but the ceiling-mounted gravity clamps were designed to restrain much greater mass than this. Even so, their straining resonance was enough to set off a dull ache behind Recker's eyes.

The *Vengeance* was partly dismantled – as much as was needed for the technicians to access the weapons and defensive modules inside. Much of its armour had been stripped away, exposing the engine modules underneath, yet without disguising the purposeful lines of the warship. Six cranes, along with an army of metal-cutting robots made Recker think of flies crawling on a corpse.

The most important components – the mesh deflector, the Fracture device, the Executor bolt generator and the processing core – had been extracted weeks ago, to be studied and reverse-engineered in order that the HPA could create its own copies and turn them against the enemies of humanity. Recker understood this was how it had to be, but that didn't make it easier to deal with the sense of loss.

A two-person gravity car – a vehicle which was little more elaborate than a ten-inch-thick slab with bucket seats and a joystick on top - floated nearby. Recker jumped up and drove it towards the *Vengeance*. Halfway there, he spotted two people he recognized amongst the throng of technicians, and he changed course towards them.

"Commander Aston, Lieutenant Eastwood," he greeted them, loudly enough to be heard over the drone of gravity clamps, the scrape of shifting armour plates and the roaring noise of laser cutters.

Aston turned. She looked fresh-faced like always and her hair was tied in its usual ponytail.

"Sir," she said.

Something was wrong – Recker saw it at once. "What is it?" he asked.

"That obvious, huh?" Aston attempted a smile.

"Yes, it's that obvious, Commander."

Recker glanced at Eastwood. The man's normally stoic face echoed whatever it was had got Aston so agitated.

"Damnit, tell me."

The news not what Recker had been expecting. He thought he was about to be told that the *Vengeance* had shut itself down during the dismantling, or that the Daklan had shown up in Earth orbit. What he got was something else.

"Haven't you heard?" said Aston, evidently feeling that her seniority over Eastwood left her with the job of telling Recker. "The rumours are everywhere, but I've heard confirmation. Fleet Admiral Solan is coming here to inspect operations on Topaz and to check progress on the *Maximus*."

Recker smiled thinly. "It's about time I saw that old bastard again." Without realizing he was doing it, he cracked his knuckles. "I promised myself I'd settle things once and for all. Maybe I'm about to get my chance."

CHAPTER TWO

IT WAS as if hearing the news about Fleet Admiral Solan was a trigger. The communicator in Recker's leg pocket started buzzing and the muffled notes of the tune he'd assigned to high-priority messages reached his ear. With a sense of foreboding, he pulled out the communicator, flipped it open, stared at the message and then flipped the device closed.

Aston and Eastwood stared at him.

"Well?" said Aston.

"Well what?"

Aston didn't accept the evasive answer. "You received a message."

"It was Admiral Telar. I have a meeting with him."

"Now?" said Eastwood incredulously.

"Yes, now."

"Coincidentally good timing."

"Don't I know it, Lieutenant."

"At least you're still on that gravity car, sir," Aston observed.

Recker shook his head in disbelief at the situation. "I've got thirty minutes to find a communication station."

"What happens if you don't?"

"In that case I'll have missed my window. Admiral Telar's a busy man."

"He's on Topaz, isn't he?" said Aston. "Why not use that pocket communicator and route through the lifter's comms?"

"He's not on Topaz."

"Mysterious."

Recker didn't answer. Instead, he turned the gravity car and steered it for the exit.

"Maybe the admiral will have some good news," Aston called after.

"I doubt it, Commander. I really doubt it."

With his spare hand, Recker opened the communicator again and spoke to an officer on the bridge of the *Maximus*. Having obtained directions to the nearest FTL comms unit, he stayed on the gravity car and drove it up the steps leading from the bay. From there, a left turn was the beginning of a two-kilometre journey to one of the lifter's internal comms stations.

The station was accessed via a door in the wall of the corridor. When Recker entered the compact, dingy room, he discovered a queue of four off-duty personnel waiting to use the communicator, with a fifth staring morosely at a screen. This woman turned in the seat and looked at Recker suspiciously.

"I'm position twenty-five in the FTL queue, sir," she said. "After that..." she thumbed over her shoulder to let Recker know that rank didn't allow him to jump in front of the others.

"I need this station, Lieutenant." Recker took a deep breath and addressed the others waiting. "In fact, I need this whole room."

With obvious reluctance, the five personnel exited and Recker closed the door behind them. He was sympathetic and got no pleasure from interrupting their efforts to speak with family and friends. Still, the military installed the comms tech for primarily military use, so he didn't feel too guilty.

Having taken the lone seat, he requested an FTL channel. He was prompted to enter a priority code, which he did. Without delay, the channel was created and the *Maximus*' comms system established an FTL stream to a concealed destination, which Recker happened to know was the Amethyst station, a short lightspeed journey from Topaz.

The comms delay wasn't longer than a few seconds and the screen turned briefly static, before resolving into a low-resolution feed which was hardly recognizable as Admiral Telar. The feed stabilised and the clarity improved.

Telar wasn't smiling. "I imagine by this moment you've heard about the impending arrival of Fleet Admiral Solan," he said.

"Yes, sir, I have. Why is he coming here?"

"Fleet Admiral Solan is performing his duties, Carl. As he is required to do."

The unspoken words were louder still. "He's trying to stamp his authority."

"Authority he has been granted by his office."

"I've been told he's coming to the *Maximus* as well as Topaz."

"That is correct."

"Will I be required to speak with him?"

"He specifically asked that you be available." Telar's expression gave nothing away.

Recker stared. "Why? Why now?"

"A schism is forming."

"We don't need one."

"A schism in which you are in danger of becoming the fulcrum."

That got Recker's attention. "Me? How?"

"You're not stupid, Carl. Do I need to spell it out?"

Recker opened his mouth and then closed it. The HPA was up the proverbial shit creek and Recker's recent, significant successes were earning him a reputation of being a man who knew how to paddle. Without doing anything more than his duty, he was polarising the military into those who were for him and those who were against.

Of course it was about more than just one man. Admiral Telar was at the forefront of efforts to upgrade and expand the fleet so that it became fit for purpose, and Recker was sure Telar had the backing of many other senior officers – those who had no intention of letting the HPA become the meek and accepting subjects of an extinction event.

"No, sir, I don't need you to spell it out."

"Expect to be surprised, Carl. That's all I can tell you."

"I'm sure you can tell me more than that, sir."

Telar's mouth flickered in what might have been a smile. "Perhaps I would like to see how you handle matters for yourself."

"You know my plans, sir. Land a spaceship on the fleet admiral's car and send a missile through his window."

"If that's what it is, then that's what it is."

"Why did you call me to this meeting, sir?"

"To gauge your mood, more than anything."

"And?"

"It seems I'll have to wait until your upcoming *encounter* is finished."

"When can I expect to meet Fleet Admiral Solan?"

"He is scheduled to arrive at the Topaz station anytime from now. When you are finished, we will speak again."

"I don't wish to be caught in the middle of what is coming, sir."

Telar narrowed his eyes. "You have no choice, Carl. Wars are fought on many fronts and often the greatest danger comes from your own side."

"Is this inevitable?"

"Nothing is inevitable." Telar gave a short laugh. "Or so my analysis teams keep telling me. I am not sure I believe them."

Recker guessed that was the best answer he was going to get. "I want the HPA to come through this Daklan war, sir. And I want us to be ready for the next one."

Even as he said the words, Recker knew they sounded

naïve – like a barrier erected by a simple man to protect himself from his fears. He steadied himself and continued.

"I'll do what's right, sir."

"I know."

Recker thought the meeting was over, but Telar wasn't done.

"Change is coming. I've told you the same before, but I want you to prepare yourself. Your preconceptions will be your greatest enemy." Telar leaned forward, his dark eyes intense. "Can I trust you, Carl?"

There it was. The question. Choose once and never again.

"Yes, sir. You can trust me, as long as you don't ask me to betray myself."

"That won't happen. Not ever." Telar leaned back in his chair. "I will speak to you again soon."

The comms screen went blank, leaving Recker alone with his thoughts. Something significant had taken place, though he didn't – yet - understand exactly what it was. Time would tell, like it always did.

He got up from his seat and exited the room. The five people who'd been queuing earlier were still waiting, most of them disgruntled and hiding it poorly. Recker didn't have anything to apologise for and he said nothing.

A person or persons unknown had made off with the gravity car and it was a long run back to the *Vengeance*'s holding bay. Recker didn't mind and he welcomed the opportunity to burn off some of the febrile energy which coursed through his muscles. He set off at a fast pace and his breathing deepened. A single phrase turned around and around in his head.

Change is coming.

Recker didn't slow until he arrived once more at the *Vengeance*. Aston and Eastwood weren't in sight. Presumably, they were somewhere onboard helping the technical teams.

One of the senior technicians – a burly individual called Douglas Frank – spotted Recker and ambled over, with the pace of a man who was never hurried. Frank was middle-aged, with a dour face and a bleakly depressing sense of humour.

"The *Vengeance* will request a biometric re-approval in the next hour, sir."

"When are you planning to sever the last tie-ins?" asked Recker.

"Still on schedule for today." Frank looked about as if he was hunting for an oily rag to wipe his visibly clean hands on. "Meaning this shift is the last time we'll need you, sir. If all goes to plan, of course."

Many of the *Vengeance*'s less critical components had already been scanned, their structures analysed and the data transmitted to the HPA's many different scientific teams. The physical components would remain here on the *Maximus*, and a huge, well-staffed workshop had already been set up behind the aft bulkhead on this upper bay. It was these hands-on teams who were taking up all the accommodation on the heavy lifter.

"Are they sending you anywhere, sir?" asked Frank, hoping for some gossip.

Recker didn't know and he said as much. With a disappointed *harrumph*, Frank wandered off back to the nearest group of technicians.

A waving arm caught Recker's attention and he saw Aston emerge from the *Vengeance*. She hurried down the forward boarding ramp and jogged over.

"Well?" she demanded.

The audacity of it made Recker chuckle. "I get to meet the big man," he said. "Maybe today, maybe tomorrow."

"What's the reason for the meeting?" Aston was worried and trying to hide it.

"Truthfully, I don't know, Commander. Even if you asked me to pick my best guess, I wouldn't have a frontrunner."

"You're about to be played like a puppet."

Recker checked his shoulders. "I don't see any strings."

"But that's what's going to happen, sir. Fleet Admiral Solan has avoided you for years and now this happens. There's a reason for it."

"There's a reason for everything. Maybe those reasons aren't always so obvious."

"So you *do* know something."

"No," Recker shook his head. "If I did know, I'd tell you I knew."

Aston grinned suddenly. "You just might not tell me what it was that you knew."

"Exactly."

"One thing's for sure – they won't leave you languishing on the *Maximus* forever. As of today, you're effectively redundant from the process of dismantling the *Vengeance*."

"I know it."

She raised an eyebrow. "And you won't have to travel far to find your crew."

Recker laughed. "We're all in it together."

His pocked buzzed and his personal communicator played its infuriatingly catchy tune. Recker flipped open the device and read the message. He didn't keep Aston waiting.

"Fleet Admiral Solan doesn't want to delay his inspection of the *Vengeance*," Recker said. "The battleship *Divergence* broke out of lightspeed about ten minutes ago, along with a second ship the comms team didn't recognize. Once the formalities are done – whatever that entails – the admiral is planning to pay us a visit."

"He isn't hanging around," said Aston. "A shame it's taken him so long to find this enthusiasm, and I mean that for the war as well." She grinned again. "I guess you're just a side-line, sir. A footnote in the life of a busy fleet admiral."

Recker didn't take the bait and recognized that Aston was trying to keep his spirits high in the face of a coming event which had been avoided for years.

"I don't feel much of anything," said Recker eventually. "If you'd asked me a few weeks ago, I'd have told you I was angry about the past. Furious, even. Not anymore. I won't allow it to control me."

"What happened to Fortune puts things in perspective."

"It does, but I think it's more than just that. Fleet Admiral Solan is fighting his own war – a war to keep himself in power."

"Do you think it's a war he's going to win?"

"I can't call it one way or another, Commander. I couldn't even guess at the outcome." Recker stared at

Aston. "But I can assure you that this time I won't be a passive spectator. The fleet admiral and his son have had their time and by hell they're going to move over and let someone else take charge."

"Whatever it takes?"

Recker hesitated for only a moment and then he nodded. "Whatever it takes."

As he considered his newfound determination, Recker came to appreciate exactly how clever Telar had been. The man had planted the seed and hardly even bothered watering it. Then, he'd sat back to see what would take root. It was the kind of manipulation that Recker couldn't bring himself to resent and, in fact, thought that just maybe, Telar had done him the biggest favour imaginable.

With a deathly calm, Recker waited for the coming meeting.

CHAPTER THREE

LIKE A BREEZE RUSTLING through a lonely forest, news of Fleet Admiral Solan's arrival in the Gygor system came to everyone. It was the first time Recker had witnessed the organic spread of rumour and fact from such a proximity. Communicators buzzed with increasing regularity, comments were shouted from person to person, while new arrivals from elsewhere on the *Maximus* carried their own take on the rumours, heard from different sources.

Within thirty minutes of Recker's return from his meeting with Admiral Telar, every single technician was talking about Fleet Admiral Solan. Senior officers flooded in, to make it seem like they were always on hand, and Recker overheard that others – currently off duty – were on their way from the Topaz station.

"Fleet Admiral Solan doesn't seem interested in keeping this low key," Eastwood observed, as he watched a new group of senior technicians arrive from the heavy lifter's main bay.

"This is a show of strength," said Aston. "I wouldn't be surprised if he's brought the TV crews with him, in order that everyone in the HPA can see how well Solan is leading the military."

"I knew I should have shaved this morning," said Lieutenant Burner, from his seated position on a metal crate. He'd sourced a coffee from somewhere and swilled the dregs around in the bottom of the cardboard cup.

"A comb through your hair wouldn't hurt either," said Aston. "Maybe that's why you're single."

"I'm naturally curly, Commander. This is what naturally curly looks like."

"Like a bird's nest, you mean?"

"Please," said Recker. "If I've got to listen to this for the next five hours, I think I'll return to Topaz."

He cast his eye over the ongoing dismantling works. The activity around the *Vengeance* was clearly at an agitated and elevated level, though Recker was sure the efficiency had plummeted. This was a stressful, artificial situation and the technicians were anxious to appear like the well-trained experts they really were.

For the next few hours, Recker paced around this part of the bay, answered questions from the technicians and generally filled in time, while hoping that the overall reduced pace of work wouldn't result in him having to provide his biometric authorisation for an additional day. Recker wanted to be away from here, fighting the war.

As the time approached, tension in the upper bay climbed so high that work almost ground to a halt.

"This isn't how to run a military," said Recker angrily. "He's one man, not a damned god."

"They don't see him as a god and that's the problem," said Eastwood. "They don't know what the hell he is."

"Just a man," Recker repeated.

Instructions came over the internal comms that Fleet Admiral Solan was on his way and that he preferred to see his personnel at work, rather than wasting time with line-ups and introductions. This was in stark contrast to Recker's own experience of the man. The Fleet Admiral Solan he remembered preferred to be treated like a visiting head of state and have rose petals strewn on his red carpet.

"Here he comes," said Aston, her head turned towards the nearest entrance to the bay. "Do you think we'll be asked to explain what a fleet warship can do?"

"Commander," Recker warned.

A line of four of the heavy lifter's gravity vehicles emerged from the stairwell. Like most others on the *Maximus*, these vehicles were designed to navigate steps, ensuring that the officers onboard wouldn't have to trouble their heartrates by walking even the shortest of distances.

With untroubled serenity, the gravity cars approached the *Vengeance*, and a squad of soldiers ran along behind. The lead car stopped about a hundred metres from Recker and the others did likewise. Doors opened and a total of sixteen officers climbed out.

"No TV crew," said Burner.

Recker didn't answer. His eyes were on one man only. Fleet Admiral Thaddeus Solan was tall and slender, his age indeterminate. For a time, Solan and his officers chatted to some of the technicians. Heads were nodded sagely and fingers pointed at places of interest.

"Feels unreal," said Eastwood.

"Only if you let it, Lieutenant."

At last, the visiting party drifted towards the place Recker was standing. Determined he wouldn't wait meekly, he strode across to meet the approaching group. Aside from Solan, Recker identified numerous faces he recognized – those who had long ago thrown in their lot with the fleet admiral and who now had everything to lose.

When he was close enough, Recker saw that Solan hadn't visibly aged at all, though his unnaturally pale skin was possessed of an unlined tightness that suggested he took one of the multitudes of available drugs which could slow the onset of aging. The fleet admiral's green eyes were piercing, his dark hair thick, his cheekbones high and his mouth thin-lipped. He looked every inch the patrician, though a striking appearance meant nothing. In fact, Recker had absolutely no idea how this man had managed to attain leadership of the HPA military at the most critical time in the history of humanity.

The group stopped in front of Recker and spread out in a semi-circle. It could have been a way to ensure that no words went unheard in the din of the bay. To Recker, it seemed like they hoped to intimidate him. He'd faced down worse and didn't flinch.

"Captain Recker," said Solan, speaking first. His voice was cool and studiously neutral. "It has been a long time."

"Yes, sir. It has."

"I keep myself updated on your progress. You have exceeded the expectations of many."

"What would the universe be without surprises?"

"A far safer place, I'm sure." Solan raised his head and studied the underside of the *Vengeance*. "This is to be our saviour?"

"Perhaps."

"You did well to bring it home, Captain Recker. It is not just the citizens of the HPA who are grateful." Solan's gaze dropped and this time it speared into Recker. "And not just the military either."

"I'm pleased to have the support of my superiors, Fleet Admiral."

"You can be assured of that." Solan half turned. "Please," he said, waving the members of his group a few paces further away. "I would like a moment to speak with Captain Recker."

The group shuffled back and Solan took a step closer.

"Change is coming," he said.

Hearing the words repeated from this different source made Recker's head swim. "What sort of change, sir?"

"The military has failed in its duty to protect our citizens. As the leader of the armed forces, the blame for this sits squarely on my shoulders. I wish to learn. I have been learning."

Recker watched the other man's face carefully, for contrition or perhaps a sign of the mask slipping. He saw neither.

"We are losing the war, sir. This is not a good time for lessons."

"Oh but it is, Captain. This is the best time to learn. I am not a man accustomed to personal failure, nor to self-doubt. Recognizing them in myself has been difficult."

Solan raised an arm and swept it the full width of the bay. "Total war – at my request. Unlimited funding for the military. New hulls, new designs, new technology." He lowered his voice. "Where did the impetus for this come?"

"I know the answer you want to hear."

"And you won't say it?"

"Had this happened two years ago, sir. Hell, maybe even twelve months."

"You think it's too late?" Again, Solan's face showed no concern, like he was entirely disconnected from the subject at hand.

"No, sir, I don't think it's too late. What I do think is that we've left ourselves a mountain to climb. And after the first mountain, there's another behind it, potentially even higher and steeper."

"Then we will climb." Solan's eyes narrowed a fraction. "With my guidance, we will emerge from this stronger."

Recker didn't want to commit an answer, so he kept his mouth shut and waited.

"Not only have I failed myself and the military, but I have failed you, Captain Recker. As this war moves into a new phase, I would like to put our past behind us. The HPA requires the service of those who can give their all. Until recently, I had not understood that you were amongst those few."

"People like me are not so few, sir. If you look around, you'll see them everywhere. In every warship, in every ground crew and in every support team."

"In which case, we might yet become victorious." Solan tried what he might have thought was a conciliatory smile. "On this day, it is you in whom my greatest interest lies. You are a modest man, Captain Recker, yet tales of your deeds are becoming widespread. People are watching and listening. They are asking questions."

Recker played along. "What sort of questions?"

"I have been asked by members of our Representation why an officer who has proven so resourceful commands only a destroyer in our fleet."

"And what answer did you give them, sir?"

"I told them I would take a personal interest and see to it that your success is rewarded."

Despite himself, Recker was keen to hear where this was leading. A carrot was about to be dangled and he didn't think it would be an out-of-shape, worm-ridden carrot of the kind dug up by the neighbour's pet dog. This one was going to be juicy.

"If you give me the tools, I will use them, sir."

"Tell me, Captain. Have you heard about the Terminus program?"

Recker hid his confusion. "No, sir, I have not."

"It's a fast-track construction program," said Solan with a thin smile. "The first of our own heavy cruisers."

"We couldn't design a whole new class of ship without everyone in the military hearing something about it, sir."

"Quite. Which is why we haven't designed from the ground up."

"I'm interested," said Recker truthfully.

"I thought you might be," Solan nodded. "Now, if you imagine a Teron class cruiser, with an additional layer of armour and another four billion tons of engine mass to bulk out the overall structure and increase the length to

2200 metres. After that, we fit some additional missile clusters and install twin push-pull processing cores, backed up by a switchable and isolated obliterator unit, in case the vessel is attacked by a core override."

Recker wasn't sure, but he thought he detected hints of genuine enthusiasm in Solan's words. He weighed up the basic tech specs in his head. "Maybe not enough to go one-on-one with a desolator, sir, but I'm impressed." He meant it.

"I wouldn't be so sure our heavy cruisers will be outclassed, Captain." This time the enthusiasm was unmistakeable. "The additional outer armour has been specifically designed to absorb the impact of a Terrus projectile – the plates crumple, leaving the surrounding armour, as well as the inner plating, unaffected."

"Meaning that the enemy are required to land two hits in exactly the same place to cause any kind of significant damage," said Recker.

"That's the idea. It works in the modelling, but, as you're aware, a simulation is no substitute for some real face-to-face battle testing. This is where you step in."

"You're giving me command of a heavy cruiser?"

"If you want it."

"Yes, sir. I am happy to accept."

"It is the only one in our fleet, thought more are planned if it performs to expectations. The best part is, we can convert an existing Teron cruiser in a third of the time it would take to build an entire new warship."

"That is good news, sir."

"We'll defeat these Daklan bastards, Captain Recker.

One way or another, we will show them what happens when they start a war with humanity."

Since the destruction of planet Fortune, the Daklan had reduced their aggression significantly. In fact, they hadn't forced a single engagement in the intervening weeks. To Recker, that seemed like an opportunity – not for war, but for peace. During the recent years in which humanity had been on the back foot, Fleet Admiral Solan had acted more like the HPA was at peace. Now the enemy might be open to discussion, he was talking a good fight.

Recker had no idea how the man could so badly misjudge everything.

"When will my command be finalised, sir?"

"I wished to speak with you before I completed the signoff. Following this discussion, I am satisfied that I have chosen the right officer." A glint appeared in Solan's eye – a flash of nastiness which he hid at once. "They say that every man has his conceit, and I am no different."

What is he building towards?

"For me, it is my son," Solan continued. "A son who has given me cause for nothing but pride. Therefore, I felt no guilt or shame when I chose his name for the first of these new heavy warships."

Shit, no.

"Therefore, Captain Recker, I give you command of the heavy cruiser *Gabriel Solan*. I trust you will use this weapon of war to bring death to our enemy and honour to the HPA. May you every day feel the same pride in your spaceship as I do in the man whose name adorns it."

With his piece said, Fleet Admiral Solan took a step

back, not for a moment breaking his locked gaze. The gleam of nastiness was gone, hidden away and replaced by the same neutrality which the admiral had displayed throughout the conversation.

Recker knew the malice was there and he didn't let his eyes drop. His jaw wanted to clench, but he couldn't give even that sign of weakness, so he held steady until Solan re-joined his officers. Here and there, one of them smirked knowingly, though not once in Recker's direction.

With simmering anger, Recker returned to where Aston and Eastwood were standing, their expressions both questioning and uncertain. Fleet Admiral Solan had pulled a masterstroke and Recker knew he'd been completely outmanoeuvred.

CHAPTER FOUR

THIRTY MINUTES LATER, Recker was inside the same FTL comms station he'd used earlier. This time, he did experience guilt when he ordered out the same five people as had been queueing for a personal FTL comm slot earlier, especially when he noticed that the woman was next in line for a connection. Some things couldn't wait and Recker told them to leave.

He got comfortable and requested an FTL comm to Admiral Telar.

"Your meeting is over?" said Telar when the link formed.

"Yes, sir."

"And?"

"Did you know about it?"

"The *Gabriel Solan*?"

"Yes."

"I am involved in the signoff process for every new warship."

"Why didn't you tell me?"

"It's only a name, Carl."

"You know damn well it's not only a name, sir. Everything I accomplish will be associated with the warship."

"You could crash it into a planet at high speed and claim it was hardware malfunction," said Telar mildly. "Or you might get shot down in the line of duty."

"Not with the Daklan holding fire, sir."

"Who mentioned the Daklan?"

Recker's ears pricked up. "A mission?" He had a sudden thought. "Does this mean I'm still under your direct command?"

"Fleet Admiral Solan proposed a swap. One of his officers, for one of mine. I declined his request."

"I'm grateful, sir."

"Don't be. I can't allow my officers to fly only the easy missions, which would have undoubtedly been the result of your transfer to Fleet Admiral Solan's command."

Recker could well enough picture those easy missions – delivering the finishing blow to already crippled Daklan warships and orbital bombardments of poorly-defended surface facilities, with every success exaggerated and spoon-fed to the waiting media, like they were war-defining victories. Played cleverly, everyone in the HPA would associate success with the name *Gabriel Solan*.

"He's preparing for a succession," said Recker in sudden understanding.

"I'm pleased I did not underestimate you, Carl," said Telar.

"Will the others in high command buy it?"

"That is a question for another time," Telar replied,

shutting down this line of questions. "Anyway," he continued. "The fleet admiral was not entirely pleased with my decision and he continues to press his case. Perhaps he will make it impossible for me to deny his wishes."

This was something Recker had no control over and it seemed pointless to repeat his preference on the matter, since Admiral Telar already knew it well enough.

"So. A mission?"

"Yes, Carl. A mission."

"You said it doesn't involve Daklan?"

"I didn't say that. Not exactly."

"In that case, what?"

"We'll get to it."

"Why not just answer the question, sir?"

"Because I choose otherwise," said Telar without irritation. "Would I be right to think you are itching to be away from there?"

"Yes, sir. As of today, I'm no longer required on the *Vengeance*. The technicians will shortly sever the last of the tie-ins and then the necessary dismantling work will be complete. I've granted security access to the lead techs, so they'll be able to run tests on any of the remaining onboard systems."

"And they'll be able to put it back together again as well."

"Are there plans for that, sir?"

"There are always plans. Plans for everything." As if to prove it, Telar lifted a cardboard folder into the comms unit's visual arc. He held it there for a moment and let it fall to his desk. "We have spent much time investigating the data you pulled from the Lavorix Interrogator."

"You told me it was all blanks so far."

"That's correct. We still have several ongoing missions to far-flung places which may yet discover signs of the Meklon and Lavorix civilisations. Other than that, we have all four deep space monitoring stations working flat-out to pinpoint locations which may bear fruit. Whatever that fruit might be. Eventually, we'll find something."

"*Eventually* is too long. We lost a planet, sir."

"And the data shows that the Interrogator failed to extract coordinates of any other of our populated planets. Still, we are building evacuation spaceships capable of carrying billions of people, but it may be that they never see use."

"We should be prepared."

"Which is why the work continues."

"We should back off this search for alien weapons and focus on rebuilding, sir. We never expected to find the tenixite converter network in the first place."

"The cat is already out of the bag, Carl. What happens if the Daklan find a functioning converter? What if they stumble upon an abandoned landing field where a dozen warships like the *Vengeance* are stationed?" asked Telar, his voice rising. "What about others in the HPA who insist we continue our search? If humanity were to gain control over these alien weapons, we would defeat the Daklan, they say. The Representation constantly tells me that we must act first and quickest."

"Even with everything that's happened, I can't believe the HPA is split," said Recker. "We should settle with the Daklan and forget about the Meklon and the Lavorix – at least until we're ready to deal with what we might find."

"We cannot," said Telar quietly.

"Why not, sir?"

"We have too many unknowns to allow us to sit back and hope for the best. What if another of our planets was destroyed by a depletion burst targeted from a place unknown? And what if a third followed it? By then whatever action we decided upon would be too late."

"Do you believe the Lavorix are actively hunting us?"

"I do."

Recker detected something else – a something which Telar was finding it hard to say. "There's more."

"Yes, Carl, there's more." Telar sighed. He visibly got hold of himself and continued. "The Daklan lost several of their warships during a mission to locate parts of the tenixite converter network."

"How do you know this?"

"A second cat escapes its confinement. I have a direct line of communication with a member of the Daklan war council. We exchange certain information."

There was only one way to ask the next question and that was bluntly. "Does Fleet Admiral Solan know you're in contact with the Daklan?"

"Let me keep that one to myself."

"Is this another new front in the war?"

"It may become one. Now please – move on."

Recker didn't press. "So the Daklan lost some warships."

"Not just any warships, Carl. These ones were carrying the coordinates for Lustre in their memory arrays."

"Just Lustre or do the Daklan know about more of our planets?" asked Recker sharply.

"My relationship with Admiral Ivinstol does not yet extend to an open exchange of military secrets."

"Except about the loss of their warships."

"This is something different. It might affect both the HPA and the Daklan equally."

"Then what are you planning to do about it, sir?"

"The mission."

"Find out what happened to the Daklan ships and discover if they ran into another Interrogator?"

"That is the core of the mission. Clearly we require someone who is capable of identifying and acting upon any opportunities which may present themselves." Telar smiled without humour. "Someone who has the respect of the Daklan."

"Why...?" Recker stopped himself before he went any further. "A joint mission?"

"That's right. A single HPA warship and a single Daklan warship. Together, you will discover what happened to these missing Daklan ships and handle whatever comes after."

"Why only two ships?"

"I'm sure you can guess the reason."

Recker's mind was turning. "The obliterator core on the *Gabriel Solan*. It's designed to take over in the event of a core override."

"I see you haven't had a chance to study the full specifications. In fact, the obliterator core is designed to purge the core override by flooding the warship's onboard systems with so much data that everything else is forced out."

"Which will shut down the entire ship."

"For a short time. And then, the obliterator core will force-inject an entire copy of the backup control software that it's holding on its own data arrays into the purged systems. We believe this is similar to the method employed on the *Vengeance*. However, we've added some refinements."

"The *Vengeance* has only one core, not two or three."

"The Meklon technology isn't the same as ours, Carl. I'm sure if you wanted details, your engine man will be happy to provide them. I hear he's been putting his nose into many places where it's not exactly welcome."

"I'm sure he has," said Recker with a short laugh. "So the *Gabriel Solan* is the only warship in our fleet that might resist a core override. Is this Daklan ship resistant to core overrides?"

"I have received assurances that the Daklan contribution will be suitably equipped and capable."

"No doubt. When does the mission begin?"

"Let me respond with a question of my own."

Recker felt a sinking feeling and wasn't sure why.

"Did Fleet Admiral Solan mention anything about a crew for your warship?" Telar continued.

"No, sir. I assumed that as commanding officer I would choose my own."

"You will, but with an additional member selected for you."

"One of his men?"

"Yes."

Recker's blood started to boil. "I won't have it! I will speak to Admiral Solan and tell him I choose my own crew!"

"I have a better idea. Lieutenant Salvatore Alexander is currently touring the *Maximus*, as part of Fleet Admiral Solan's party. He is due to return to the *Gabriel Solan* in approximately two hours."

Recker was already halfway from his seat when Telar called for him to sit.

"You are not yet assigned as commanding officer."

"Shit."

"I can make the arrangements."

"You'll get some heat for that, sir."

"I've got plenty already."

Once again, Recker attempted to leave his seat.

"One more thing," said Telar.

"Sir?"

"Before it was subject to its recent modifications, the *Gabriel Solan* was a cruiser by the name of *Axiom*."

"Thank you, sir."

"Good luck, Captain Recker. The mission documentation will be with you soon."

With the meeting over and two hours before Lieutenant Alexander was due to return to the *Gabriel Solan*, Recker knew time was tight. He sprinted from the room.

CHAPTER FIVE

RECKER DIDN'T HOLD BACK and steered the gravity car along one of the main corridors which ran the full length of the *Maximus*. Luckily, most of the personnel were elsewhere, and he was able to achieve a speed that stuck up a proud two fingers to every health and safety guideline pertaining to the use of gravity vehicles within an enclosed space.

With him were Commander Aston, along with Lieutenants Eastwood and Burner. Circumstances didn't allow Recker to provide any more than a brief outline of the situation, which was enough to instil a sense of great urgency in his crew.

"Here's our target," said Aston, having called up the file image of Lieutenant Alexander on her pocket communicator.

Recker glanced at the picture and remembered him from Solan's group.

"Excuse my language, but the man looks like a cock," said Burner.

"Contemptuous curl of upper lip...check. All-knowing expression...check. Slightly oversized forehead...check," said Aston.

"He could have the appearance of a heavenly cherub and I wouldn't want him on my spaceship," said Recker, guiding the gravity car around a group of surprised technicians.

"I just spoke to the comms team on the bridge and they won't divulge his location," said Burner, snapping shut his own communicator.

"If you hadn't gone missing, we'd have plenty of time," said Eastwood.

"I didn't go missing. I went for a coffee."

"Three thousand metres from the *Vengeance*," said Aston. "And not answering your communicator."

"I didn't hear it. I was running."

"All three thousand metres?" said Eastwood doubtfully. "That would pretty much double your previous personal best."

"I told you I'd get in shape and I meant it."

"Save it for later," said Recker. "Like when we've got a six-week lightspeed journey to fill."

"We've got a six-week journey?" asked Burner in horror.

"I've got no idea where we're going, Lieutenant. Just be quiet."

Burner took the unsubtle hint and cut the chat. Not far ahead, Recker spotted the airlift which would take him to a bay where he'd been informed he might find a vacant shuttle. It was just his luck that Solan's arrival, alongside a shift change, had significantly increased the demand for transport.

Recker brought the gravity car to a halt adjacent to the lift, just as the door opened and a group of personnel exited. Once inside the lift, he checked the time. The diversion to find Lieutenant Burner had cost many minutes and there was no guarantee that Fleet Admiral Solan's party would depart at the exact two hours mentioned by Admiral Telar.

As a result, Recker was feeling the strain.

"If Lieutenant Alexander gets there first, couldn't we, you know, knock him out or something?" said Eastwood. "Maybe have the squad onboard arrest him for a crime we made up."

"The idea is to get the mission started and let Admiral Telar handle the political crap," said Recker. "I don't want to be involved."

"Too late for that," said Aston. "You're up to your neck in it."

"I'd have said the shit-line was somewhere closer to his forehead," said Eastwood. "Maybe even a little higher."

"The captain is wondering if he'd be better off with Lieutenant Alexander and a whole different crew onboard," said Aston. "I can see it in his face – the exact question going through his mind right now is *what did I do to deserve this?*"

Recker was saved by the opening of the airlift door and he sprinted into a short connecting corridor which led directly to a brightly lit mid-sized rectangular room, with two airlocks leading to separate shuttles clamped behind the bulkhead.

"Shit, there he is," said Aston quietly.

A group of five were talking next to the closest of the airlock doors. Three members of the group were from Solan's party, with the other two being technical crew from the *Maximus*. Lieutenant Alexander wasn't paying any attention to the conversation and he looked utterly bored with the proceedings.

Keeping his head down and his face directed at the opposite wall, Recker jogged past to the far airlock.

"In a hurry?" asked one of the technicians.

Recker didn't answer. Impatiently, he activated the access panel and the door opened to reveal a short corridor leading directly to the shuttle.

"Uh-oh, they're leaving," said Aston, taking one final look into the main area of the bay.

"Not before we are."

Once the airlock lights turned green, Recker opened the shuttle door and ran for the cockpit, with Aston taking the second seat.

"Everything's ready," she said.

"Let's disengage the clamps." Recker punched in the command and swore at the outcome. "Shuttle one in the bay has priority departure," he said. "I can't override, so we'll have to wait for Lieutenant Alexander to leave."

"Maybe he's got some things he needs to collect from Topaz station," said Burner from the cockpit doorway.

"Like hell, he's going straight for the *Gabriel Solan*," said Eastwood.

"The *Axiom*," said Recker. "I'm damned if I'm calling it the *Gabriel Solan* while I'm flying the damned thing."

"Two obscenities in one sentence. He's pissed," said Burner.

As it happened, Recker wasn't angry, he simply recognized how much harder the coming mission would be if he was required to look over his shoulder every time he wanted to speak his mind.

"Shuttle one has departed," said Aston.

"Thirty seconds and we can do likewise."

It was a long thirty seconds and Recker spent it staring at the rear feed which showed the sealed door leading to the launch tunnel. At last, a status update indicated the shuttle was free to depart. With feeling, Recker stabbed his finger at the launch button. The gravity clamps holding the vessel in place detached and he took manual control.

Since the shuttle had been docked front-first, he was required to pilot it out in reverse, which he did at speed. An alarm chimed softly to let him know he'd breached a launch velocity threshold and then the shuttle emerged from the heavy lifter's outer skin into the coldness of space.

Recker requested maximum power from the engines and flew the shuttle along the length of the *Maximus*, in close enough proximity to earn him another advisory chime.

"There's the *Gabriel*...I mean the *Axiom*," said Aston. "Four hundred klicks dead ahead. Lieutenant Alexander got a good head start on us."

A small green dot on the tactical – shuttle one – was

on a vector that would take it straight to the *Axiom*, and it was travelling fast. Recker performed some mental calculations and concluded that it would be close as to who arrived first. Shuttle two was at full thrust and he couldn't do any more than that.

"Bring up the *Axiom* on the sensor feed," he said.

"You got it."

A broad-beamed spaceship appeared on the forward feed. At first glance, it looked exactly what it was – an elongated Teron class cruiser with enormous quantities of additional plating fixed to the hull. When Recker stared for longer, he began to appreciate that rather more thought had gone into the design. Now the warship's overall appearance put him more in mind of a massive, angular, blunt-ended battering ram than the sleek and low-profile original which lay somewhere underneath.

"A bruiser, not a fencer," he said. "Looks like it could punch through anything even without weapons."

"I like it," said Aston.

"Me too." Recker pulled his attention back to the task at hand. "And it's only got one docking bay."

At fifty kilometres from the *Axiom*, Recker overtook the other shuttle, so close that it would likely have been visible to the naked eye. He wasn't watching his opponent and instead had his attention entirely on the *Axiom*.

"The shuttle dock," he said, spotting the opening midway up the portside flank.

"We're getting some attention from the crew on Topaz, the *Divergence* and the *Maximus*," Aston warned. "People asking what the hell we're playing at. And here's a comms request from Lieutenant Alexander's shuttle – wanting to know the same thing."

"Ignore everything."

"And now I've got Lieutenant Larson from the *Axiom*, sir."

A request from the heavy cruiser was something Recker couldn't ignore, not unless he wanted to risk the crew onboard denying him access to the bay.

"Tell them their new commanding officer is in a hurry."

"Yes, sir."

Recker didn't wait to hear the outcome - the shuttle was travelling fast and the much bigger *Axiom* filled the sensor feed with grey. In the centre of the screen, the docking bay was a tiny square which grew quickly. Holding his nerve, Recker decreased speed at the last moment and guided the shuttle into a docking tunnel which was far longer than the equivalent on a normal cruiser.

"Fleet Admiral Solan wasn't exaggerating about the armour," said Recker, bringing the vessel to a halt. Immediately, the gravity clamps engaged and a green light appeared to indicate the docking was successful.

"Lieutenant Alexander sure is persistent," said Aston, pointing at a flashing light on the comms panel.

"A good trait to find in an officer. Now let's move," said Recker.

He ushered Burner and Eastwood away from the cockpit door and hurried to the exit. The airtight seals were in place, so he wasn't required to wait for another green light. The door opened when he touched the adjacent panel and Recker dashed into a short tunnel which led to an intersection. He paused at a wall-mounted console and sent a command to close the outer docking bay doors, an action which gave him an entirely explicable feeling of satisfaction.

"The bridge," he said, stepping away from the console.

At the intersection, he headed left into another short passage and then took the first right. Recker hadn't visited a fleet cruiser for a few years, but nothing had changed. The corridors were a little wider, such that two personnel could almost pass sideways without making contact. The ceiling was higher, though not so much that it allowed taller people to achieve a flat-out sprint without risk of injury. Otherwise, it was the same old design which placed functionality on a pedestal and left comfort in the gutter.

Not far from the bridge, Recker nearly collided with a figure coming around a corner from the opposite direction.

"Private Drawl."

"Yes, sir."

"I wasn't expecting you."

"In which case you've got a whole lot more surprises ahead of you, sir. Sergeant Vance and the rest of the squad are here somewhere." Drawl shrugged to indicate he wasn't exactly sure where the other soldiers were hiding themselves. "We got the order to come onboard maybe a couple of hours ago. Maybe less. And here we are."

"I'll speak to Sergeant Vance," said Recker, squeezing past Drawl.

"Say, are we going someplace nice, sir?"

"Always."

"Admiral Telar's got a real eye for detail," said Aston, once the crew were away from Private Drawl.

"I'm just beginning to understand how much so," said Recker.

He arrived at the steps leading to the bridge, climbed and opened the protective door. Familiar blue-white light spilled into the darker corridor and he narrowed his eyes instinctively. The bridge floorspace was approximately fifty percent greater than that on a riot or destroyer, with seats for a total of seven personnel.

Two officers already present were standing and they saluted Recker as he entered. He took it as a good sign that they'd followed his progress through the warship and were ready for him.

"Lieutenant Jo Larson, sir. Sensors and comms," said the closest, a blonde woman in her mid-twenties with a confident air and a face that could have launched a thousand warships.

"Lieutenant Larry Fraser, sir. Engines." In appearance, Fraser was about ten years younger than Eastwood, but with the same broad shoulders and similarly craggy features, like they were a prerequisite of the specialisation.

"Backup comms, backup engines," said Recker at once, pointing at each in turn. "Where's the rest of the stand-in crew?"

"They left shortly after Lieutenant Alexander, sir. We received a high-priority message from Topaz station and a shuttle came for the pickup."

"Who sent the message?"

"Admiral Telar, sir."

Recker was not taken aback by the disclosure. "Do

either of you know Lieutenant Alexander? Was he stationed on the bridge?" He watched closely for their reactions.

"Yes, sir," said Fraser, with scrupulous neutrality.

Larson's eyes flashed dangerously and her shoulders drew in defensively, so fractionally that Recker would have missed it were he not already looking. "Yes, sir," she said.

"What's his specialisation?"

"I'm not sure, sir," said Fraser. "All of them, from listening to him speak."

"Where did he sit?"

"Over there on weapons, next to Captain Ramirez."

"So his specialisation was weapons?"

"I don't know, sir. We were part of the *Axiom*'s original crew – along with Captain Ramirez - before it got renamed. Lieutenant Alexander came onboard shortly before lift-off and that console is where he mostly sat."

Both Fraser and Larson had plenty to say about Lieutenant Alexander, that much was clear from their expressions. However, they didn't know Recker and they weren't about to badmouth another officer just yet. Doubtless they'd find their tongues at some point and Recker had yet to find anyone who could resist Commander Aston's efforts at persuasion.

"Everyone to your stations," Recker ordered, heading for the command console. "This is my usual crew – I'll leave them to make introductions."

Recker sat. The *Axiom* had been heavily modified on the outside and the refit extended to the bridge hardware.

The console in front of him was the latest available, though nothing about it was unfamiliar.

"Sir, Lieutenant Alexander is requesting a channel," said Larson.

"Deny the request and any others you receive from him."

"Yes, sir."

Instead of waiting around, Recker took the warship's controls and accelerated directly away from both Topaz station and the battleship *Divergence* which was stationary nearby. The effects of the additional propulsion mass were immediately noticeable and under full thrust the engines pushed the life support utilisation gauges far higher than normal. One of the sensor feeds showed the Lapus-1 gas giant sliding steadily by as the warship gained speed.

"Where are those mission documents?" Recker muttered to himself, taking one hand off the controls to check the messaging system. He wanted to get into light-speed before news about the situation reached Fleet Admiral Solan. If that happened, the crew on the *Divergence* battleship would take a much closer interest.

Before his eyes, an encrypted document arrived, keyed to his own command codes. He opened the file and scanned the contents.

"Lieutenant Eastwood, I'm sending you some coordinates. That's where we're heading."

"Got them, sir, and they are now entered into our navigational system."

Recker hauled back on the controls and the *Axiom*

came to a halt. Straightaway, the ternium drive activation timer appeared and started counting down.

"What's our destination?" asked Recker.

"Nowhere near anything," said Eastwood. "Five days out."

"What's the mission, sir?" asked Larson.

"I'll let you know once we're at lightspeed," said Recker. If he told them they were off to a rendezvous with a Daklan desolator, he risked them thinking he was a traitor.

Then, he realized that Admiral Telar wouldn't permit such a loose end to jeopardise the mission. If Larson and Fraser were here, it was because they were trusted. Even so, he kept the details quiet for the moment.

"However, there's one fact I will make clear before we jump to lightspeed," said Recker, raising his voice. "If I hear anyone referring to this warship as the *Gabriel Solan*, I will have them incarcerated in the brig."

"This warship does not have a brig, sir," said Larson.

"In which case, I'll order Sergeant Vance to shoot anyone who ignores my order and have the body ejected into space along with the waste from the septic tanks."

The expressions on Fraser and Larson's face indicated they didn't know if Recker was joking. He let them stew on it.

When the ternium drive countdown reached zero, and without interference from Topaz station or the *Divergence*, the *Axiom* entered a high multiple of lightspeed.

CHAPTER SIX

ONCE THE POST-TRANSITION status checks were complete, Recker played it straight.

"We're heading for a rendezvous with a Daklan desolator," he said.

The reactions of Fraser and Larson dispelled any doubts he might have had about their allegiances.

"About time we settled our differences," said Fraser. "Hell, the HPA's been fighting for survival these last five years I reckon, and now with these new aliens blowing up our planets, it seems to me that we're running out of road."

"I don't think we're friends with the Daklan yet, Lieutenant."

"It's a start, sir," said Larson. "The fact that this mission is happening means people on both sides are giving serious thought to the future. The Daklan lost a planet, we lost a planet. We've got to stop it happening again."

Recent events - from the Daklan attack on Lustre to

the fact that the enemy had suffered in the same way as the HPA - had become widespread knowledge, so Recker wasn't surprised to learn that these officers knew the background and had formed their own opinions.

"What do you know about the Meklon and the Lavorix?" he asked.

"Bits and pieces, sir," said Fraser. "A bunch of aliens fighting it out with technology that's in advance of our own."

"We believe the Lavorix used a network of tenixite converters – these are weapons which extract the energy from ternium ore and convert it into something called a depletion burst – to destroy both Fortune and the Daklan planet. We also believe the Lavorix are in the ascendency against the Meklon. Maybe they've already won."

"Are we treating the Meklon as allies, sir?" asked Larson.

"I don't think we can make that assumption, Lieutenant," said Recker. "It would be in the best interests of the HPA and the Daklan if these new aliens just went away. But that's not going to happen, so we're obliged to deal with the situation."

"What's the scope of the mission?" said Aston. "I assume we're planning to do more than shake hands with a Daklan captain and return home?"

"I don't think even a handshake is on the cards just yet, Commander. The Daklan lost some ships. Their war council and our high command agree there's a possibility they ran into another artifact like the Interrogator. If that turns out to be true, then we've got plenty to worry about."

Recker was hesitant to mention that the coordinates of

planet Lustre were in the databanks of those Daklan warships and he waited to see if any of his crew would make the connection.

"Lustre," said Aston at once.

Understanding dawned in the faces of the other crew members.

"We can't afford to lose another planet," said Eastwood.

"Even if it meant the Daklan potentially lost several more planets at the same time?" said Recker, trying to gauge the mood. "Those missing warships might hold location data for their entire civilization."

"I don't know what I think," Eastwood said. "I want the best for the HPA and I guess I don't care too much what happens elsewhere." He grimaced, like he wasn't sure what else to say.

"I'm not judging, Lieutenant," said Recker. "I don't think we can guess our future. What we can do is keep pushing. That doesn't necessarily mean fighting – I mean we search for every opportunity and we make the best of them. It could be that this joint mission with the Daklan leads to something bigger. It might be that we need the Daklan's help in order to survive, or it might be that they lose all of their planets to depletion burst attacks, leaving the HPA alone to face whatever's coming."

"I never did like guessing games," said Burner.

"Then let's stop playing," said Recker, who had only a tentative appreciation of them himself. "Lieutenants Larson and Fraser – what can you tell me about the *Axiom*? I haven't had time to check out the full technical specifications."

"We've got the same standard comms system that you'd find on a Teron class, sir," said Larson. "The bulked-out hull required some repositioning of the sensor arrays and at the same time, the shipyard upgraded all the lenses and the processing units. Plus, the *Axiom*'s main cores have so much grunt between them, the sensors can scan further and faster than most ships in the fleet."

"A good start," said Recker. "Lieutenant Fraser?"

"The propulsion has enormous output, as you've already gathered," said Fraser. "I've been reading up on the new armour design and it looks promising."

"It's meant to soak up explosives and Terrus projectiles," said Recker.

"That's the basic outline, sir. The intention is that the outer armour buckles and stays in place so that it still offers protection. We could take a few big hits and end up looking like we're ready to fall apart when the reality is that we're as tough as we ever were. That's the theory, anyway."

"Somebody's got to test that theory, Lieutenant," said Recker, cracking his knuckles. "It might as well be us." He pointed at Aston. "Your turn, Commander."

"Not much to tell you, sir. We're fitted with eight Hellburner tubes and sixteen clusters of ten Ilstrom-6 missiles, which have a higher maximum velocity and slightly higher lock range than the Ilstrom-5s. Other than that, we have enough Type 2 Railer turrets to make a Daklan surface installation resemble a piece of cheese. That's if they hadn't just become our good buddies."

Recker wasn't disappointed. He knew the realities of bringing new tech and weapons into service, and even switching the HPA's entire society to total war wasn't going to produce a new super-weapon as quickly as everyone would prefer. He was aware of numerous ongoing projects, none of which had evidently produced results fit for installation on the first of the military's heavy cruisers.

"We've got armour, missiles and countermeasures," Recker said. "We should be able to soak anything this side of a depletion burst and emerge from the explosion with our weapons firing. As far as I'm concerned, that makes the *Axiom* a success."

"I agree with you, sir," said Fraser. "And I didn't mention the Daklan lightspeed missiles earlier, so I'll tell you the destruction models indicate that their warheads should detonate between the outer and inner layers of armour. We'd lose the outer plating and end up with a big crater in the hull, but not enough to make a breach."

"I like it," said Eastwood.

"Yeah, it feels good to be onboard a warship that isn't going to break apart as soon as the missiles start flying," added Burner.

Recker felt it too. Although the *Axiom* wasn't a technological masterpiece, it didn't need to be. It was fast enough, tough enough and with large enough magazines to survive an extended campaign away from base. For this mission it might well be a near-perfect tool, given the options available.

"So where are we heading after the rendezvous?" asked Burner. "Is this going to be another long journey?"

"I don't know where we're going afterwards," said Recker.

"The Daklan haven't told us?" said Aston in shock.

"Nope. This is something we're taking on trust."

"They haven't earned any!" said Burner.

"We've got to start somewhere and this is the time and the place."

Nobody disagreed – not out loud, anyway - and Recker spent another thirty minutes talking with his crew, to ensure that both Fraser and Larson were aware of the current information regarding the Meklon and Lavorix. They had some gaps in their knowledge, where the military was still trying to keep a lid on things, but nothing that Recker couldn't fill in. Few secrets existed these days – when an entire planet was reduced to dust and twelve billion people died with it, there wasn't any hope of keeping things under wraps.

Once the crew's questions had dried up, Recker headed for the mess area, ready to answer plenty more. Most of the soldiers stationed on the *Axiom* were here and he located Sergeant James Vance sitting at a table near the replicator.

Vance seemed to have more good humour about him than usual, or maybe it was just because Recker knew him better.

"Sir," said Vance, almost smiling.

"Sergeant," said Recker, almost smiling in response. "Glad to have you back."

"I don't think I ever left, sir."

"What do you know about this mission?" asked Recker, testing the waters.

"Nothing more than I've been able to guess."

"Fly out, shoot some Daklan, fly back," said Corporal

Hendrix. She'd lost family on Fortune – more than most others - and it was obvious she was carrying a burden.

"You're right to say we'll be flying out and flying back, Corporal. This time we won't be shooting the Daklan. In five days, we'll rendezvous with a modified desolator and we'll head out in search of some missing Daklan warships."

"Does that mean the Lavorix are now public enemy number one?" Hendrix asked.

"I think that's the best way to describe it."

"The enemy of my enemy just became my friend," said Private Ken Raimi.

"I wouldn't go so far as to say that," Recker warned. "This is the first tentative step. If it goes wrong, we might well be trading blows with that Daklan heavy."

"And we've got our own heavy to do it with," said Raimi. "The *Gabriel Solan* – a tough son of a bitch, ready to pound the crap out anything that stands in its way."

Hendrix looked up from the table and squarely into Recker's eye. "I heard they called it the *Axiom*, once. I think I prefer that. Feels right, rather than naming a mean-ass ship after a man who didn't fire a gun in the last ten years."

Recker smiled at Hendrix and she smiled back.

"I just came down here to let you know that things have changed," he said.

"What if we're required for a surface mission, sir?" asked Vance.

"It might happen," said Recker with a nod. "I might need you to fight with the Daklan against a common enemy."

Vance sighed, leaned back and ran a palm over his buzz cut. "Things really are changing," he said in acknowledgement. "Ride the wave or get pulled under."

Those two short sentences were enough reassurance for Recker. Vance and his squad would adapt to whatever circumstances they faced – it was how they'd survived the war for so long.

"Hey, look on the bright side," said Raimi, his face brightening. "I bet Drawl a week's pay that we'd be propping up a Daklan bar sometime this year. Maybe I'm in with a chance of collecting."

"Good luck with it, soldier," said Recker.

He eased himself out of the gap between the bench and the table and stood. The smell of replicated food wasn't enough to stimulate his appetite, so he exited the mess room in order to check out his quarters.

A short distance from the mess, he was brought up short by a voice from behind.

"Sir?"

"Corporal Hendrix," he said, recognizing the voice. He stopped and turned.

She looked uncomfortable – strangely vulnerable, considering she was dressed in combat armour and carrying a gauss rifle.

"I just wanted to thank you for keeping us all informed, sir," Hendrix said defiantly, like it had taken an immense effort to speak. "Nobody says it, but we appreciate being treated like we're more than dumb grunts."

"I remember how it is, Corporal," said Recker. "I used to sit with my squad, playing the guessing games, while the senior officers kept the intel to themselves. I've lost squadmates because of it and I won't allow myself to become part of the same problem."

Hendrix hesitated. "When the sergeant first told us we were being assigned to Captain Carl Recker's ship, everyone was asking what we'd done to deserve it."

"And now?"

"Now most of the squad would say we got exactly what we deserved. Me with them."

"Thank you, Corporal. I appreciate what you've said."

"I just didn't want you to think nobody recognized..." Hendrix tailed off, looking uncomfortable again. She took a deep breath. "How did it happen, sir?" she asked, the words coming quickly. "I mean you and Admiral Solan falling out."

Recker didn't usually speak about it. Maybe, he worried, it was because he'd lost trust in people. He shrugged.

"It was years ago. A lifetime. Back then Gabriel Solan was being fast-tracked for high command – he was flying a shard class when he was fresh out of the simulators. I was a ground lieutenant, commanding troops on a planet called Rar-42132. *Choker* we used to call the place on account of all the sulphur dioxide. After a couple of weeks trying to take a Daklan ternium plant intact, my squads were ready to finish the job. The last building to fall and in we went, to flush out what was left of the enemy. Solan saw a chance for glory when we'd already won and he sent a plasma missile into that building. Killed five of my soldiers and took out the ternium control hardware at the same time, making the whole facility useless."

Recker felt the fury come. Even now, the memory had the power to affect him.

"What happened after?" asked Hendrix.

"As soon as I saw *Captain* Solan, I laid him out cold. Broke his jaw in three places." Recker's hand clenched into a fist. "He'd screwed up – a court martial grade screw up - and everyone knew. It didn't matter. The incident was whitewashed and gradually the people who'd been on Choker died or pretended they'd forgotten."

"But not you," said Hendrix softly.

"I don't forget, Corporal – I can't. I've been told it's one of my failings."

"It's not a failing, sir."

Recker couldn't think what else to say and he suddenly felt self-conscious. "I'm coming to accept that, but it's taken a long time."

With an expression Recker couldn't interpret, Hendrix turned and walked back towards the mess room. He headed off to view his quarters, agitated and full of nervous energy. Those quarters were exactly as anticipated and he didn't linger. Having completed an inspection, he returned to the bridge, carrying a used tray and a cup that Captain Ramirez had evidently been unable to dispose of given the rapidity with which he'd been called away to the Topaz station.

Once more in the command seat, Recker mentally prepared himself for the journey ahead.

CHAPTER SEVEN

THE JOURNEY TIMER ticked down to ten minutes and Lieutenant Eastwood called out his traditional warning. None of the crew scrambled for readiness since they'd been waiting five days for the coming moments. Those five days were more than enough for Recker's usual crew to familiarise themselves with the hardware and for everyone to learn about each other.

So far, it was going swimmingly and Recker had no doubts about the battle-readiness of his warship, especially since both Fraser and Larson appeared to be remarkably accomplished officers. Given Telar's apparent hand in their selection, that was not a cause for amazement.

Having heard Eastwood's warning, Recker offered a quick summary of the immediate goals.

"We'll break out of lightspeed, scan the area and make contact with the Daklan. They aren't known for posturing, so if things are really going south, we'll learn about it quickly."

"I think the Daklan turned up for the same diplomacy lesson as you did, sir," said Burner. "The one that got cancelled."

"And it comes as a great relief for me to think so, Lieutenant," said Recker, who took no pleasure from verbally dancing around a subject, using flowery compliments to achieve a result that would have been quicker accomplished in two honest sentences. The Daklan might be warmongering alien bastards, but when it came to diplomacy, they were cut from the same tree as Recker.

"You were telling us the plan, sir," Aston reminded him.

"I thought I'd finished," said Recker, feigning surprise. "Scan the area, contact the Daklan, and see what happens after."

"That next part being a journey into a hitherto unexplored section of the universe where we will engage in deadly combat with a Lavorix construct or something equally deadly," said Eastwood.

"I didn't want to look so far ahead, Lieutenant," said Recker, watching the lightspeed timer drop to two minutes. "Any other questions?"

Everyone knew the score – this was a time for quick thinking and reactions, rather than forward planning. In the initial dealings with the Daklan, Recker would be the one doing most of the heavy lifting. He called up the mission documentation again.

"Our contact is a Daklan captain named Jir-Lazan and he commands the desolator class *Aktrivisar*," he said. "And that is the sum total of the HPA's knowledge of both this officer and his warship."

The lightspeed calculations were a few seconds out and the *Axiom* shuddered into local space. Recker sucked in deep breaths to quell the nausea and threw the controls forward. The warship accelerated strongly and the propulsion thundered.

"Status reports!" he yelled.

"Local area scan commenced," said Burner.

"I got the fars," added Larson.

"No errors or failures to report on the propulsion or any linked system," called Eastwood. "Everything's at one hundred percent."

"Local area scan complete. Running a sweep for open comms receptors. Got something! Sir, the *Aktrivisar* is showing a green receptor."

"I've located the desolator on our sensors," said Larson. "They're a quarter of a million klicks from our position."

Considering the distances both warships had travelled to get to this lonely part of the universe, they'd arrived with remarkable proximity.

"Put them on the tactical."

"Done. They're stationary."

"No sign they're preparing to fire," said Aston.

"A visual confirms their Terrus cannons are not trained on our spaceship, sir," added Burner. "Here's the *Aktrivisar* up on the comms. Doesn't look much like a desolator."

Not wanting to be the only one dancing at the party, Recker slowed the *Axiom* and stopped the evasive manoeuvres. At the same time, he kept one eye on the sensor feed of the Daklan heavy cruiser. Like Burner had said, the vessel was different to other desolators. The *Aktrivisar* was longer and bulkier, with four twin-barrel Terrus cannons instead of the usual two.

"It's not just the HPA that's been working on something new," said Recker. "That desolator's been loaded up with extra armour just like we have."

"Most desolators have a mass range between eight and ten billion tons, depending on when they were constructed," said Eastwood. "I reckon that one's at fifteen billion tons. Five billion up on the *Axiom*."

"And four hundred metres longer than normal," said Aston. "What's the old terminology? A pocket battleship? A battle cruiser?"

Recker didn't know if the Daklan had created a whole new class of warship, or if the *Aktrivisar* was just a modified version of their existing heavy cruisers – a desolator on steroids. One thing was certain – he didn't want to get into a slugging match with it.

"Watch them closely. Lieutenant Burner, request a channel."

"Channel request accepted. Captain Jir-Lazan would like to speak with you, sir."

"Bring him through on the bridge speakers."

Jir-Lazan had a voice that was so rough it bore a striking resemblance to low-octave white noise.

"Captain Carl Recker," said the Daklan.

"Captain Jir-Lazan," Recker returned. "We have come as agreed."

"So I see. You are the Carl Recker who destroyed our fleet at your planet Lustre."

"Yes."

"Then perhaps the HPA has chosen a suitable officer for this mission."

"They have. I was told you have information for me."

A raucous sound emerged from the bridge speakers – a sound which made Recker think of two immensely heavy slabs of abrasive stone rubbing together. Jir-Lazan was laughing.

"I have a destination, Captain Recker. That is all. A place far from here – we name it the Lanak system."

"What were your ships looking for?"

The laugh came again, this time lasting for only a couple of seconds. "Weapons."

"It sounds like they found what they were looking for."

"That is our conclusion. Were the choice mine, we would send a hundred Daklan warships to Lanak. Unfortunately, the war council sees it otherwise. They are wary of the core override."

"You are familiar with the weapon?"

"Of course! Do you believe we Daklan have only encountered the Lavorix in places familiar to your HPA? This has been going on longer than you know, human."

"What defence does the *Aktrivisar* have against the core override?"

Jir-Lazan didn't answer at once and Recker guessed he was considering how much he was permitted to give away.

"We have a defence against the core override."

"Is it tested?"

Another hesitation. "No. The hardware is experimental."

"Well that puts us both in the same position," said Recker.

"If we allow our vessels to be affected by a core override, the fault will be ours."

Having seen the Interrogator fire an override into his warship *Expectation* from fifteen million kilometres, Recker didn't agree with the Daklan's assessment. He didn't mention it. "Does your species count itself at war with both the Meklon and the Lavorix?"

"The Lavorix, yes. The Meklon, no."

"So if we encounter the Lavorix, you will attack them without provocation, assuming the situation warrants it?"

"That is correct."

"The HPA has not yet declared war on either Meklon or Lavorix."

"This might cause problems on our mission."

Recker mentally cursed the lack of communications between the HPA and Daklan which might well have attached a ball and chain to the mission before it even got underway. He required guidance and that meant an FTL comm to Admiral Telar. He muted the channel.

"How long to get an FTL message to Admiral Telar and receive the response?"

"In excess of twenty-four hours," said Burner promptly.

"Damnit!" Recker took the comms off mute. "Have the Lavorix specifically declared war on the Daklan?" he asked. "Or have they simply been destroying your vessels without dialogue?"

"We have had no dialogue."

From experience, Recker knew the Daklan treated negotiation as an optional distraction, or at least they did when it came to their dealings with the HPA.

"Have the Daklan attempted to speak with the Meklon or Lavorix?"

"That is not our way."

Upon hearing the response, Recker closed his eyes for a moment. "You're fighting and you don't know why?"

"We are fighting because our initial encounters were hostile. The Daklan do not back down from a confrontation."

That was something Recker knew all too well. "Are they an opponent you can overcome?"

"We lack sufficient data to reach a conclusion. The known network of tenixite converters is abandoned, perhaps because the Lavorix were forced to do so, or perhaps because they had eliminated their Meklon enemies in that area of space."

"The Lavorix could have an empire which spans a thousand worlds, or they might have suffered catastrophic losses in their war."

"You are familiar with the concept of uncertainty," said Jir-Lazan.

"It's something I've learned to live with."

"But not to love." Once again, the Daklan erupted into laughter, which persisted for many seconds.

Recker exchanged a glance with Aston and waited for Jir-Lazan to settle himself.

"The Lavorix destroyed our planet Fortune without provocation," said Recker. "On this mission, I will treat them as the enemy and act accordingly."

"I am glad that your Admiral Telar sent an officer capable of making decisions," said Jir-Lazan. "You know how the Daklan fight and I know how the HPA fights. We will offer a formidable challenge to the Lavorix shit-faces."

"However, we will engage only where necessary," said Recker firmly.

"I agree," said Jir-Lazan at once. "There is more than one way to tear the skin from a bleeding corpse."

The language module was clearly having a problem with the Daklan vernacular, but Recker got the message. Not only that, but the speed of the response told him that the Jir-Lazan wasn't so blinded by the need for combat that he would rush into every engagement. Or so Recker hoped.

"From our conversation so far, I have learned that we are heading into the complete unknown," he said.

"Perhaps that is no bad thing," Jir-Lazan replied. "If our futures were written in a list and handed to us at birth, where would come the pleasure of discovery?"

"There are times when it's better to know."

"Given that we have no choice in the matter, all living species should embrace the chaos. From it, we can bring order."

"A discussion for later."

"Of course. I will have the destination coordinates and a synchronisation code sent across to your warship. We should depart immediately – our destination is approximately three days from here."

"Closer than I was expecting."

"The enemy once lived on our doorsteps, human. Where they are now, perhaps we will find out."

"Indeed." Unwilling to abandon this opportunity to learn more from the Daklan, Recker had one last try. "Is there anything else you can tell us before we depart? This is the first joint HPA-Daklan mission that I'm aware of. Our success or otherwise will be remembered."

"I am not keeping anything from you that I am permitted to speak of," said Jir-Lazan, showing a talent for evasion. "I will send you some basic data concerning the *Aktrivisar*'s capabilities, if you will do the same for your own vessel."

"Agreed." Recker turned and nodded at Burner to indicate his should proceed.

The comms went quiet as if the conversation was over, but Jir-Lazan had something else to say. "This may be the beginning of the end, human. The Daklan will fight to the last."

The words made Recker shiver and he knew Jir-Lazan was waiting for a response. "As will the HPA."

"I am not so sure."

"Then you are wrong."

"In which case, it bodes well for you." Another laugh. "Perhaps, should our own differences be too great to overcome and our war resumes, you may yet offer the Daklan a challenge." More laughter.

Recker held in a sigh and turned to find Lieutenant Burner with his thumb in the air to indicate he'd received a synch code.

"We've got what we need, Captain Jir-Lazan," said Recker.

The laughter stopped. "This place is as empty as the balls of a rutting [translation unknown]. Let us depart at once."

Abruptly, the comms channel went dead, leaving

Recker unable to decide what to make from the conversation.

"Accept the synch code," he said.

"Done. We're warming up for a departure," said Eastwood. "It looks like a dead-heat between our processing cores and theirs."

"A tie feels like a victory," said Fraser.

"I didn't want to say it, but I agree," said Aston.

"Does the Lanak system appear on the HPA charts?" asked Recker.

"Yes, sir," Burner confirmed. "We've mapped the central star but assigned it one of those letters-and-numbers names that no human brain can easily memorise. We haven't visited the place and none of the monitoring stations have taken a closer look. Luckily, the Daklan sent us some details along with the information on their warship."

"I'll check it out once we're at lightspeed."

"Yes, sir."

The timer counted down, while Recker pondered the future of this mission. His conversation with Jir-Lazan had been in some ways enlightening, though it had also raised many questions. It was clear the Daklan were worried and too damn proud to come out and say it. Not only that, the aliens clearly had a greater knowledge of the Lavorix than the HPA, but that still didn't seem to be much. Jir-Lazan had scarcely made of an effort to hide the fact.

As the lightspeed drive activated, Recker felt more troubled than ever.

CHAPTER EIGHT

THE THREE-DAY JOURNEY passed quickly and the crew spent much of the time engaged in speculation. As usual, little came from it other than frustration and, for Recker, the arrival at the Lanak system couldn't come soon enough. His intuition told him that answers lay there and he fully intended to live long enough to carry the information back to high command.

And, while the HPA wasn't strictly at war with the Lavorix, Recker couldn't see a downside to blowing up a few of the aliens' facilities and warships, should the opportunity present itself. For once, he could apply the word *enemy* to a species which wasn't the Daklan, which left him wondering exactly how humanity's relationship with its most longstanding foe would turn out.

Any thoughts of them being friends was completely misguided, though Recker admitted that Jir-Lazan had left him with a positive impression. The fact the Daklan was in charge of a powerful warship like the *Aktrivisar* meant his superiors held him in high regard, and he therefore had the potential to be a useful ally in the coming mission.

An hour before arrival, Recker called up the mission documentation again, though he already knew it word for word. One of the final paragraphs described the agreement to share all data equally between the two parties, except as it pertained to locations of populated worlds and planets with significant installations or ternium processing facilities.

How anyone thought he'd be able to make the distinction, he had no idea. If enemy data was stolen during the mission, it was likely to require dedicated facilities to interpret, rather than guesswork on the battlefield. It was a problem for later, along with the instructions on what he was expected to do in cases where the Daklan became excessively difficult to handle or refused to share.

Trust was in short supply everywhere and Recker didn't want to be the man responsible for re-igniting the Daklan war at a time when the HPA really needed the breathing space. With an effort, he kept his face neutral and closed out of the file.

Aston didn't miss much and, as Recker's backup, she was privy to most of the details in the mission documentation. "It might never happen, sir."

"If it does, we won't be the driving force."

"Captain Jir-Lazan had something about him."

"He did. That only suggests he's a competent officer, rather than having the HPA's best interests at heart."

"I disagree, sir," said Aston. "This mission is happening because, for once, the Daklan need us as much as we need them. Jir-Lazan isn't here to betray us, though

I'm sure there are circumstances in which he might do so. Both parties have an equal stake and this is the moment when we discover if this one-off alliance will result in bigger things."

"Peace with the Daklan in order to fight the Lavorix," said Recker.

"You know what tough bastards the Daklan are, sir. Whatever happens, I'd rather have them on our side for the coming war."

"You're convinced it's happening?"

"We all know it." Aston exhaled, as if saying the words had made a secret thought tangible. "No species can suffer the loss of a planet and accept the perpetrators as anything other than an enemy to be defeated."

"And here we are. The burden of a few hundred billion souls – human and Daklan alike – resting on the outcome of one mission."

"I know you're being facetious, sir, and I also know you believe it's true."

"It's a lot to deal with. I can handle it." He laughed bitterly. "I've got no choice."

The conversation ended and the *Axiom*'s crew prepared for re-entry into local space. Lieutenant Burner ran through the information provided by the Daklan about the Lanak solar system. It was light on details.

"The Lanak star has a diameter approximately four hundred times greater than that of Earth's sun," he said. "It has absorbed any close-in planets, leaving a bunch of others much further out. We're heading for a planet named Qul, which is between forty and forty-five billion klicks from Lanak and thought to be covered in ice."

"And that's as much as we know about Qul," said Larson. "The Daklan recorded the presence of other satellites further out from Lanak, but they weren't interested in them and didn't gather any useful data."

"Meaning they were pretty sure what they were looking for was on Qul," said Aston.

"Weapons," said Recker. "Weapons that were enough to capture or destroy a Daklan fleet."

"Did you ever learn how many warships they lost, sir?"

"No. That's something they've been keeping to themselves."

"Anyway, the lightspeed calculations for this journey aim to land us fifty million klicks from Qul," said Eastwood. "We know the planet's orbital track, so we shouldn't end up on the wrong side of Lanak. That's if everything goes to plan."

"After that, a softly-softly approach," said Recker. "I'm damned if I'm going to be taken unawares by another alien weapon we have no defence against."

"What if Captain Jir-Lazan decides to go for the frontal approach, sir?" asked Burner.

"I don't think he will. It's his synch code that'll bring us to fifty million klicks. If he wanted all guns blazing, he'd have argued for a much closer arrival point."

Although he spoke the words, Recker wondered if he really believed them. He knew he'd find out soon enough if the Daklan captain was capable of adopting a measured approach.

When Eastwood called out his two-minute warning, the crew settled in anticipation of their arrival. Fifty million kilometres was theoretically enough to ensure safety out of lightspeed, but Recker knew they were dealing with many unknowns, not least of which being the missing Daklan warships.

"Any second!" yelled Eastwood.

Right on time, the *Axiom*'s ternium drive shut off and the warship entered local space. Recker barked a few commands and began his usual evasive pattern of banking and rolling the warship in case anything hostile was close by.

"Local scan clear," said Burner.

"I'm scanning for open receptors," said Larson. "I've located the *Aktrivisar*!"

Recker couldn't deny his relief. "Where are they?"

"Checking…half a million klicks from our current position."

"Speak to their comms team and obtain their status."

"On it, sir."

Meanwhile, Burner expanded the scope of his sensor sweep. "These twin processing cores are churning through this data as fast as I can throw it at them," he said. "I've located Qul – we're forty-eight million klicks out, so we came in a little closer than planned."

"Forty-eight is fine," said Recker. "Keep scanning."

"There's nothing in our vicinity, sir," said Burner. "I have transmitted my findings to the *Aktrivisar*."

"The Daklan ship reports no problems, sir," added Larson. "They're fully operational."

"Good – I want to establish a battle network for our two ships. Do it quickly."

"Our systems aren't designed to speak to their systems," said Burner. "I can think of a potential work-around, but the data passing between our two ships will be delayed."

"I wasn't expecting perfection, Lieutenant. If you can think of a solution, speak to your counterparts on the *Aktrivisar* and put it into action."

"Yes, sir."

Recker had no doubt that the two comms teams would figure out a method that worked. While they got on with it, he reduced the *Axiom*'s speed and set it on a low-velocity course towards Qul. At forty-eight million kilometres, the sensors on a riot class wouldn't have detected anything more than a cold-blue disc. The *Axiom*'s arrays, with their access to the warship's twin main processors, were far more accomplished and Recker saw many surface imperfections which made him believe Qul was mountainous and – like the Daklan had suggested - entirely cased in ice.

It was difficult to obtain promotion to the bridge of a fleet warship if you couldn't solve problems quickly, and Recker wasn't left waiting long for his comms team to create a viable battle network.

"That's our ships linked, sir," said Burner. "The battle network will show positional data with a short delay and the Daklan have also set their missiles to broadcast their positions to our comms antennae. Their turrets can't be set to broadcast a discharge and neither can their countermeasures."

"What about ours?"

"Done for the Ilstrom-6s, negative on the countermeasures. The Hellburners aren't so easily reprogrammed and I've asked Commander Aston to work on those."

"Well?" asked Recker, turning her way.

"Done." She shrugged like it was nothing and then offered a grin. "Easy when you know how."

"That means we're set," said Recker.

"I've spoken to Captain Jir-Lazan and he confirms his readiness," said Burner.

"First we scan, to see what we can find."

"Yes, sir. Already on it. Focusing on the planet and ignoring everything else."

"Please," Recker confirmed.

"For a planet with a rocky composition, Qul is larger than average," said Larson. "Twice the diameter of Earth, all of it covered in ice, except one big patch on its central band."

"The atmosphere isn't hospitable but the surface conditions aren't completely terrible," said Burner. "If you wanted to take a walk about down there, all you'd need would be a standard-issue spacesuit."

"I'm not planning on sightseeing," said Recker. "What're the chances you can detect any visible side surface facilities from here?"

"Slim, depending on size and composition. I've detected clouds in the planet's atmosphere and they aren't helping."

"This is to be expected from our current range, sir," said Larson.

"Don't I know it, Lieutenant."

Recker got comfortable in his seat, anticipating an extended period of scanning, during which he would have little input. Lieutenant Burner came up with an idea.

"Sir, I've been thinking about this. The Daklan sent

some warships out here, but Captain Jir-Lazan hasn't given us much to work with."

"What are you getting at, Lieutenant?"

"If we knew their lightspeed vector, we might be able to determine exactly where they arrived. Since we're close enough to Qul to work out its speed of rotation, we might be able to calculate which side of the planet the Daklan fleet was facing when it first came to the Lanak system."

"That's a good idea," said Recker, rubbing his chin. "Surely the margin of error in those proposed calculations is going to be enormous given the distances involved?"

"There will be a margin of error, sir," Burner confirmed. "However, it'll give us something to go on. The alternative is that we scan from here, inch closer, scan again and repeat. It'll take time."

"It can't hurt to give it a try. Speak to the Daklan comms team and ask them to provide the data."

A minute later, Burner announced his success. "They've sent us the flight plans for their ships, sir. They're going to work on the calcs as well."

"How long?"

"If you're happy with me tapping both processing cores, a few minutes."

"Do it."

A moment later, the utilisation on the twin cores jumped to ninety-five percent and Recker stared at the gauge, waiting for it to drop again.

"I've got an estimate of the Daklan fleet's arrival point," said Burner, as the core utilisation plummeted to its usual out-of-combat level. "Now I've got to overlay the arrival point of the Daklan fleet onto the orbital track of Qul, adding in the rotation of the planet."

Recker drummed his fingers.

"Got it! Sir, from this, the Daklan only arrived ten days ago."

"Sounds like Admiral Telar didn't have much time to arrange this joint mission," said Aston.

"Which implies the Daklan were particularly keen to get things moving," said Recker.

"Their fleet broke from lightspeed on the planet's blindside, sir," said Burner. "Almost directly opposite from us."

"What chance of error in the calculations?"

"Not as much as I was expecting, sir. It appears the Daklan were being far more cautious than normal – they exited lightspeed about thirty million klicks from Qul. Here's an overlay on your screen."

The image Burner had generated showed the planet as a large sphere and the alien fleet as a dot. A series of red lines and overlapping cones showed the likely margins of error.

"We're looking in the wrong place," said Recker.

"Yes, sir."

"Communicate your findings to the *Aktrivisar* and recommend we execute an in-out lightspeed jump to the current blind side of Qul."

A short time later, agreement was reached and the sound of the ternium drive warming up filled the bridge. Frustration gnawed at Recker, though he knew that Lieutenant Burner had saved this mission potentially many hours of fruitless surface scans aimed at the wrong side of Qul.

The ternium drives on both warships fired simultaneously and then shut down within a second. The double transition made Recker feel like shit, but he got on with business, ordering sensor scans of the vicinity at the same time as he flew the *Axiom* evasively. The tactical screen indicated that Captain Jir-Lazan was doing likewise.

"Nothing on the near scan," Burner announced.

"I'm expanding the search sphere," said Larson.

Shortly, the comms officers reported their confidence that the *Axiom* was not under any immediate threat. Recker reduced the warship's speed and Captain Jir-Lazan did likewise with the *Aktrivisar*.

"Scan the planet," said Recker. "Tell me if we're in the right place."

He spoke the words, not expecting an immediate answer.

"Crap," said Burner. "Look at this."

An enhanced sensor feed of Qul appeared on the centre section of the bulkhead screen. Once again, Recker was impressed by the detail, which wasn't perfect, but was enough for him to clearly see the pattern of imperfections on this side of Qul where the ice had been shattered by multiple collisions from massive objects.

"Impact craters," he said.

"Not only impact craters, sir," said Burner. "See these tiny specks in between and in the area around? I'm convinced they were made by a tenixite converter, except some of these ones are way bigger than anything we saw on Oldis."

"Way bigger?" said Eastwood. "That doesn't sound like a positive development."

"No, it doesn't," said Recker. "How many impact craters?"

"Thirty, maybe more. Some are overlapping and it's not easy to separate them."

Recker couldn't take his eyes off the screen. The planet had suffered enormous damage and he knew he was viewing the outcome of a large-scale confrontation.

"Daklan?" said Aston.

"Impossible to tell from here, Commander," said Larson.

"We're not going any closer," said Recker. "Not yet." He took a deep breath. "Get me Captain Jir-Lazan. We need to have a talk."

CHAPTER NINE

"WE EXTRACTED data from a tenixite converter one of our heavy lifters salvaged from a planet," said the Daklan, his words becoming easier to understand through repeated exposure. "The cylinder was not operational and had suffered both internal and external damage. Many of its arrays had been forcibly wiped clean, but not all. We located an accessible backup which was only partially erased."

"It sounds like you weren't expecting the internal damage," said Recker, getting side-tracked despite himself.

"We believe the cylinder was subjected to a raid by ground forces, as well as a warship attack."

"Meklon soldiers?"

"That is the conclusion we reached, though we found no sign of bodies."

"What did you find on this functioning backup array?"

"Encrypted files. We broke the encryption and discovered a list of coordinates, some of which we believed were

Lavorix installations and others which the Lavorix had categorised as belonging to their enemies."

"What made you send warships to Qul instead of one of the other locations?"

"Intelligence which I am not allowed to divulge."

Recker held in a sigh. "Yet here we are in the Lanak system, presumably because the Daklan thought something of greater significance was to be found here."

Jir-Lazan didn't respond at once and only a faint background hum indicated the comms channel was still open. "The Lavorix had assigned the target at Qul a higher priority than all the others," he said at last.

"Which is why you sent a whole fleet."

"Yes."

"How many, exactly?"

Again, a pause. "Forty, including two of our primary lifters."

"That's a serious amount of firepower to lose."

"It is."

"Did your fleet have any idea what it was looking for?"

"No."

Recker paced up and down on the bridge, trying to grasp the motives which had driven the actions of the Daklan war council. Jir-Lazan wasn't being obstructive, but he was clearly unable to speak openly.

"Why did your war council agree to such a limited response by means of our mission?" asked Recker. "They've only committed one ship. And why did they choose to collaborate with the HPA on this in particular?"

"I cannot speak for the war council, human."

"No, but you can speak for yourself."

"I imagine the war council did not wish to risk more than the *Aktrivisar*," said Jir-Lazan. "It is the only warship we believe is equipped to handle a core override. As for why they agreed an HPA warship could accompany my desolator, that is something I'm sure you can work out yourself."

As it happened, Recker did have a good idea – he suspected the Daklan were so worried about the Lavorix that they were willing to take a gamble on working with the HPA. That meant they were considering a formal ceasefire and this mission would likely have never happened if it weren't for the Daklan's recent losses here at Qul. Assuming those forty spaceships really were lost and, at the moment, it seemed like a safe bet to say that they were.

He asked the big question.

"I am wondering what action you have been instructed to take should this mission stumble upon a weapon or artifact that your war council would prefer to keep for itself."

Jir-Lazan laughed and Recker had no idea if it was genuine or an act. He suspected the former. "Our two species have fought for many years, human, yet you know so little about us."

"I disagree."

"Then you know that the Daklan have no need for subterfuge. When a situation calls for war, we will fight. When it is time for peace, we will settle. There will never be a time when we talk peace while planning for war."

"Your war council has learned enough about the Lavorix to make them believe they are the greater enemy."

"Perhaps the Meklon also, though we suspect they are either extinct or on the brink of it."

Recker had no way to be sure if Jir-Lazan was telling the truth, yet his intuition made him think the Daklan was on the level.

"What happened to the strategy of neutralising the HPA quickly so that the Daklan could focus entirely on the Lavorix?"

"I am not party to such high-level discussions. For the HPA, the reality is that our attacks have stopped. That knowledge should be enough."

"Perhaps." Recker felt somehow invigorated by the words of the Daklan, but it was time to move things along. "What does your sensor team make of the surface cratering on Qul, Captain Jir-Lazan?"

"The same thing your sensor team makes of it. Warships have recently crashed into the surface. From this distance, we are unable to identify the wreckage."

"We have found cylindrical holes, consistent with those made by a tenixite converter, except these ones are much bigger."

"Yes, my comms team are now searching for another cylinder."

"You said your fleet came looking for a Meklon weapon or installation."

"Does it seem so unusual that both sides in this faraway conflict would be equipped with equivalent technology?"

"The Meklon use their Fracture weapon to achieve the same ends as the depletion burst. The effects are not identical."

"We have many unknowns, Captain Recker. If you are right, these cylindrical holes on Qul suggest that the Lavorix have been here before and may yet retain a presence."

"Something took out your forty ships. Perhaps the wreckage on the planet's surface comes from different sources. If so, we will find clues."

"Yes, that is a possibility. We must continue scanning."

"I recommend we maintain our current distance."

"I agree, though my patience is thin."

"This is not a time for risks."

"We will see."

The channel went dead and Recker gritted his teeth. Everything had been going well until the very end of the conversation and now he was concerned that Jir-Lazan might not be prepared for the slow and steady approach.

"Keep scanning," he ordered. "Find something before our ally decides it's time to load up the missile clusters."

A few minutes later, Lieutenant Larson spotted something that provided a clue as to recent events at Qul.

"I've detected an object, sir," she said. "Approximate mass, twelve billion tons, and coasting at fifty-one klicks per second. It'll pass by within eight hundred klicks of our current position."

"What kind of object?" said Recker sharply. "Get it up on the screen."

The object was debris from a spaceship and when Recker squinted, he thought he noticed similarities with the stern of a Daklan annihilator. It was difficult to be certain because the armour plates of this section had suffered an intense missile bombardment, leaving hardly any part of the surface untouched.

"No open receptors," said Larson. "I doubt there's anyone onboard that's alive, even if the comms hardware was functioning."

"Captain Jir-Lazan confirms it's Daklan in origin, sir," said Burner. "I've reverse-plotted the trajectory of the debris and its point of origin was Qul, or more likely somewhere above the planet."

"This confirms a recent engagement," said Recker. He watched the slowly tumbling wreckage for another few seconds and then ordered Burner and Larson to re-focus on Qul.

Bit-by-bit, a picture emerged. When – at Lieutenant Burner's request – Recker held the *Axiom* stationary relative to the rotation of Qul, some the larger pieces of surface debris became visible to the sensors.

"Not much of the wreckage originated from Daklan warships," said Burner. "The rest of it must be Lavorix or Meklon. Take your pick which one it is."

"I'll choose Lavorix," said Recker, adding things up in his head. "The Daklan came here looking for a Meklon target which the Lavorix had classified as high priority. What the Daklan found was a bunch of warships waiting for them. They fought and this is the outcome."

"Which leaves several questions unanswered," said Aston. "Namely, did the Daklan fleet destroy all of the Lavorix warships and secondly, what happened to the Meklon target that got everyone interested in the first place?"

"And since the Daklan seemed to be on top, where is their fleet?" said Eastwood.

Recker didn't want to guess and he requested a channel to Jir-Lazan. The Daklan had similar questions regarding the recent engagement but was no more successful in producing answers.

"It seems increasingly unlikely that any of the fleet survived," said Jir-Lazan, his voice heavy. "My sensor officers believe they have identified fragments of between five and eight of our warships on the surface of Qul."

"That leaves plenty still missing."

"Indeed, but those ships have neither returned home, nor contacted the *Aktrivisar*. Therefore I must assume they are lost."

"What do you propose?" asked Recker.

"I cannot leave without learning more."

"I feel the same. It's just figuring out how to do it without getting blown to pieces. Do you believe the Meklon artifact will be hostile to us?"

"If it is a weapon, we would be foolish to imagine otherwise."

"I agree." Recker scratched absently at the stubble he'd forgotten to shave before coming on shift. "We should approach to thirty million klicks and resume scanning."

"Yes – let us do so immediately."

Recker cut the channel and took the controls. Following a brief period of hard acceleration, he allowed the *Axiom* to coast through the vacuum.

"This is the second time we've found the Lavorix lying in wait at a Meklon facility," said Eastwood.

"And twice the Daklan have been caught out," said Burner with no note of satisfaction.

"The Lavorix have already won their war," said Recker. "At least that's what the Daklan believe and that's what our own evidence suggests. This is the cleaning up operation."

"No quarter," said Aston.

"Doesn't seem like it."

Thinking about the Lavorix's ruthless pursuit of their last few enemies made Recker even more worried. He thought it inevitable that the HPA would eventually, and without any desire, find itself embroiled in a new war. At Lustre, the Daklan's actions had gone a long way to proving they weren't interested in mass slaughter. When it came to the Lavorix, Recker had already seen their methods in the destruction of Fortune. The Daklan had fared no better.

Having settled himself for an extended time on the sub-light engines, Recker was interrupted by a frantic wave from Lieutenant Burner.

"Sir, we've received a written comms message. You need to read it - I'll send it to your screen."

A line of glowing text appeared on the leftmost of Recker's console screens.

Excon-1> Unknown warship, this is Meklon Station Excon-1. Please identify.

Recker twisted in his seat. "Has the *Aktrivisar* received the same message?"

"Yes, sir," said Burner.

"Can I send a response from my console?"

"Yes, sir. I'll transmit it for you."

Recker thought quickly and then typed, his fingers racing across the keys.

Axiom> Meklon Station Excon-1, this is HPA warship Axiom. We have no hostile intent.

"Transmitted," said Burner.

The next response came quickly.

Excon-1> Your hostile intent is unproven. You are not welcome here. Please depart immediately.

Recker swore under his breath. He could repeat what he'd already typed with some extra feeling, but he doubted a computer would suddenly believe him just because he added a pinkie promise. An idea sprang into his head.

Axiom> I am Captain Carl Recker, commanding officer of the terminator class warship: Vengeance.

Excon-1> Acknowledged. Security tier increased. Welcome, Captain Recker. Please transmit biological profile data to complete authorisation process.

"Damn!" Recker thumped his fist on the console.

"Can't we do what it asks, sir?" asked Larson. "The *Axiom* has got biological identification markers for everyone in the HPA military stored in its databanks."

Recker swore again. "It's not the same thing, Lieutenant. The *Vengeance* stored its biological profile data in an encrypted array that we haven't dared try to crack open in case it somehow screws up my ability to operate the warship."

"We could send what we have anyway? Maybe it'll be enough to link you to the *Vengeance*."

"No," said Recker firmly. "More likely the mismatch in how the data is arranged will make the Excon-1 station think we're trying to gain access by deception. At that moment, things will turn nasty - most likely for us."

Recker typed again.

Axiom> I am unable to transmit biological identification markers. Request permission for re-scan.

Excon-1> Permission for re-scan granted. Be aware that hostile action against this station will not be tolerated. Be aware that Lavorix warships are in the vicinity. Be aware that this communication link is corrupted. Be aware that the Lavorix may have determined your location from the vector of the transmission. Recommend you prepare for engagement. Recommend you dock for biological re-scan. Recommend you be aware of imminent arrival of Lavorix Galactar. Recommend you...

The stream of incoming text ended and Recker yelled for Burner to find out what had gone wrong.

"The link got cut from the far end, sir. I can't tell you any more than that."

"Shit! Pass on the details to Jir-Lazan. The Lavorix are coming for us."

"Shouldn't we get the hell away?" said Aston.

It was the right course of action, given the complete lack of information regarding the numbers and capabilities of the enemy warships. Jir-Lazan agreed, though his intention wasn't necessarily to avoid an engagement.

"We must assume the Lavorix are many millions of kilometres from our position and will therefore require several minutes to load up their ternium drives. We should fly half a million kilometres from here on our sub-lights. That will leave us well-placed to surprise the arriving enemy while they scan for our position."

Recker knew that at some point, he would have to fight and this seemed like as good a time as any to test the waters. "Agreed – half a million klicks it is. If we're outgunned, we withdraw."

"Yes. Whatever you may think, I have no desire to lose the *Aktrivisar* so early in the mission, Captain Recker."

The decision was made and Recker took the controls, intending to pilot the *Axiom* to the location which Burner put up on the tactical screen.

"Crap!" shouted Eastwood. "I've detected a combined particle wave, incoming at fifty thousand klicks! I don't recognize the type, which likely means we've got Lavorix warships inbound. They'll be here any second!"

"How?" said Aston.

Recker guessed the answer. The *Vengeance* could execute an instant, short duration lightspeed jump and it appeared the Lavorix could do likewise. While his comms team spoke to the *Aktrivisar*, Recker prepared for combat.

CHAPTER TEN

RECKER AIMED the *Axiom* directly for the centre of the particle wave. The propulsion growled and the bridge walls creaked with the strain of acceleration.

"As soon as the Lavorix appear, give them everything, Commander," he said.

"Yes, sir."

Dozens of green dots – missiles from the *Aktrivisar* - appeared on the tactical and sped past the *Axiom* towards the ternium cloud. Without a target lock, Captain Jir-Lazan was relying on good fortune to achieve a few successful detonations.

"Hold," Recker said, not wanting to take the same chance himself.

"Twenty second travel time on those missiles," said Aston.

For short lightspeed transits, the ternium waves didn't usually last long. Four Lavorix warships appeared in local space, stationary and within five hundred kilometres of each other. Burner got a sensor lock and Recker glanced at the feed.

The Lavorix warships were identical types – square-nosed, long bodied and with stubby wings that were fitted with huge turrets and likely housed missile clusters as well. Each craft was about the same length as the *Aktrivisar*, but with additional bulk suggesting they had a greater mass. Not one was undamaged – their armour plates were pocked and cratered.

"That fourth one looks like it might fall apart," said Aston.

"Lightspeed missile strike," said Recker.

A vast, ragged hole about four hundred metres in diameter left the rear section of the fourth Lavorix ship in a terrible state and its facing gauss turret was completely missing along with most of the portside wing. Not only that, numerous smaller missile craters indicated that the craft had survived its previous engagement by the skin of its teeth.

Without delay, the four enemy craft accelerated ferociously on diverging courses and Recker saw pieces of debris rip away from the hull of the most damaged warship.

"Fire!" he said.

"Forward Hellburners one and two locked and launched. Forward and upper Ilstrom clusters one through four launched."

Sound filled the bridge – engines and the detonations of missile propulsions. Recker banked hard, to bring the *Axiom*'s rear launchers to bear and the creaking of the walls became a groaning and pinging of flexing alloy. From the corner of his eye, he saw the *Aktrivisar* also banking as it gathered speed.

"Set the Railers on auto and aim them at that fourth Lavorix ship, Commander."

"Yes, sir. Railers targeting."

"Switch back to missile track and destroy the moment you detect a launch."

Recker prepared himself for the cacophony. Many metres separated the bridge from the Railer turrets, but the sound waves swept through in a roar interspersed with a heavier bang-bang-bang that made him think of explosives, rather than metal slugs being hurled from a barrel. Such was the brutality that it seemed to Recker as though the air pressure in the bridge increased and he experienced a droning, buzzing sound at the extremes of hearing.

On the bulkhead feed, streaks of white lanced into space, connecting with the damaged enemy warship. It accelerated with noticeably less urgency than the other three and the *Axiom*'s multiple Railers pounded its armour. A moment after the Railer fusillade started, four much larger projectiles sped across the feed with such velocity that they left trails like white-hot meteorites behind them.

"Terrus," said Aston.

The Terrus projectiles tore into the most damaged Lavorix warship, smashing away huge sections of the already shattered armour.

"That's got to be enough," said Eastwood.

The enemy warship's acceleration ended and it started coasting, though Recker didn't think it was entirely out of action. He checked the tactical and counted twenty Ilstroms locked on the stricken vessel. That would have to be enough.

Recovering from the short period of surprise, the Lavorix warships unloaded missiles and countermeasures. Recker was waiting for the gauss slugs and he threw the *Axiom* around, hoping it would be enough to turn a direct hit into a glancing blow.

The closest enemy ship fired its gauss cannon. Given the angle, it could only discharge from its portside wing and the projectile skimmed the *Axiom*'s upper armour. A moment later, a second projectile struck the *Axiom* a crunching blow topside, not far from one of the sensor arrays. Recker caught a glimpse of crumpling armour and a trace of heat.

"Minor damage, sir," said Fraser.

A third enemy slug hit the *Axiom* a reverberating blow. Recker didn't see the impact and tried to ignore the distraction as he piloted the ship in a series of increasingly erratic turns.

"Hellburners on boost," said Aston. "The *Aktrivisar*'s launched another wave of missiles."

The Hellburner missiles were capable of a short-duration final approach burn, designed to help them evade countermeasures and to give their armour-piercing warheads some extra punch. Twin plasma explosions erupted on the flank of one Lavorix warship, engulfing a large section of its hull in flames.

At the same time, ten or twelve Ilstroms crashed into the most severely damaged of the four enemy craft. Pieces of wreckage flew everywhere and the spaceship broke in two, splitting where the Daklan lightspeed missile had exploded. A second later, twin Terrus impacts and a wave of Feilars finished the job, turning the Lavorix warship into eighteen billion tons of dispersing wreckage.

Nobody had time to celebrate. The surrounding area of space was filled with missiles flying in both directions. Multiple tracers lanced through space, coming from both the *Aktrivisar*'s Graler turrets and the *Axiom*'s Railers. Spheres of white flashed from the Daklan pulse-shock countermeasures. Aston released a wave of disruptor drones and they glittered like sunlight on a pure ocean.

Fifty thousand kilometres away, the Lavorix ships become surrounded in what appeared to be an intricate spiderweb of white and blue lines, which formed a gradually expanding sphere. Ilstrom, Hellburner and Feilar missiles entered the web and were destroyed in a series of tiny explosions, each one leaving a gap in the Lavorix countermeasures.

"Ilstroms launched," said Aston. "Setting all Railers to track and destroy. Second wave of drones launched."

The enemy missiles entered the storm of drones and gauss slugs. Many were destroyed or fooled into detonating against the disruptor drones.

"Hellburners launched."

Not every enemy missile was taken out by the countermeasures. One struck the *Aktrivisar*, exploding in a huge burst. Another crashed into the *Axiom*'s stern, where it penetrated the outer layer of armour and detonated, ripping out a few million tons of alloy.

"Damage report," growled Recker.

"Checking," said Eastwood.

With missiles flying and the fighting at its most intense, Recker was in his element. Several of the *Axiom*'s Ilstroms struck the Lavorix craft which was still glowing hot from the Hellburner strikes only a short time before. A second enemy spaceship was lit up by a swarm of Feilars, along with four simultaneous Terrus impacts which inflicted colossal damage.

The decaying spiderwebs of the Lavorix countermeasures faded and were instantly renewed. Two Hellburners were destroyed by the cloud of tiny interceptor missiles and Recker cursed the timing.

"Ilstroms on their way."

"No hull breach from that missile, sir," said Eastwood. "We've got a hole in the outer plating and the inner plating is intact."

"Forward Hellburners one and two launched. Upper Ilstroms fired."

Recker banked again.

"Rear Ilstroms fired."

The *Axiom* suffered another gauss impact and two missiles evaded the disruptor drones and the Railers. Explosive sounds came like thunder and Recker clenched his teeth as a row of green lights on his console turned amber.

"Terrus strikes on the third enemy ship," said Aston. "The *Aktrivisar* took two shots in return."

At that moment, something entirely unexpected happened. A message appeared on his screen – directly this time, rather than being forwarded to his console by Lieutenant Burner.

Excon-1> Captain Carl Recker. Prepare your ship for core override.

Recker took the warning at face value. "Core override incoming!" he shouted, turning the *Axiom* so that it would drift away from the Lavorix ships, rather than coming closer to their weapons.

"Disruptor drones launched," said Aston immediately. "Rear Hellburners locked and away."

"I have advised the *Aktrivisar*," said Burner. "Comms now offline. Shit."

The core override came and the last thing Recker saw on the tactical was a few dozen enemy missiles heading towards both his ship and the *Aktrivisar*. Then, the screen stopped updating, leaving the green and red dots unmoving.

"I'm frozen out of my console," said Eastwood.

"Me too," said Aston.

"Sensors offline," said Burner. "The arrays are powering down."

"The enemy aren't messing about this time – they're going to shut everything down and blow the crap out of us. Be ready to give the obliterator core access to our onboard systems," said Recker.

Even as he spoke, the propulsion note and the pounding of the Railers stopped, bringing an overpowering silence to the bridge. In fury, Recker watched the rapid progress of the core override as it infiltrated the last few minor subsystems. In seconds, it was done.

The technical teams who'd installed the obliterator core had provided vague guidelines as to the best time to introduce its purge function. The truth was, they didn't really know and Recker couldn't blame them. However, he was the one in the firing line and he was acutely aware that a purge of the core override wasn't going to help much if his spaceship was subsequently destroyed by enemy warheads.

"Switch over the core," he ordered.

"Done," said Eastwood.

At first, nothing happened. Recker counted down the seconds in his head before the inbound enemy missiles would hit the *Axiom*. Even with the heavy cruiser travelling fast and in the opposite direction, the warheads would catch up in less than thirty seconds.

Something new appeared on one of Recker's displays. It was a graphical representation of the *Axiom*'s internal systems, with each one coloured in red and labelled *Core Override Status: 1*.

In the middle of the schematic, a green square was labelled *Obliterator Core*, and the accompanying utilisation gauge was stuck at 100%. Recker closed his eyes for a split second. These core units were something new. They could only run a reduced set of instructions, which made them currently unsuitable for main duty on a warship. But those instructions they *could* run were executed at many times the speed of any other processing unit in the HPA.

The rectangular block representing the life support system changed to green and the label updated. *Core Override Status: 0. Backup: Burst Restore: 80%.*

"It's happening!" said Lieutenant Eastwood excitedly.

"It's not happening quickly enough," said Aston. "Missiles impacting any second."

With the sensors shut down, Recker and the crew

were blind, but they didn't require sight to know when the missiles hit the armour. The sound of numerous overlapping blasts came to them and Recker held tightly to the controls, knowing the designers and the shipyard had gone to town with the extra plating, and hoping it would be enough.

"We had more incoming than that," he said in realization. "The *Aktrivisar* must be operational and their countermeasures took out some of the missiles which were coming our way."

The explosions died and Recker listened for the bone-deep rending which would indicate the *Axiom* was breaking up. It didn't come, though he didn't get his hopes up that the warship was about to emerge from this intact.

"Life support restore complete!" said Eastwood. "The core override is purged from the control system, the engines and the sensors! Restore in progress. Damn this obliterator unit is fast!"

"It's prioritising the most critical systems," said Recker. "If we pull through this, I might just have to find the team responsible and buy them all a drink."

He tried the controls. They shifted along their runners but without affecting the direction of the ship. A tremendous bang against the hull was followed by a second straight after.

"Gauss slugs," said Aston. "They haven't forgotten about us."

Suddenly, four red lights on the schematic diagram turned green.

Backup: Burst Restore: Complete.

Three more reds turned green. The propulsion kicked

back into life with a rumble and the controls started responding. Recker banked the *Axiom* steadily, listening for the sound of distressed alloy which would indicate it was breaking up. The hull groaned more than usual, though it didn't sound terminal. He banked harder and the *Axiom* held together. Another gauss projectile racketed off the armour.

"Weapons panel available!" said Aston. She stabbed one of the buttons with a straight finger. "Disruptor drones away."

The drones were the only autonomous countermeasures – everything else relied on the sensors for targeting.

"What's the status on the sensors?" asked Recker.

"Not yet online."

A faint glow on the bulkhead screen indicated the sensors were almost back. Three of the feeds came up, showing nothing but darkness. Recker kept an eye on the tactical to find out if the sensor arrays had started gathering target information yet. So far, nothing.

"Comms systems are back!" said Burner. "I'm relinking us to the battle network."

The news brought a surge of relief and hope to Recker. If the battle network was available, that meant the *Aktrivisar* was operational.

"Come on, folks. We're in with a chance," he muttered.

"Battle network data now available!"

"It's not accurate," said Recker, glancing at the tactical. "I'm not reading any positional data for the enemy warships."

"Sir, it's definitely..." said Burner. He interrupted himself. "I have Captain Jir-Lazan on the comms."

"Bring him through," Recker ordered, not letting up on the controls.

Daklan laughter came through the speakers. "Captain Recker, it is over. You have nothing to escape from!"

"We suffered a core override attack and lost our sensors. What happened?" Recker asked, not yet ready to believe the engagement was over.

"The *Aktrivisar* is a mighty warship, human. We destroyed the Lavorix and saved you from certain death!"

Recker pictured the situation at the time of the core override. One of the Lavorix spaceships was carrying two impressive Hellburner craters, along with a series of smaller ones. The other two opponents had taken moderate damage in addition to that which they'd suffered during their earlier engagement with the Daklan fleet.

The *Aktrivisar* was a powerful ship, but Recker didn't think it had the firepower to finish off three equivalent sized Lavorix opponents in less than two minutes.

"I've got a sensor lock on the *Aktrivisar* for you, sir," said Burner.

A feed of the desolator appeared. The heavy cruiser hadn't escaped unscathed – far from it. Large sections of its armour glowed and in other places was missing entirely. Heat-edged furrows and indentations spoke of multiple gauss projectile impacts.

Recker muted the comms channel. "Find the wreckage of the Lavorix ships and show me that as well."

"I've already got one for you, sir," said Larson.

The enemy warship was beyond repair, with a

burning hull and dozens of missile craters. As the drifting hull turned, Recker caught sight of a much larger opening in the warship's mid-section, where the alloy was still white with retained heat. He rubbed his chin as he realized what had caused so much damage.

Taking advantage of the muted comms, Lieutenant Eastwood gave a brief, preliminary damage report for the *Axiom*. "No hull breach, no major system failures. I'm sure we've lost much of the outer armour."

Recker nodded his acknowledgement and took the comms off mute. "Captain Jir-Lazan, I see the *Aktrivisar* is carrying lightspeed missiles. You have not mentioned this capability before, nor was it in the data you sent before our departure."

"I omitted it from the specification file," said Jir-Lazan, with something Recker hoped was genuine regret. "I was not permitted to disclose details of their presence, and to only deploy them when there was no other choice."

The outcome was starting to make sense. "You destroyed all three enemy spaceships with your lightspeed missiles?"

"I cannot claim full credit," admitted Jir-Lazan. "In truth, your final two Hellburners were enough to cripple one of the Lavorix vessels. The *Aktrivisar* launched two lightspeed missiles, which were enough to turn the tide." The Daklan's voice dropped conspiratorially. "Alas, the production expense of the missiles is such that my warship started this mission carrying only four in total."

"Now you have two."

"That is correct. Should I return to base having fired

them all, I will be required to deal with a mountain of paperwork to explain my profligacy."

"Does that mean you're holding onto them?"

"If necessary, I will empty every single one of the *Aktrivisar*'s magazines and then set fire to the debriefing paperwork!" Jir-Lazan laughed again. "Your warship looks like shit!"

"I'm sure it does," said Recker dryly. "Were you attacked by the core override?"

"No," said Jir-Lazan, just quickly enough that Recker couldn't be sure if the Daklan was trying to hide something. "Though I am not sure why the Lavorix targeted the weaker ship, when the *Aktrivisar* is clearly vastly more capable."

"I received another message from Excon-1," said Recker. "It warned me about the core override."

"That is a positive sign, is it not?" mused Jir-Lazan. "The Meklon facility might provide us with assistance or technical data."

"I'm sure it has been infiltrated," said Recker. "Without knowing exactly what Excon-1 is, I don't know what this infiltration might entail."

"I will attempt to make contact," said the Daklan. "Though last time it didn't respond after issuing an initial warning."

"The facility won't give you any information."

"Why is that, human?"

"Because it doesn't recognize you or your ship. It knows me as the commanding officer of the Meklon warship *Vengeance*."

"Very well. You will lead. Update me with your findings."

"Agreed."

Recker cut the channel. Before attempting contact with Excon-1, he had other matters to worry about. "I need additional status reports," he said. "Double check the core override is gone. Lieutenant Burner, show me what my warship looks like."

"Yes, sir."

The *Axiom*'s sensors were nearly flush with the hull, limiting their ability to provide a comprehensive view of the exterior. Following some adjustments, Burner put up a variety of feeds on the bulkhead.

"I think the Daklan was being kind when he said we look like shit," Eastwood remarked.

"Yeah," said Aston.

Seeing the indentations, the splayed metal, the missing plates, the patches of orange and red, and the cooling rivers of hardening alloy, made Recker wonder how the *Axiom* hadn't broken into pieces. He had to keep reminding himself that this was how the heavy cruiser was designed.

"It's only superficial," he said.

"Of course it is, sir," said Eastwood. "I'll put on my suit helmet and go outside with a laser welder. It shouldn't take me longer than a couple of hours to patch things up."

"What happened to respect for a superior officer, Lieutenant?" asked Recker.

"I have complete respect, sir."

"See that you don't forget." Recker flexed his fingers.

"I'm going to send another message to the Excon-1 station. I've got plenty of questions I need answering."

He poised his hands over the keyboard, only for a new message to appear and this one was even less welcome than the core override warning.

Excon-1> Captain Carl Recker. Prepare your ship for Fracture.

Recker stared at the writing and, in that instant, he didn't have the faintest idea what to do.

CHAPTER ELEVEN

RECKER'S single experience of the Fracture told him that it had an almost instant warm-up and discharge. He was certain the Lavorix had partly corrupted the Excon-1 onboard systems and was also sure they used the station's weaponry against the Daklan fleet. How the enemy had accomplished this, he had no idea.

Almost without conscious thought, he typed.

Axiom> Excon-1. Cancel Fracture discharge.

Seconds passed.

Excon-1> Fracture discharge cancelled.

Recker grasped this opportunity. He dropped his hands onto the controls and gave the *Axiom* maximum thrust. At the same time, he shouted orders to ensure that Jir-Lazan was made aware. Within seconds, the desolator was accelerating with similar urgency.

Excon-1> Captain Carl Recker. Prepare your ship for Fracture.

A darting motion of Recker's hand set the *Axiom* on autopilot, allowing him to type a response.

Axiom> Excon-1. Cancel Fracture discharge.

Excon-1> Fracture discharge cancelled.

Seconds passed.

Excon-1> Captain Carl Recker. Prepare your ship for Fracture.

"Shit!"

Recker typed out the cancellation command and added some additional text.

Axiom> Excon-1. Cancel Fracture discharge. Set Fracture to offline state.

Excon-1> Request denied. Security tier too low.

"How the hell are the Lavorix able to active the weapon?" asked Larson, watching the exchange.

"I don't know," said Recker grimly. "Either they pulled off the same trick as we did with the *Vengeance,* or they've got some hardware that allows them to activate the Excon-1 weaponry."

He typed quickly.

Axiom> Excon-1. Provide your location coordinates. Set Fracture two million kilometres off target.

Excon-1> Location coordinates provided. Second request denied. Security tier too low. Prepare your ship for Fracture.

Axiom> Excon-1. Cancel Fracture discharge.

Recker felt like he was back in the training simulator, in one of the thumbscrew scenarios designed to ratchet up the pressure to find out if the poor bastards in the pod would crack, fail, quit the military or any combination of the three.

The Excon-1 station recognized his authority to cancel a Fracture activation, but not do anything else. It said something about the Meklon that they'd made it easier to prevent their weapons discharging than to fire them in the first place.

"I've received coordinates for the Meklon station, sir," said Burner. "It's an orbital – currently geostationary five million klicks above Qul. You won't believe how big this thing is."

"It's about fifty klicks in length, with a fifteen-klick diameter," said Larson, just in case Recker needed it spelling out.

The station targeted the Fracture again and once more Recker issued the cancellation order. He knew they were running out of time – whoever was on the station ordering the Fracture activation, they'd be trying their damnedest to figure out a way to block the cancellation commands.

Axiom> Excon-1. End sensor tracking of Axiom warship. Place Fracture into maintenance mode. Elevate security tier: Captain Carl Recker. Recognize Lavorix security breach. Shut down data cores. Shut down Excon-1 station.

Every idea Recker could think of, he tried. Each one was met by the same warning that his security tier was too low. All the while, his crew offered suggestions, and Burner was getting his ear chewed by Jir-Lazan, who wanted to know why the situation wasn't resolved.

And then, a new idea came to Recker. If it worked, there'd be ramifications, though he'd far rather be alive and dealing with them than dead and not knowing.

Axiom> Excon-1. Please provide location coordinates of Fracture hardware.

Excon-1> *Location details provided.*

"Lieutenant Burner, send those coordinates to the *Aktrivisar* and request that Captain Jir-Lazan hits them with his last two lightspeed missiles."

"Yes, sir."

Recker cancelled another Fracture activation and kept his eyes glued to the screen for the next warning.

"Captain Jir-Lazan is concerned that his warship might become the target for an overwhelming response from the Excon-1 station, sir."

It was a definite concern and one which Recker had not considered given how many plates he had spinning.

Axiom> Excon-1. Your systems have been infiltrated by the Lavorix.

Excon-1> Yes. They have control of the Fracture. My protocols have also been corrupted. My AI module tie-ins are severed. I am no longer capable of acting upon evaluation of known data. Fallback rules implemented. I cannot elevate your security tier without biometric scanning. This channel is discovered. Switching to new channel.

Excon-1> New channel.

Axiom> What happens when Excon-1 is attacked?

Excon-1> A defence response is initiated.

Axiom> Is that response governed by the fallback rules?

Excon-1> No. The discharge of weaponry is governed by the AI module.

Axiom> Your AI module is disconnected.

Excon-1> That is correct.

Axiom> Does that mean you can't fire these other weapons?

Excon-1> Yes. Unless they are manually operated by the Lavorix infiltrators.

Axiom> Can they do so?

Excon-1> Insufficient data to confirm.

Axiom> We intend to destroy the Fracture weapon with missiles.

Excon-1> Good luck.

Recker blinked at the response and then shouted an order for Lieutenant Burner to relay. A few seconds later, he got the answer he wanted.

"Captain Jir-Lazan has agreed to fire his last two lightspeed missiles. Apparently, he's going to send you the paperwork."

"Tell him I'll hit it with a plasma missile," Recker smiled. Another Fracture warning appeared on his screen. His smile vanished and he sent the cancellation command.

The Daklan didn't earn their reputation of being competent enemies by waiting around meekly for an invitation to unload copious quantities of explosive weaponry. Hardly ten seconds after Jir-Lazan had agreed to launch the *Aktrivisar*'s missiles than the first one was ejected from its launch hatch beneath the desolator.

Burner had a sensor array focused on the place and Recker got his first good look at a Daklan lightspeed missile. It was little more than an enormous grey cylinder, which appeared, boosted ahead of the *Aktrivisar* on a standard propulsion and then vanished into lightspeed, leaving a small ternium cloud as evidence of its transition.

Ten seconds after the first missile disappeared, a second launched from the same place. Soon, it too was gone into lightspeed.

"The *Aktrivisar* can fire them quicker than any other Daklan ship we've seen," said Recker. It was a concern, but one for another day.

He looked at Burner and Larson. "Any way we can confirm successful detonations?"

"As it happens, Captain Jir-Lazan's comms team have just advised me that both missiles hit their target," said Burner.

Axiom> Excon-1. Please confirm destruction of Fracture weapon.

Excon-1> Status report for Fracture weapon: disabled.

Axiom> Can the Lavorix reactivate the weapon?

Excon-1> This outcome has a low-low probability.

Recker suddenly remembered how the Excon-18 station at planet Vitran had brought the *Vengeance* in under direct control.

Axiom> Requesting permission for manual approach for biometric re-scanning.

Excon-1> Request denied. Security tier too low. At thirty million kilometres, the flight controller will take over. You will be brought into the upper dock for biometric re-scanning.

Recker didn't like it, but recognized he had no other choice.

Axiom> Request for Daklan warship Aktrivisar to also dock.

Excon-1> Request denied due to hostile action from Daklan warship Aktrivisar.

Axiom> Will the Lavorix infiltrators fire the Excon-1 station's other weaponry at the Axiom while we are brought in by the flight controller?

Excon-1> Negative. *The weaponry cannot target spaceships held by the flight controller.*

It was information which might have been useful to know before the desolator hit the Fracture weapon with two lightspeed missiles, though the *Axiom* was a long way from the thirty-million-kilometre activation range for the flight controller. Recker put it from his mind.

Axiom> Do protocols permit the Aktrivisar to be brought in by the flight controller, without docking at Excon-1?

Excon-1> Yes.

"Lieutenant Burner, relay the details to Captain Jir-Lazan," said Recker, looking up from his screen. "I want to know his opinion." He remembered something else and the memory brought with it a sudden shiver of fear.

Axiom> Excon-1. You warned about the imminent arrival of a Lavorix Galactar. Please provide details.

Excon-1> The Lavorix Galactar. The deciding force in this section of the conflict sphere. The probability model suggests that a threshold has been breached as a result of recent warship activity in the Lanak system. The Galactar may investigate.

Axiom> What capabilities does the Galactar possess?

Excon-1> It is equipped with step-change technology. It is impervious to harm. It is impervious to Fracture. It is impervious to depletion burst. It destroys life.

Even the computer seemed to be getting emotional about the Galactar and Recker was already one hundred percent certain he didn't want to encounter this warship. He had a thought.

Axiom> The Meklon raided the tenixite converter network. Was this to aim a depletion burst at the Galactar?

Excon-1> Yes. The raid was successful. The depletion burst was not.

Recker sat back, thinking. He was gradually learning snippets from the Lavorix-Meklon war and he was fascinated.

"Sir, Captain Jir-Lazan wants to talk," said Burner.

"Bring him in – open channel."

The bridge speakers hummed. "I do not like this, Captain Recker," said Jir-Lazan, cutting to the chase. "What happens if the flight controller will not relinquish control of the *Aktrivisar*?"

"I believe it will – once you're close enough to the space station. Other than that, you must have command codes you can try. If all else fails, I guess your core override protection systems allow for a purge of the control systems. At which point, you'll have your ship back."

Jir-Lazan made a growling noise which left no room to misunderstand his opinion of the situation. "If you complete your biometric re-scanning, will you have access to the station's data repositories?"

"I'll have access to the files which the captain of a primary warship would be expected to access."

"That should be enough," said Jir-Lazan. "I am worried, human. This Galactar sounds like an opponent we should avoid."

"The *Axiom* has in-built systems to purge the navigational computer," said Recker. "And the shipyard has given my crew access to the physical tie-ins, which can be severed if needed. The enemy will gain nothing from this spaceship."

"The HPA has been as cautious as the Daklan," rumbled Jir-Lazan. "The *Aktrivisar*'s star charts can also be disabled. However, my concern is for the fleet which preceded us."

"I believe they had almost defeated the Lavorix and were destroyed by the Fracture before they could finish the job. There will be nothing left of them. Scans of the wreckage on the planet indicate the possibility something could be salvaged from the destroyed Daklan warships."

"It is possible, but from our own scans I do not think it likely," said Jir-Lazan. "It pains me to say it, but this is a time when the deaths of my fellows and the destruction of their warships is the most favourable outcome."

"Will you allow the flight controller to fly the *Aktrivisar*?" asked Recker.

"Yes, though with one condition. I will send a shuttle with my soldiers onto the *Axiom*. When you dock, they will assist with overcoming any Lavorix resistance. Once the re-scanning is complete, they will extract a second copy of the data from the space station's memory arrays."

It was a condition that Recker didn't much want to comply with. Under the circumstances, he understood that the Daklan wanted reassurances they were getting a fair share of the spoils and in the interests of the mission, he couldn't deny them.

"I agree," said Recker. "Fifteen of your soldiers and no more. And I expect absolute discipline while they are onboard my warship. Once we are inside Excon-1, my lead officer Sergeant Vance will command."

"My soldiers will not follow orders from a human."

"I can't accept two forces operating independently once we're inside the station."

"This may present a problem for us, Captain Recker." Jir-Lazan made another of his rumbling sounds, which Recker guessed indicated the Daklan was thinking. "I can compel them to accept orders from a senior officer. You will be required to disembark for re-scanning and your authorisation will be needed to access the Excon-1 data arrays. Captain Recker, you will command them."

"I accept," said Recker.

"We are working together, human! I will send a shuttle across within the next few minutes. Then, we will find out what the Meklon station offers."

"And escape before the Galactar shows up."

"That is imperative."

"Once we arrive at the station and the *Axiom* is in the bay, you should bombard the surface debris with missiles. Just to be sure."

"You are convinced this will not produce a hostile response from the space station?"

"Excon-1 can't fire its weapons, so yes I'm certain."

"Very well."

Recker cut the channel and exhaled loudly, while mentally reassuring himself he was doing the right thing. Time would tell.

He opened an internal comms channel to Sergeant Vance and let him in on the news.

CHAPTER TWELVE

THIRTY MINUTES LATER, the Daklan soldiers arrived and used one of the *Axiom*'s emergency docking hatches to enter the warship. Recker was there to greet them, along with Sergeant Vance and the rest of the *Axiom*'s soldiers – or at least those who could fit in the airlock-sized room at the end of the access passage. The others had fortified the nearby stairwell in case the Daklan proved untrustworthy, and Private Titus Enfield had rigged up a few remote-activated explosive surprises. Meanwhile, the bridge crew watched through the internal monitors, ready to switch on the anti-hijack miniguns dotted around the warship.

The first of the Daklan emerged from the access passage and straightened to a height well in excess of seven feet. Like most of his kind he was a broad-shouldered, muscular brute, and dressed in a bulky grey combat suit. This Daklan had thick, dark grey hair and piercing green eyes that almost seemed to glow with an inner light. His skin was red-brown and, like all Daklan, he had two small, upturned fangs which protruded between his lips and gave him the appearance of a demon, though perhaps without the savage cruelty. In one thick-fingered hand, he carried an angular helmet and in the other, a gauss cannon that Recker knew could put a hole through a thin sheet of warship-grade alloy, but which became much less effective over longer ranges.

"I'm Captain Recker," said Recker, striding forward confidently. He stopped in front of the Daklan and met the alien's gaze.

The Daklan stared back. This was the closest Recker had come to a living Daklan without gauss slugs skimming past his head, and it felt strange.

We need each other. Whatever happens later doesn't change the present.

"I am Sergeant Shadar. I am to obey your orders."

Shadar's voice was as rasping as Jir-Lazan's and when he spoke, a language module converted the words and sent the translation through the chin speaker in the helmet he carried at his side.

"There will be no trouble," said Recker. He glanced past Sergeant Shadar and saw the other Daklan waiting in the access tunnel.

"No trouble," Shadar confirmed. "On this mission, we act as one."

Recker introduced Sergeant Vance and Corporal Hendrix. Shadar nodded at each in turn and then beckoned out the first of his own squad.

"Itrol," he said.

The next came.

"Lumis."

The lack of space made these first minutes awkward, and Recker waved the nearest of his own soldiers away in order to make room. Any hope of controlled combat was gone, but this was a time for trust, not gunfire.

Shadar reeled off the names as the Daklan filed inside and the aliens headed deeper into the *Axiom*. Mostly they were armed with gauss rifles, but one carried a shoulder launcher, another a compact data-extractor and a third was laden with a brutal-looking repeater.

"Unvak, Litos, Ipanvir, Zivor, Reklin," said Shadar, pointing at each in turn.

The Daklan didn't return the greeting, only nodded in acknowledgement as their names were spoken.

"They have no other names?" asked Recker.

"None that you will hear, human."

The words weren't spoken insultingly – or Recker got no impression they were - and he didn't question the statement. If the Daklan preferred to keep part of their names secret, so be it.

"I have a warship to fly. Sergeant Vance will take you to the mess room. I don't anticipate you'll be onboard long enough that you'll require quarters." He didn't drop his gaze. "I will not tolerate any action which might break the peace. Is that understood?"

"That is understood," Shadar confirmed.

"I trust you've been briefed. I'll see you on Excon-1."

With that, Recker exited the airlock room and returned to the bridge. He felt no tension from his first meeting with the Daklan. In fact, he'd recognized the competence of the alien soldiers and that had allowed him to fall back into his old mantle of ground commander.

"Well?" said Aston when he took his seat.

"They're on our side for the moment."

Recker didn't need to say anything more. He got on the comms and arranged the next moves with Captain Jir-Lazan.

"It'll require more than two hours on the sub-light engines to reach the thirty-million klick range of the Excon-1 flight controller," he said. "I've contacted the station and advised that we will execute a lightspeed jump to one million kilometres."

"That is acceptable," said Jir-Lazan. "My officers have scanned the location of the space station and have been unable to learn anything. We believe it is equipped with sensor deflection technology."

"That's the conclusion reached by my own team," said Recker. "The Lavorix Interrogator was similarly protected."

"We are going in blind and I do not like it, any more than I like relinquishing the control of my warship."

"We're aiming for the prize, Captain Jir-Lazan. Both the Lavorix and the Meklon possess weapons technology we lack. Should their war come to us, I would prefer to fight as an equal."

"It seems we agree on many things, human. The desire to fight and survive is a trait of all sentient creatures."

With nothing further to say, Recker cut the channel and ordered Lieutenant Eastwood to create a lightspeed synch code for the two warships. Shortly after, the *Axiom*'s ternium drive started warming up and Recker drummed his fingers on the edge of his console. He glanced over at Aston – she looked cool and calm on the surface. A quick smile reassured him that she was ready for whatever was coming.

The timer counted down to zero and the two warships launched into the shortest of lightspeed journeys. Shaking off the resulting nausea, Recker threw the controls forward in case he'd somehow been tricked into arriving amongst previously undetected hostile warships. The controls didn't respond, though the propulsion grumbled and he could feel the acceleration.

"The flight controller has hold of us," he said.

"Captain Jir-Lazan's comms team confirm likewise," said Burner. "I'm still waiting on the sensor feeds."

The *Axiom*'s arrays came back all at once and Recker waited impatiently for Burner and Larson to finish their local area scans so that they could focus their efforts on the Meklon station.

"The *Aktrivisar* is ten klicks to port," said Larson. "It's mirroring our course and velocity."

"There's Qul," said Burner. "Still searching for Excon-1."

The facing side of the planet was a mess and the damage inflicted by impacting warship wreckage extended for thousands of kilometres. For so much debris to have landed, the engagement must have been close to the planet and Recker wished he'd been there to witness it, if only to learn something about the Lavorix spaceships and how they fought.

"No sign of Excon-1, sir," said Larson. "We're still

receiving location data, so we know where it is and we know it's massive."

"We just can't see it," said Recker.

"I'm trying some different lens filters, sir," said Burner. "I might be on to something."

"You haven't got long," said Recker, checking the velocity readout. "Ten minutes and we'll have arrived."

Three minutes later, Burner worked his magic on the sensors and he obtained a feed of Excon-1 which made the space station appear semi-transparent like it was an imprinted memory of something which had been here long before.

For a time, Recker stared at his destination. Excon-1 was a complex structure; four fifty-kilometre cylinders were connected to a central cylinder of equal length and diameter. Other modules were attached to these outer cylinders, all of them rectangular. Recker saw vast antennae arrays, and dozens of smaller modules which he suspected had been added over the years. The overall impression he got was that the Meklon had constructed a vast, impressive technological masterpiece and probably one which had played a central part in their war against the Lavorix.

However, the space station wasn't undamaged. Its outer surface had suffered colossal damage, from a variety of missile and energy weapon strikes. Parts of it had been melted in heat and then solidified into shapeless masses of alloy. Two of the main cylinders looked as if they might snap free at any moment and drift away into the infinite depths of space. On one of the outer rectangular structures, heat still glowed with a burning fury and Recker peered closely at the feed.

"That's where the lightspeed missiles hit," he said. "The first one pierced the armour and the second flew right through the hole."

It made Recker feel a peculiar sadness to stare at the reduction of this massive structure to a shadow of what it must have been. He doubted the Meklon would have been friends of the HPA, yet he couldn't help but feel empathy for the species capable of such wondrous feats as the construction of Excon-1 and the *Vengeance*. And it hadn't been enough to save them from defeat.

"Where are we expected to dock?" said Eastwood.

"This section," said Recker, pointing at an area two thirds up. Here, the central cylinder and the four surrounding ones were cased in additional housing which made that part of Excon-1 appear more like a square.

The flight controller banked the *Axiom*, clearly intending to bring the warship around to an opening that was currently out of view. On the portside feed, the *Aktrivisar* did likewise, while maintaining a constant distance of ten kilometres from the *Axiom*.

"You might want to check this out, sir," said Burner. "I'm magnifying part of the feed."

One of the arrays which was aimed at the midsection of Excon-1 zoomed to an irregular, darker patch on the shroud which encompassed the central cylinders. The angle wasn't perfect and at first Recker couldn't understand what he was looking at.

"A hole?" he asked.

"Yes and no, sir. I'll try an outline and enhance."

The feed cleared and then Recker knew. There *was* a hole in the side of Excon-1 – a massive hole. Not only that, the stern of the spaceship which had created it was still protruding a few hundred metres into the vacuum.

"An annihilator," he said.

"Yes, sir. What we're looking at is consistent with the shape and size of a Daklan battleship."

"Get me a channel to the *Aktrivisar*."

"Captain Jir-Lazan is already waiting."

Recker spoke first. "One of your annihilators crashed into Excon-1."

"By its markings, I know it to be the *Raxinal*," said Jir-Lazan. "It's not responding to comms requests."

"What's it doing there?" Recker guessed the answer to his own question. "Core override at the wrong time."

"The fleet which came here would have no defence against that weapon, Captain Recker."

"Does this change anything?" asked Recker. He knew the answer already and dropped to his seat, with his eyes on the sensor feed. The flight controller was slowing the *Axiom* and bringing it in a wider arc towards an out-of-sight docking place. Recker typed.

Axiom> Is there anything you can do to remove the core override from the battleship which is embedded in your structure?

Excon-1> Negative. The warship's internal systems were completely purged. I could inject the Meklon equivalent control systems, but the results would not be positive.

Axiom> Is the core override still active within the annihilator?

Excon-1> The core override is gone.

Axiom> Did it breach the warship's encrypted data arrays?

Excon-1> Impossible to determine.

It was a question which Recker desperately wanted answering, but since the Meklon station didn't know, he wasn't going to spend time thinking about it. If the core override was gone from the annihilator, that meant the Lavorix had either plundered the battleship's navigational system or they hadn't, with no way to alter the outcome. He typed again.

Axiom> Did the warship's crew escape?

Excon-1> Negative. The core override shut down the life support system and subjected the occupants to a sustained burst of acceleration.

Axiom> And then crashed the battleship into the Excon-1 station.

Excon-1> The Meklon war against the Lavorix is almost concluded. The enemies of my species have little further use for the Excon-1 facility.

Axiom> They'll destroy Excon-1?

Excon-1> Eventually.

Recker was drawn from the conversation by Lieutenant Burner.

"There's the bay, sir. About five thousand metres above the annihilator."

A pair of immense, rectangular doors came into sight and they were sliding open slowly and laboriously. Both doors had suffered numerous missile strikes and the walls all around were similarly cratered. Nevertheless, the doors drew apart, revealing an internal space large enough to accommodate several warships of the *Axiom*'s size. The bay was unlit like the exterior, but the *Axiom*'s sensors were capable enough to determine that it was empty.

"The doors have stopped," said Burner. "They must have jammed or lost power."

"Plenty of room to get through," said Aston. "Eleven hundred meters."

"The *Aktrivisar* is now stationary," said Larson. "I'm speaking to their comms team."

Recker drummed his fingers again and watched the forward sensor feed as the flight controller flew the warship towards the Excon-1 main bay. The inner walls were partially hidden by the doors and he wasn't sure where the *Axiom* would end up.

"Captain Jir-Lazan reports he has regained control of the *Aktrivisar*," said Larson, relief evident in her voice. "He has received no communication from Excon-1 and will commence bombardment of the surface as soon as we are docked."

"What's the plan, sir?" said Aston.

"I'll lead both squads off the *Axiom*," he said.

"What about the biometric re-scanning?"

"Excon-1 said it would bring us into the bay so the process could be completed." Recker suddenly wondered if he should have given the matter more thought. "I assumed it would happen once I disembarked. If the process happens twenty klicks below us, we're screwed unless this station is fitted with a long airlift."

"You could wait here and see what happens. The station might offer guidance once we're docked."

"I'll just ask it instead," said Recker.

Axiom> Excon-1 - where does the biometric re-scan take place?

Excon-1> The nearest security station is within eight hundred metres of the docking bay exit. Be warned, Lavorix infiltrators are present in the area.

Axiom> Numbers?

Excon-1> 653.

"Damn," said Recker.

Given the size of the space station, the Lavorix may well be spread out, or indeed nowhere near the place Recker needed to go. Somehow, he didn't think it likely.

Axiom> Please provide directions to the security station.

Excon-1> I have placed the map data in your warship's databanks.

Time was running out and Recker broke off the conversation. He called up a list of most recent files and downloaded a copy of the Excon-1 map data. When he loaded it onto his screen, he found what he expected – an intricate, multi-level map of a structure that contained hundreds of levels, along with thousands of corridors and internal spaces.

This upper docking bay was the largest of the internal spaces and Excon-1 had highlighted the route to the security station in red. Recker zoomed the map and determined that the forward boarding ramp was likely to provide the closest exit when the *Axiom* finally docked.

He picked up his suit helmet and grabbed the rifle he'd propped against his console a few minutes ago. The moment the seals around his neck tightened, he accessed the squad open channel.

"Sergeant Vance, head for the forward boarding ramp."

"What about the Daklan, sir?"

"They aren't in the same channel?"

"No, sir. They refused."

In no mood for any further delay, Recker ordered his suit comms to hunt for receptors. He located a single green light and requested a connection. A moment later, he was speaking to Sergeant Shadar and Recker told the alien in no uncertain terms what he expected. Shortly after, the Daklan soldiers joined the squad comms and Recker counted a total of thirty soldiers at his command.

He took one last look around the bridge and then handed over to Commander Aston. The flight controller had guided the *Axiom* between the two half-open doors and it wouldn't be long before the warship touched down.

"Take care, sir," said Aston.

Recker nodded, fully aware of how important his life was since he was the only person in the HPA capable of accessing the Meklon hardware. He ran for the forward boarding ramp as quickly as the confines of the passages allowed. Being last to arrive, Recker found the passage leading to the airlock crammed with hulking Daklan and smaller humans.

No sooner had he joined the back of the pack than Recker felt the *Axiom* touch down and the propulsion note dropped to little more than a whisper.

He got on the open channel. "I've made the map data available to every one of you. We're following the red line to the security station, where I'll have my biometric data re-scanned. Once that's done, we're going to extract whatever data our species might use against the Lavorix. Anything moves, assume it's hostile and kill the bastard. No quarter. We've got 653 enemies arrayed against us and that means we have to fight with our brains."

"Yes, sir," said Vance.

"We will succeed," growled Shadar.

"Does anyone know what these Lavorix look like?" said Private Drawl, trying hard not to sound nervous.

"I hear their asses look exactly like your face, Drawl," said Private Redman, bursting into laughter at his own joke. "So we know they're ugly."

"Enough!" shouted Recker. "Any more of that crap and you'll be dealing with me. Is that understood?"

"Yes, sir."

"Good. We've got two mean-as-hell squads of soldiers here and this is a chance to start getting even for what happened to our planets. In case you hadn't heard, we're running against the clock. The Lavorix have something called a Galactar inbound. A game changer. When it breaks out of lightspeed, I want to be six hours in the opposite direction and that means we can't piss about."

Nobody asked questions and the air had a sudden electric quality to it, like the soldiers of both species understood what was coming and were eager to get on with the mission.

"First man, lower the boarding ramp," shouted Recker.

"I've got it, sir," said Vance.

The boarding ramp gears clunked and the motors whined. Air was sucked past Recker and into the vacuum of the bay. He glanced over his shoulder to reassure himself the *Axiom*'s inner door twenty metres behind was closed.

And then, he was moving, following the burly figure of Private Hunter Gantry with his MG-12 repeater, towards the top step of the ramp. Moments later, Recker was on his way to the bay floor, his mind turning fast and conjuring up endless possibilities for the path ahead.

CHAPTER THIRTEEN

THE DARKNESS of the bay was absolute and the temperature was far enough below zero that Recker felt the chill through his suit's insulation. On another occasion, he might have worried about concealed threats to his soldiers. Not now – he knew the *Axiom*'s crew would be watching and the darkness was no impediment to the warship's sensors.

His night vision enhancement activated automatically, lending a tinge of sickly green to everything. Turning 360-degrees, Recker tried to make sense of his surroundings. The flight controller had landed the *Axiom* near to the bay's left-hand wall, while the right-hand wall was a long way in the distance. Peering through the heavy cruiser's landing legs, Recker could see that the bay doors were still open and he guessed their motors had failed.

Under guidance from Sergeants Vance and Shadar, the soldiers had taken positions of cover amongst the warship's legs.

"Move!" Recker ordered. "The *Axiom* is watching out for us - head for the bay exit."

The soldiers got going without hesitation, darting from cover to cover like it was a habit they couldn't break. Without air to carry the sound, everything was done in silence, except for the occasional word on the comms. As he passed one of the retractable landing legs, Recker planted his palm against the alloy and looked up to where it vanished high overhead into its socket. The extent of the damage from the earlier engagement was visible even from this vantage, and splayed pieces of metal jutted outward like fingers of a taloned hand.

Once the soldiers emerged from the warship's underside, they broke into a fast-paced jog, heading for the chosen exit. The night vision enhancement wasn't perfect and Recker struggled to identify the precise location of the door. The best he could make out was a lighter patch on the wall, about eight hundred metres ahead.

With the life support system on Excon-1 maintaining a gravity level roughly comparable to that on Earth and Lustre, Recker found it easy to pace himself and he arrived at the exit with his heart rate only moderately elevated. He counted himself lucky that he wasn't carrying a data extractor, a medical box or Gantry's MG-12, but those soldiers with a heavier loadout hadn't dropped back.

"This is the way," said Recker.

The exit door was huge and clearly designed for loading vehicles to pass through. At one side, the access panel showed a tiny red light.

"Sergeant Vance, you give it a try," said Recker. "This

mission will be off to a bad start if I have to open every single door."

"Yes, sir," said Vance. He reached out and touched the panel.

For long moments, the light remained red. Then, it switched to green, which made Recker believe a far airlock door had closed automatically to isolate the rest of the interior. The metre-thick outer door slid silently into a left-hand recess, to reveal a fifty-metre passage leading to another – closed - door. It was what Recker had expected.

"Sergeant Vance, go."

Beckoning six soldiers to come with him, Vance sprinted along the corridor and crouched at the next panel, which was also red.

"I don't like it, but the whole squad should enter this airlock, sir," said Vance. "It's better than getting separated."

Recker gave the order and the other twenty-three soldiers hurried into the passage. The moment he was satisfied with their positions, he joined Vance and signalled for him to open the inner airlock. In the same eerie silence as before, the outer door closed and Recker lifted his gauss rifle as he waited for the inner door to open.

When it happened, he found himself looking into an expansive storage area, resembling a warehouse in size and contents. Alloy crates of many different shapes and sizes were stacked in an orderly fashion, towering to the ceiling a hundred metres overhead. When Recker stared upwards, he spotted an intricate pattern of grooves, along with blocky gravity cranes which likely did the heavy lifting.

An aisle ran straight through the middle of the storage area and joined a tunnel which continued deeper into Excon-1. On the left-hand side, an enormous, utilitarian flatbed was parked. The vehicle floated a metre above the smooth floor, indicating it was still operational.

Bodies lay everywhere – in the main aisle, along the side routes and in front of the doorway. They were bipeds and wore combat suits of a colour Recker couldn't easily determine with his night sight active. The way they'd fallen made him think their life switches had been turned off and they'd simply dropped to the ground.

The storage area was pressurized, allowing the distressed sounds of tortured metal to carry through the air. Screeches, groans and distant booming noises made it difficult to hear anything else, and Recker abandoned hope that he might hear the approach of the enemy.

"As dead as the grave," said Sergeant Shadar.

Recker glanced at the Daklan officer, unsure if he was referring to the corpses or the lack of movement. The alien's face was hidden by the side of his helmet, making it hard to guess what he was thinking.

"Let's watch and wait," said Recker. Sensing the already tense soldiers nearby becoming edgy at the delay, he warned them to be calm. "This is nothing you haven't seen before," he said.

"These look like the same type of aliens we found in the cylinder on Oldis," said Vance.

"I remember," said Recker, casting his mind back to the pile of burned corpses in the tenixite converter. At the time, he'd thought they were part of the cylinder's crew, but subsequent discoveries made him think they may have been Meklon attackers. "No sign of injuries on these ones."

"None that I can see," Vance confirmed.

"Another mystery."

"This place is going to be full of them, sir."

Recker double-checked the map - the main corridor diverged from his intended destination and eventually ended up at another, even larger space than this storage bay.

"We should find another passage over that way," said Recker, pointing towards the right-hand corner of the bay. "After that, it's another two hundred metres to the security station." He cursed. "A thousand soldiers could be hiding in this warehouse and we wouldn't hear them."

"And they won't hear us either, Captain Recker," said Sergeant Shadar.

"In which case, we'll surprise the bastards and shoot them first," Recker replied. He waved the squads forward. "Move in."

A stack of much smaller crates offered cover ahead and to the right of the aisle. Sergeant Vance, along with five members of his squad broke free from the wall and sprinted towards them.

"Clear," said Vance.

Recker rose from his half-crouch, ready to join them, when he spotted movement about three hundred metres closer to the main exit tunnel. A shape emerged from behind a pile of crates, gangly and moving with an erratic gait. At first, Recker thought he was looking at more than one creature and then he realized it was, in fact, something with more than four limbs.

The squad was exposed in the corridor, leaving him with no option. Muscle memory took over and Recker aimed and fired his gauss rifle in one easy movement. The gun coils whined softly and the barrel thudded into his shoulder. He heard two other gauss discharges, along with the louder crack of a Daklan gun. In a sprawl of flailing limbs, the target fell in a heap.

"What the hell was that?" asked Private Gail Baylor.

"What do you think it was?" asked Corporal Givens, his voice dripping sarcasm.

"Quiet!" said Recker.

He gave a couple of brief orders and allowed the squad officers to put them into operation. Soldiers sprinted into the storage area, while Recker and three others watched, unmoving. No other aliens appeared and no matter how hard he tried to make sense of the distant corpse, he couldn't figure out its exact form. A metre-long, metallic shape on the floor nearby indicated it had been armed, but otherwise, the creature was no more than a heap of flesh.

"Think it got out a warning?" asked Private Wayland Steigers.

"I don't know," said Recker. "It didn't have time to shout, but its suit might have issued an automatic life signs warning." He tapped Steigers on the shoulder. "Time to move."

The last few soldiers in the airlock darted across to the smaller crates ahead. Sergeant Vance had already led the rest of the squad across another, narrower aisle and was about eighty metres closer to the intended exit. The most efficient route was self-evident and the Daklan ran with the human soldiers.

Recker dashed over the second aisle, which continued to the opposite wall. Stacks of other crates loomed high, making him feel like an insect in a pantry. A dead alien lay at his feet and he stopped only briefly to examine it, finding a grey-skinned, vaguely human face behind a clear visor, its features twisted in pre-death agony and its mouth locked open in a silent scream.

No injuries. What the hell caused this?

Comms discipline was immaculate and the soldiers made rapid progress, without encountering any more living aliens. Even so, Recker's internal alarm bells were ringing and with each passing moment their clamour become louder.

The storage area was logically arranged in a grid, so progress was not stalled by unexpected dead ends. With his breathing deepened from the run, Recker arrived at his chosen exit, the size of which indicated it was intended for use by foot personnel. The crates here didn't reach the wall, meaning the door was exposed to gunfire across the full width of the bay, so he didn't delay. A thump of his palm on the access panel got the door open.

"Clear," growled Sergeant Shadar, his gauss cannon aimed into the space beyond.

Recker heard a sound he recognized as a door motor. Shadar's gun fired twice with a crack-crack and the Daklan sprinted into the opening.

"Not clear," he said.

Itrol and Zivor charged in afterwards, followed by Raimi and Vance. No further gunfire came and then

Shadar confirmed for a second time that the way was clear.

Recker hurried through the doorway, which led directly to a ten-metre square room. On the left and opposite walls, he saw racks of alien rifles, along with two larger pieces of hardware which might have been Meklon repeaters.

"Arsenal," said Shadar, not taking his eyes from the single exit doorway.

An alien body lay across the threshold, preventing the door from closing, and the night sight enhancement made its blood glisten darkly. Recker stooped briefly to examine the corpse. The alien was facing away from him and it was dressed in a near-black suit made from a material that appeared to be made of ultra-fine links, like chain mail but with three millennia worth of technological know-how built in to make it vacuum proof.

"Four arms," said Vance in obvious disgust. He nudged the corpse with one foot.

The topmost pair of limbs were attached to broad shoulders and the second, longer pair erupted lower down the creature's torso. Two disproportionately short legs appeared muscular, though it was impossible to be certain of anything given the bulkiness of the combat suit the creature was wearing.

"Two different species fought over this space station," said Recker. "These four-armed ones came out on top." He stared at the corpse for a few moments longer. "This one's Lavorix," he said. "All these others are Meklon."

"How do you know, sir?" asked Vance.

"The Meklon lost the war, which make me think they're the dead ones."

Recker didn't confide that a large part of his certainty came from intuition. With a hesitant movement of his arm, he placed a hand on one side of the creature's suit helmet. The head protection was hemispherical at the back and when he turned it over, Recker discovered that the front and visor were flat and wedge-shaped.

The strangely pudgy face inside was pale white, perhaps with a tinge of putrid green, though again the night sight made things different. Two milky white eyes with near-invisible pupils stared outwards, and just below them were two holes instead of a nose. Thin lips were partially open and the teeth within were numerous and sharp, indicating the Lavorix had a diet predominantly consisting of meat.

"That *is* an ugly bastard," Drawl confirmed from nearby. "My ass is a whole lot prettier than that."

Recker hadn't spent more than five or six seconds examining the Lavorix and he rose to standing. Ignoring the Meklon weapons – which might be of interest to the HPA labs but weren't important right now - he joined Shadar and peered along the exit corridor to a closed door at the end.

"They're coming," said the Daklan.

"I know it," said Recker, his internal alarms now sounding with such urgency that he couldn't shut them out.

He got on the comms and provided Aston with an update. Already the signal was degraded, though he hoped to piggyback the Excon-1 internal comms as soon as his biometric re-scan was complete.

Without warning, the far door opened and movement flickered in the room beyond. Sergeant Shadar fired and Recker did likewise. The Lavorix vanished from sight and the found of its rapid footsteps was akin to a rhythmic pattering.

"Go!" Recker ordered.

Sergeant Shadar growled out a command to the nearest soldiers and they responded, following him at a sprint along the short passage. Recker spotted orange flickers on his movement sensors and he heard the discharge of human and Daklan weaponry.

The rushing soldiers reached the end of the corridor before the door closed, crouched briefly to check out the room and then they disappeared inside. Recker hated having to wait for the conclusion, but his death would guarantee the same fate for everyone on this mission.

"Clear," said Shadar.

Vance was crouched nearby, waiting for Recker's command. So far, he'd been admirably restrained and hadn't turned the incursion into a competition with the Daklan.

"Let's go."

Recker dashed into the ten-metre room and scanned the contents. A low-level console was fixed to the left-hand wall and another to the right. Three additional exits led away at the cardinal points. Two more Lavorix were dead to the recent gunfire, while Meklon corpses were on the floor near each of the consoles.

Like everywhere else, the room was in total darkness.

The consoles might have been worth investigating, but they didn't respond to input and Recker couldn't even hear the hum of power in their circuits. He was struck by the sudden worry that this entire area in Excon-1 might be offline, and, though he expected the control computer would have warned him, with the AI tie-ins severed the backup might lack the intelligence required to anticipate and forewarn.

The only way to find out was to press on. Another reference to the map informed Recker that the opposite door was the way to proceed. That would lead to another - larger - room and after that, the security station.

He considered briefly and then ordered five human soldiers to secure this room, in case the Lavorix were familiar enough with Excon-1 that they could attempt a flanking move. Once that was done, he issued a new order.

"Sergeant Shadar, advance and secure the next room."

The Daklan hardly waited long enough to acknowledge the words. Without any obvious communication, he separated five of his soldiers from the others and opened the opposite door. The next passage was clear and ended at a second door – the Meklon had built the place to be resilient to decompression.

Given the arrangement, it was impossible to open the next door without becoming exposed to potential enemy fire. The moment Shadar touched the panel and the door started opening, Recker heard the clattering of inbound projectiles and he saw the orange of movement. One of the Daklan soldiers fired into the room beyond but then went down under a hail of bullets. The others dropped to the ground.

"Ipanvir!" roared Shadar.

One of the Daklan, who was mean-looking even compared to his peers, was still in the room near Recker and he appeared to be waiting for the order, like it was prearranged or something the Daklan had practised numerous times. In a split-second, he spun his heavy rocket tube onto his shoulder, the coils already whining. The projectile was ejected from the barrel with a whump and it flew along the corridor just as Shadar fell flat with the others. In a blur of movement and shimmering propellant, the missile streaked into the next room.

Reaching up, Shadar smashed his hand onto the door panel. The door started closing, though not nearly quick enough to seal in the detonation of the rocket tube. A flash of light and plasma was enough to incinerate anything living in the room and the extremes of the blast washed into the passage, turning sub-zero air into blistering heat.

"Nice shot," said Raimi in admiration, his own shoulder launcher held vertically.

Ipanvir didn't answer, he simply rolled the rocket tube off his shoulder and checked the ammunition readout like nothing was a concern.

Along the passage, Sergeant Shadar wasn't slowed by the heatwave and nor was he dissuaded from finding out how it had affected the Lavorix. He opened the door and surged into the room, his high-grip soles making an audible squeal as they gained purchase.

"Move!" he yelled.

"Corporal Hendrix!" said Recker, indicating the fallen Daklan.

For whatever reason, Jir-Lazan hadn't sent a medic,

leaving Hendrix to look after all thirty soldiers. She darted forward with her med-box in one hand and an injector in the other. Dropping low, Hendrix unceremoniously jabbed the alien with her needle, using force to drive the sharp point through the material of the combat suit.

"Let's hope the Daklan can handle Frenziol." Hendrix raised her voice. "Too late, he's dead."

"Damnit! Sergeant Shadar, please report!" said Recker.

"No hostiles remain. More will come."

Recker joined Shadar in a thirty-metre room, filled with more tech. Another rack of alien rifles was bolted to one wall, with several missing, and four exits led to other places. The blast from the rocket had torn several floor-mounted consoles away from their moorings, and others were half-melted. A layer of char unevenly covered a large area of the floor, as well as parts of the ceiling. However many Lavorix had been in this room, the blast had killed them all and left no recognizable trace, not even the scent of burned flesh.

"Too many approaches," said Sergeant Vance, using hand movements to direct his soldiers to various parts of the room.

"Through that door," said Recker, pointing at one of the two exits in the left-hand wall. "Another passage, another door and then the security station."

"And once the re-scan is complete, we go hunting for data," said Vance. "The pressure is increasing on us, sir."

"Only if we let it, Sergeant. This is a big place and even with 653 troops – less those we've killed – the Lavorix can't be everywhere."

The doubt in Vance's expression reflected Recker's own feelings. Whatever his worries, they didn't matter. The job had to be done regardless, otherwise everything would be a waste.

Recker assigned another five to guard the room – this time choosing only Daklan. The place to experiment with social cohesion was in the mess area off duty, rather than in the middle of a critical mission.

The squads encountered no further resistance on the short journey to the security room, though Recker's instinct told him it was only a matter of time, and not much time at that. He tested the connection to the *Axiom* and found it had degraded too far to carry voice comms. The discovery made Recker curse inwardly.

He entered the security station warily. It was in darkness, but his helmet night sight allowed him to see what he needed to see. Like in the security station on Excon-18, a huge, antenna made from a dark, unknown material, extended from floor to ceiling, with its base ringed by a single wraparound console. The room itself was huge and square, with multiple exits and multiple dead bodies.

"Not good," Sergeant Vance commented as he directed his soldiers to cover the doors.

Recker hurried to the console and flicked the switch to bring it out of sleep, hoping desperately that the hardware wasn't severed from the Excon-1 power supply. For long moments, the panel remained dark. He gave the metal base an encouraging kick and the lights came on, illuminating the keys and the screens, and the face of the Meklon lying on the floor at Recker's feet. Again, the expression on its face made him ask what had killed it so painfully.

He averted his eyes and, shortly, the machine was ready for input. With confident hands, Recker called up the relevant menu.

Excon-1> Welcome Captain Carl Recker. Request approval?

"What the hell do you think I'm here for?" Recker growled, entering an affirmative response.

Excon-1> Request submitted. Biometric re-scan in progress.

Recker remembered how it worked from Excon-18. On that occasion, the installation had attempted to contact Excon-1 to obtain clearance. Now that Recker was on a primary Meklon facility, he didn't expect his request to be bounced around numerous approval centres.

He was right.

Excon-1> Biometric re-scan successfully completed.

And that was it.

"Done," said Recker. Somehow, he didn't feel much relief. "Now let's plug in and steal some data."

"Is there a port on this console?" asked Vance.

"Several ports, Sergeant." Recker turned and found who he was looking for. "Private Halsey, bring that data extractor here." He racked his brains to remember the name of the Daklan pack-carrier. "Litos!" he called.

The two soldiers hurried across, unslinging heavy cloth-wrapped packs from their shoulders. A noise made Recker turn in time to see a door on the left-hand wall slide open, revealing dark shapes.

"Hostiles!" he shouted, bringing up his gun.

Gauss rifles fizzed and Daklan weapons snapped with discharge. From the doorway, Recker heard a deeper sound more like a dunt-dunt-dunt and he ducked instinctively. The two Lavorix in the passage went down and Recker heard the door behind them open to admit others.

Nearby, Drawl whipped his arm in a blur, sending a plasma grenade into the passage. A second door opened further along the same wall and a Lavorix surged out with incredible speed, using its two lower arms in conjunction with its legs to run and leaving its upper arms free to hold a gun. Recker put a bullet through its head and saw another one behind it. He fired and the second Lavorix died. More came and suddenly everything was a tumult of movement and gunfire.

CHAPTER FOURTEEN

WITHIN THIRTY SECONDS of the first shot being fired, it was clear this was a concerted effort by the Lavorix. The first few died quickly, but those coming after managed to keep the passage doors open and they fired from positions of cover.

Unfortunately for the aliens, they were limited by the bottleneck of the passages, which cut their firing angles significantly. Not only that, they faced a determined, ruthless and prepared defence in the form of the human and Daklan squads. Recker bellowed orders. Vance and Shadar backed him up, ensuring the soldiers concentrated their fire where it was needed most.

Recker pictured the engagement in his mind. Nine of his twenty soldiers were on the opposite side of the wraparound console, covering the security station's other exits. Six more were on this side of the room and exchanging fire with the Lavorix. The remaining five were effectively trapped because they were close to the doors through which the enemy were attacking.

"Move back!" said Recker. The wraparound console wasn't ideal cover, but it was better than none and he urged the soldiers to make for it. "Gantry, where's that MG-12?"

"Lock down the left door!" bellowed Shadar, the harsh volume of his order making Recker's earpiece vibrate.

"Rocket out!" said Ipanvir.

A missile screamed from the tube of the Daklan's launcher into the left-hand tunnel. Even before it detonated, the three soldiers by the wall were running – either to reach positions of cover or to avoid incineration when the rocket exploded.

Raimi was handy with a rocket launcher, but Ipanvir was a master. The Daklan landed a tight-angle shot against the far wall of the next room, filling the space with plasma fire. The extreme edge of the blast sphere was channelled along the passage and roiled eagerly into the security station. Recker's helmet sensor registered the spike in temperature, but neither he nor any of the other soldiers were harmed, while any Lavorix in the room were certainly carbonized.

Recker kept low and walked backwards around the perimeter of the wraparound console, keeping his rifle trained on the doorway and passage twenty metres to his left. He could see orange-enhanced movement in the second room, but with each step, the Lavorix's firing angle decreased. The pinging ricochets and the constant duntdunt-dunt made it clear the aliens were spraying blind shots around the corner without showing enough of themselves that they made easy kills.

Drawl threw in another grenade, bouncing it off the side wall. It detonated in a flash and he hurled a second with equal accuracy.

"Their attack stalled," said Recker. "If they've got the numbers or explosives, it won't be long before they start pushing again."

"What's the plan, sir?" asked Vance, calm as ever.

"We're not leaving. Not yet. We'll plug in the data cubes on the far side of this console and hold the enemy until we're done."

"Yes, sir."

On the comms, Recker spoke to the soldiers he'd left to guard the other rooms and ordered them to reinforce the security station. No sooner had he given the command than the furthest group reported a sighting and the sound of gauss fire was audible across the channel.

"They're coming from the left, sir," said Private Ossie Carrington.

"Numbers?"

"We killed two. We've got more incoming."

"Enemy sighted," reported Unvak, one of the Daklan in the next closest room. "We will support the withdrawal of Private Carrington's squad and then advance to the security station."

A moment later, Private Carrington reported an increase in pressure on her position. "They're attacking from two directions, sir," she reported. "We killed another four, but they're still coming at us."

"Do what you can to withdraw," said Recker. "I need you here."

"Hostiles back in the left room," said Steigers. "A shitload of them."

"Rocket out," said Raimi.

He aimed a missile along the left tunnel towards the next room in which the walls already glowed a dull patchwork of red from Ipanvir's shot. Recker didn't have an angle and he kept walking backwards, not taking his eye off either tunnel. A prone figure on the ground nearby was Private Hunter Gantry, with his MG-12 on its tripod before him.

"We are pressed," said Unvak. "Private Carrington has joined us and we are awaiting an opportunity to withdraw."

Under his breath, Recker cursed. He was beginning to feel like he'd been sucker-punched. He'd led the soldiers to this security station, expecting the Lavorix to be spread throughout Excon-1 and unable to mount an effective response to the incursion. Now it was clear the enemy was more organized than he'd anticipated.

An explosive went off ten metres from Recker and the orange-red of the blast wasn't like anything produced by an HPA or Daklan grenade. A Lavorix appeared at the doorway, one of its upper arms drawn back to throw. Gantry was ready and his MG-12 clinked with rapid-fire discharge, cutting the alien bastard to pieces and sending it backwards in a spraying cloud of blood. The grenade it had been holding went off, producing a second blast which Recker hoped took out a few more of the enemy.

"Sir, they've got gravity repeaters," said Carrington.

"Shit! Redman shoot it! Left door, left door!"

"Numbers building in the right-hand room," said Vance. He was on the opposite side of the wraparound console and evidently with an angle to see.

"Raimi to the rescue," said Raimi, dashing counter-clockwise around the console.

Recker heard the whump of a Daklan rocket blast. The central antenna concealed the explosion, but the walls were lit up in vivid white.

"Too late, human. Ipanvir the Incinerator burns all."

"Shit, man," said Raimi, stumped for a better response.

The entrance door opened and four soldiers dashed through, followed by others walking backwards and shooting at the same time. One part of Recker's brain counted them and he got as high as nine. He clenched his teeth and then Private Redman emerged. The soldier under-armed a grenade and then threw himself away from the door.

"Repeater!" he shouted.

Redman was too slow. Chunks of flesh exploded in every direction as bullets pulverised his legs. When Redman hit the ground, he was only head, torso and arms. Unbelievably, he clung onto life and produced a gurgling laugh.

"Hold!" snapped Recker, as Corporal Hendrix broke from cover. "He's gone."

Reluctantly, Hendrix slowed and returned to her place.

"Ah shit, this is going to hurt in the morning," said

Redman. The soldier's gun was forgotten and he tried to claw his way across the floor.

Recker closed his eyes.

Die, damnit and have done.

With a hissing exhalation, Redman died in a pool of his own blood. The engagement didn't stop and Recker urged the soldiers nearby to move further around the console.

"Pack up that MG-12, Private Gantry. Move!"

As Gantry hauled the heavy weapon further around the console, Recker listened for the sound of the repeater's gravity drive. It was coming, but he couldn't hear anything above the louder gunfire and the distressed notes of the Excon-1 station.

A grey, waist-high shape raced through the doorway, travelling as fast as a champion sprinter. Recker saw the turret's six-barrelled gun adjust as its control computer attempted to acquire a target. He dropped low at the same time as Ipanvir fired a rocket from the far side of the antenna.

A short burst of high-calibre repeater fire drummed against the console a few metres from where Recker crouched and then the rocket exploded. With his eyes narrowed to slits, he was only dimly aware of a dark shape flying sideways through the air. The automated turret made a crunching impact with the wall and dropped to the floor, its deflective plating ablaze and its gun barrels torn free by the blast.

"Another turret on its way!" yelled Private Montero.

"Raimi!" bellowed Recker.

"On it, sir."

A second rocket blast followed Ipanvir's and the gunfire intensified. Recker inched his way further around the antenna and by this point, he was thinking about a withdrawal. Any hope of plugging in a couple of data extractors and then strolling back to the *Axiom* was long gone.

Several Lavorix came in a rush through the visible doorway, firing wildly. One of them was carrying a chain gun or something similar. Luckily, the alien's high-speed sprint prevented it from keeping the weapon level and the spray of bullets cut through the air above Recker's head. Staying low, he shot it three times, and then the roaring torrent from Gantry's repositioned MG-12 mowed the others down.

The Lavorix didn't give up easily and Recker spotted a metallic shape arcing through the doorway.

"Grenade!" he shouted, hunkering closer to the console.

The explosive went off mid-air, so near that Recker was stumbled by the blast wave. The heat from it momentarily peaked at a thousand degrees, turning the arms and exposed shoulder on his suit brown and producing a stinking acrid smoke of burning polymers.

He crawled rapidly away, wiping at the layer of grime which had formed across his visor. A hand grabbed his upper arm and pulled him along.

"Move, sir!" shouted Hendrix. "Are you injured?"

"I'm fine, Corporal," said Recker.

Hendrix released her grip and scrambled away, leaving Recker trying to formulate a plan. The Lavorix were attacking from three entry points and when he called up the Excon-1 map on his HUD, Recker was able to form links from those adjacent rooms to one other entrance to the security station. And that entrance was directly to his left.

"Private Gantry, cover that doorway!"

"Yes, sir."

Gantry shuffled round and the door opened. An extended burst from the MG-12 caught a group of Lavorix completely by surprise, killing six or seven and leaving a pile of mangled remains in the corridor, which prevented the door from closing. The door at the end of the exposed passage opened and Gantry killed another bunch of the enemy before they even realized the danger.

It was time to withdraw, though Recker couldn't see an easy way back to the *Axiom*. He spoke to Vance and Shadar, who were at the far side of the console and able to see into two of the rooms which were hidden from Recker's sight. The news wasn't good.

"We keep killing them and more show up, sir," said Vance. "I'd say the enemy numbers are increasing. Private Raimi – hit that turret."

The blast came a moment later and Vance resumed talking.

"I don't know how many of these turrets they've got on Excon-1, sir. Raimi's got one rocket left and it's the same for Ipanvir."

The MG-12 fired again and a return hail of slugs smashed into the console and antenna, sending wicked shards of alloy in every direction. One of them hit Gantry in the shoulder and he swore with feeling.

A Lavorix charged through one of the far doors and

Recker shot it. The next alien went the same way and then a third. A glance behind told Recker that escape through one of the remaining doorways was becoming an increasingly tough option. The soldiers couldn't hold here much longer and Recker didn't want to gamble that the enemy attack would break. A retreat would mean running further from the *Axiom*, with no guarantee the squad could return without being overrun.

"Sergeant Vance, Sergeant Shadar!" said Recker. "We're leaving through that exit over there."

"I will open the door for us," said Shadar.

The Daklan sprinted across the floor, his size making him appear more lumbering than the reality. Elsewhere in the room, a rumbling detonation told Recker that Ipanvir had shot the last of his missiles. Before the sound of it faded, a Lavorix turret opened fire, somewhere out of sight. Recker turned just as the armoured gun sped into sight, its barrels spinning in a blur. A rocket hit it dead-on and the weapon was engulfed in flames.

"The way is open," said Daklan.

Recker backed towards it, not taking his eyes off the visible entry points. On the comms, he gave orders without thinking, the skills and experience of his past life coming to the fore without conscious effort.

The Lavorix sensed the retreat and they became bold. Recker shot one in the chest, catapulting it through the doorway and tripping the soldier behind. This second alien tumbled into full view, six limbs flailing for balance. Recker put a slug into its head and another into its chest. Something clipped his arm. He felt nothing and didn't spare it a thought.

"Sir, move!"

The way was clear and Recker hurtled through the doorway, where Sergeant Vance and Private Montero remained to provide cover. Only Litos and Itrol were left to come and, as they sprinted for the exit, the Daklan ripped grenades free from their waist belts and threw them behind, where they clinked off the floor and then exploded.

"This way," yelled Corporal Hendrix.

Recker didn't slow - he ran along the short passage to an intersection and followed the others left. Green-outlined shapes sprinted into the darkness, voices shouted and footsteps pounded. He darted right into a room, with Private Montero directly behind.

The last few entered, Sergeant Vance coming last.

"Close the door," shouted Recker.

Vance spun and thumped his hand on the access panel. The door closed.

The squad had taken cover in a large room. Several members of the squad were already checking the exits and the rest were either reloading or watching the retreat.

"We hold here for a moment," said Recker.

"We've got to lose the enemy, sir," said Vance. "I've tried to figure out a way that'll take us around them, but we're in for a long trip."

"The Lavorix know this place better than we do," said Recker. "It might not be so easy."

An idea came and it was the kind of idea which made him giddy with the plain savagery of it.

Recker acted on it immediately. He sent his comms unit in search of the Excon-1 open receptors which had been hidden before his biometric re-scan. The search found green lights – lots of them – and Recker linked to the first. With that done, he requested a channel to the *Axiom*.

Burner responded immediately. "Sir?" he asked, all business.

"We're in the shit, Lieutenant. I've sent you the coordinates of the squad and the direction of our attackers. Tie them in with the map of Excon-1. After that, I want Commander Aston to aim one of the Railers at the enemy positions."

"The Railers...?" Burner recovered quickly. "I'll pass on the order, sir."

Recker cut the channel and got on to the squad. "We've got some Railer support fire coming any time now. Keep low and stay alert."

"Aren't the Railers designed for..."

The rest of Private Enfield's question was drowned out by a noise of such thunderous intensity that Recker felt like his skull was going to split open. Thousands of overlaid metallic impacts came at once, their interval so short that the sound became a single overwhelming pressure wave. The worst part was that the Railer slugs weren't hitting anywhere close – the reverberation was travelling from back in the antenna room and still it was enough to cause physical pain.

The ongoing noise battered Recker and a high-pitched humming built in his head, as if a tiny buzzing insect was trapped next to his eardrums. He wanted to drop to his haunches and put his hands against the sides of his suit helmet – for all the good it would do. With the Lavorix so close, Recker couldn't take a hand off his rifle and he clenched his jaw as tightly as he could.

After five seconds, the Railer fire stopped and the relief was incredible.

"Damn, shit," said someone on the comms, the sentiments similarly echoed by other voices which Recker's scrambled brains didn't recognize.

With a snarl, he gathered his wits. A channel formed in his comms unit.

"Sir, do you need further Railer fire?" asked Burner.

"I don't know, Lieutenant," said Recker. The buzzing in his ear hadn't gone away and he shook his head, hoping to clear it. The buzzing remained and it was already irritating as hell. "Sergeant Shadar – check the corridor."

The Daklan ran to the access panel, accompanied by Reklin and Private Gantry. When the door opened, shimmering air from the corridor made the soldiers' outlines appear indistinct.

"Hot," grunted Shadar. He peered cautiously into the passage. "Clear."

Recker crossed to the door and the air temperature climbed to eighty degrees. The impact energy from the Railer slugs had likely turned much of the security station into a no-go area and he wondered if he should order the squad to wait.

A nagging, throbbing pain in Recker's arm distracted him. When he checked, he noticed a discoloured furrow in his suit where the material had been damaged and then automatically sealed over both the suit breach and the wound underneath. Self-healing combat suits was how the military referred to them – like a personal medic for every man and woman wearing one.

"Sir, you're hurt," said Hendrix, noticing the expression on his face.

"A bullet caught me on the way out of the room."

In a flash, Hendrix had a wire from her med-box plugged into the port under his chin.

"Vital signs fine. I should give you a shot."

"No shot," said Recker, wondering why he was so reluctant. He raised his voice and spoke to the squad. "This is the best time to find out what damage we did to the enemy," he said. "While they're still wondering what hit them."

With the order given, Sergeant Shadar arranged for a scouting party of five to go on ahead. They didn't have far to travel and returned a few minutes later.

"The place is a mess," said Gantry, showing no discomfort from the injury he'd suffered earlier. "No sign of the enemy and the air is disappearing faster than Private Drawl's pocket money at a country fair."

"Let's go check it out," said Recker.

The squad left the room and headed back to the security station.

CHAPTER FIFTEEN

PRIVATE GANTRY'S assessment was an understatement of the devastation wrought by the *Axiom*'s Type 2 Railer burst. At four hundred degrees, the air was blistering, though it was cooling rapidly as the atmosphere was sucked all the way back towards the docking bay. The droning sound of the evacuating air was dull and already the creaking of the Excon-1 station was becoming muffled.

"Depressurisation will be finished soon," said Shadar.

Recker turned his attention to the room. Debris in all shapes and sizes covered what remained of the floor and he spotted pieces of the console, along with fragments of the antenna which had broken in such a way that he believed the construction material was brittle instead of yielding. The top half was still attached to the ceiling and it hung precariously overhead like a technological stalactite, just waiting to crash down onto anyone foolish enough to walk underneath.

Not far from the threshold, identifiable Lavorix body

parts were strewn liberally, along with other Lavorix biological matter that wasn't so easily named. Sticky blood and clear fluids were spread like jam on most surfaces, along with crimson gobbets stuck to both floor and wall. The scents were disappearing with the air, but the harshness lingered like putrid meat on a barbecue.

"Stay alert," Recker ordered, advancing slowly across the floor.

The Railer had left nothing untouched. The closest wall was indented and ruptured, while the places where the Lavorix had sought entry were utterly ruined by the fusillade of high-velocity slugs. One wall was almost gone, revealing the empty spaces between the inner skins of Excon-1, and the alloy glowed with the heat of multiple impacts. A second wall hadn't fared much better and the rooms beyond it were exposed – at least what remained of them.

"That's where the Lavorix were coming from," said Vance, pointing with the end of his gun.

"They are dead," said Shadar. He spun slowly around and then burst into laughter. "What carnage!"

Recker advanced deeper into the room, trying to figure out if he'd been too clever in ordering the Railer attack. The angle of the upper turrets meant the projectiles had torn through the warehouse at a diagonal and then smashed into the floors. Although the Railers were precise, and Aston had been given exact coordinates, the slugs had come through many obstacles and many had deflected. If they'd caused too much incidental damage, the way back to the *Axiom* might be impassable.

At Recker's feet, a two-metre-diameter flattened disk

of metal – a Railer projectile - smoked gently and he could smell the odour of heated alloy coming from it. The torn and broken floor was littered with them – hundreds or more, crushed into different shapes and sizes, most of them far too hot to touch. Recker stepped around the slug and proceeded, his eyes roving everywhere. Nearby, Private Steigers did likewise and the man's expression was one of shocked awe.

"This was like a five-second discharge," he said.

"Yeah," said Private Haley. "Technology is great when it's on your side."

"Come on," said Recker. With half an eye on the HUD map and the rest of his attention on the space around, he passed the mid-point of the room. Here, the floor was in an even worse state. None of the stress tears were wide enough to fall through, but Recker trod evermore carefully.

By this point, he had a view along the path made by the Railer slugs. Had the intervening walls not folded in such a way when the projectiles came through, or been so jagged, he guessed he could have seen all the way to the *Axiom*.

"No way we're getting back this way," said Sergeant Vance.

"There's another route," said Recker. "This door here – the last place the Lavorix came through – it looks like we can get along the passage. A couple of rooms further in and we can cut right to join the room which links to the storage bay."

"Let's do it," said Vance.

The place Recker indicated wasn't much of a passage

anymore. Sharp intrusions from the sides and above made the way hazardous and the squad had to advance single file for a short distance, avoiding two large openings in the floor.

Soon, they were beyond and into the next room, without encountering any living enemies. Char, blood, bones and broken alien weapons lay plentifully about and Recker ignored them on his way to the opposite door.

The next passage was completely undamaged, except for one noticeable bulge in the side wall and the following room was cold, pressurized and untouched, its four maintenance consoles quiet and unlit. Recker was not lulled by the calm. If anything, his wariness increased and he made sure Vance and Shadar kept the soldiers ready for a possible renewed attack.

Another corridor led to a new room, square and much larger than the one which preceded it. Recker advanced a few paces and then stopped, so he could better evaluate the hardware. One of the walls was covered in screens and a long console intended for use by ten or twelve personnel was positioned in front of it. Elsewhere in the room, other smaller consoles faced the same way.

"Sergeant Vance, Sergeant Shadar, please secure this room."

"Can we fill the data extractors in here?" asked Vance.

"This looks like a flight control room," said Recker. "In fact, it looks like a high-level command station. If I'm right, we should be able to plug into a console and get a data link to some of the secure storage arrays."

Recker hurried to the main console, which was covered in keypads, switches, touch-sensitive panels and many smaller displays. Confidently, he brought the hardware out of deep sleep and waited for it to reach an operational state. The top panel lit up and a moment later, the wall screens did likewise, though they only showed static.

"Are those the external feeds, sir?" asked Vance. The pale light from the screens made him appear ghostly – more dead than alive.

"I think so," said Recker. "It'll take a few seconds for the link to stabilise."

He didn't wait for the link and called up the menu on one of the console displays. Scrolling through the list told Recker he was in the right place, and he spotted several options he wanted to explore.

"Bring over those data extractors," he said on the comms. "There's a wide bore port to my left and another further along. Plug in and I'll see what I can find."

"What data are you targeting?" asked Sergeant Shadar, rising from a crouch over by the furthest exit.

"Primarily weapons schematics and technical files. The flight logs shouldn't take up much room, so I'll take those as well. Rest assured, Sergeant – the human and Daklan requirements are aligned. Whatever I choose will benefit both our species."

The response was enough for Shadar and he dropped out of sight again. Recker got on with it, finding that he was becoming so familiar with the Meklon control software that he could operate it without too much thought, allowing him to focus on sifting through the available files.

Meanwhile, the sensor links stabilised and the wall screens displayed images of space, along with numerous feeds of Qul and other planets in the Lanak system. This revealed that the Meklon had deployed an extensive network of monitoring satellites. Two of the sensors were locked on the missile cratered *Aktrivisar* and tracked its slow path around the space station. Recker was interested, but he couldn't spare the time to study the feeds.

Corporal Hendrix was crouched low nearby, her medbox on the floor and her gauss rifle aimed at the entrance door. "How long will it take to fill those cubes, sir?" she asked through the chin speaker on her helmet.

"Got a date, Corporal?"

"Unfortunately not, sir."

"The extraction shouldn't take longer than five minutes through these interface ports. It's finding the right data to feed them with that's going to take longer. We've only got this one chance and if we leave with junk, the mission will have failed."

"You think the Galactar will destroy Excon-1 when it arrives?" This time Hendrix made no effort to hide her nervousness.

"I don't want to run into the Galactar either, Corporal," he assured her. "But yes – when it gets here, I think it'll destroy Excon-1. Even if it doesn't, I can't recommend to my superiors that we return to the Lanak system. The risks are too high."

While he talked, Recker continued his search. He'd already confirmed this was one of three main flight control stations on Excon-1 and, while it had no access to the space station's weaponry, it did have access to the central file repository. It also controlled something called a Gateway, which Recker was determined to check out.

He identified a few thousand files which looked interesting and he copied them to the two data boxes, noticing that Litos remained close by to watch for any funny business. Recker didn't even pretend to be upset. He certainly wasn't intending a betrayal and he continued his search for useful data.

"Can you access everything, sir?" asked Hendrix.

"Everything we need."

"That's good."

Recker located an enormous, encrypted file relating to the Gateway. While he couldn't access the contents, it wasn't copy-locked which meant he could put it onto the data cubes. Unfortunately, this one file would occupy sixty percent of their storage capacities.

"Let's move this over first," he said to himself, selecting an alternative technical file relating to tenixite conversion.

While that copied, he accessed the Gateway section of the control menu. Immediately, the wall screen directly in front of him changed to what he recognized as a map of sorts. A dozen blue circles – locations - were linked by orange lines. Not every location was connected to every other, though each had three or four destinations.

Lines of text appeared on one of the console screens.

Warships Aktrivisar and Axiom. Gateway locked.

Tenixite requirement: 23 to 4091 billion tons, destination dependent.

Approximate tenixite available: 10468 trillion tons.

Warning: Aktrivisar and Axiom lack mesh deflector protection.

Select destination?

Recker knew at once that this was something of

incredible importance and he quickly ordered the Gateway file to copy over to the data cubes.

"What's that you've found, sir?" asked Hendrix. She was either naturally inquisitive or chosen by the squad as the one most likely to obtain information from their commanding officer. Recker didn't mind which.

"The Excon-1 station operates something called a Gateway." He tapped his fingers on the console in thought. "From what I can tell, it converts ternium ore into energy and opens up a fast-travel route to other places in the Meklon empire. Or what's left of the Meklon empire."

"That's...amazing."

"It is," Recker confirmed. It was so amazing he wondered if he understood the hardware correctly. "It uses a lot of ternium ore, which I assume it extracts from Qul when the Gateway is opened."

"Are we going on a trip?" asked Hendrix.

"Not a chance of it, Corporal. We're going to fill those data cubes and return home."

Recker exited the Gateway menu, just as the flight control room became bathed in a deep red colour. The sound of a low volume, yet insistent siren came from several hidden speakers. Turning rapidly, Recker thought he might see Lavorix coming through one of the doorways, before sense kicked in and told him the alarm was triggered by one of the monitoring systems in the Lanak system. The moment he followed that thought to its logical conclusion, Recker felt his skin tighten.

"Shit," he said, and ordered an end to the questions coming his way. He called up the list of satellites and accessed the one which had triggered the alarm and he swore again when he realised the monitoring station was less than fifty thousand kilometres from Excon-1. With a stab of his forefinger, he opened the target list and felt a chill of fear at the words.

Lavorix Galactar.
Gateway exit: 25,000 kilometres.
Lavorix Galactar: preparing for lightspeed.

Recker called up the feed from the monitoring satellite and all he saw on it was empty space. The alarm on the satellite ended and another – this time thirty million kilometres from Excon-1 - started flashing red.

Lavorix Galactar.
Lightspeed exit: 13,000,000 kilometres.

"What the hell?" said Recker, switching the feed to the second satellite. He raised his voice. "Sergeant Vance, Sergeant Shadar, I think we've overstayed our welcome. Get ready to move out." A moment later, he spoke to Lieutenant Burner and told him the same thing. Burner had questions and Recker lacked answers.

The visual stream from the second satellite came up on one of the wall screens and Recker could see the sensor lens going through a process of adjustment, zooming and focusing as it tried to lock onto a distant target. He caught a hint of an immense shape, stationary and almost as dark as the void around it.

A thought – a terrible thought – made adrenaline pump into Recker's body like someone was squirting it into directly into his system through a thick hose. He called up the tactical data being fed into Excon-1. A red dot representing the Lavorix warship appeared, way out in space – almost fifty million kilometres out.

"It arrived on top of us and then went straight to where the *Axiom* and *Aktrivisar* first exited lightspeed," he said.

Hendrix wasn't a warship officer, but she understood the significance. "How did it do that?"

"A short-duration lightspeed jump. Some of the Lavorix and Meklon warships have the capability. Zero ramp-up, go from here to there and start shooting. I'm more worried about how it knew where to go."

"Should we leave, sir?"

"Absolutely." Recker glanced at the progress for the Gateway files. "80%. We'll go once this is done."

He estimated the copy operation would be finished in less than thirty seconds and he passed on a couple of orders. While he was doing so, he discovered that he could access top-level data for acquired targets and he called up the Meklon file on the Galactar. What he read instilled him with a sense of even greater fear.

"We can't leave," he said. "Even if we somehow make it to lightspeed, the Galactar will follow us. This is one opponent we can't outrun." A thought came to him. "Unless…"

He opened the Gateway menu option.

Select destination?

Wondering what the hell he was getting into, Recker entered his choice.

CHAPTER SIXTEEN

GATEWAY OPENING: 10 *minutes.*

Destination: Kemis-5.

Warning: Aktrivisar and Axiom lack mesh deflector protection.

Warning: Axiom docked. Gateway activation not possible for docked vessel.

Warning: Gateway activation requires maximum distance between target vessels: fifty kilometres.

Wasting precious seconds, Recker attempted to exert some level of manual control over the Gateway hardware, so that he could trigger the opening by remote command. The method wasn't obvious and he soon abandoned the effort.

"What's that about mesh deflector protection, sir?" asked Hendrix, acting like she'd only read the words by accident.

"Another question I can't answer, Corporal. I'm

assuming if it were a big problem, Excon-1 wouldn't allow the Gateway to activate." He stepped away from the console and noticed the file copy operation was at 100%. "Pick up those data cubes and let's go!" he yelled.

"Where is the Gateway taking us?" Hendrix asked, shrugging into the med-box shoulder straps.

"Damned if I know, Corporal. A place called Kemis-5. It's away from here and away from that Galactar."

The soldiers were ready for the order and Vance opened the door which led most directly to the *Axiom*.

"Clear!" he shouted, darting into the passage.

Other soldiers followed and Recker heard the next door open. Once more, Vance gave the all-clear. Following closely behind Private Halsey and Litos as they laboured with the burden of the data cubes, Recker emerged into a room where the soldiers watched the redundant exits and Sergeant Vance waited to activate the panel for the door leading to the *Axiom*.

"Go!" said Recker.

Vance didn't need to be asked twice. The door opened to reveal a group of Lavorix advancing along the passageway. A hail of bullets from the edgy soldiers sent the aliens dead to the floor and Vance was in the corridor almost before the enemy had hit the ground. One of the Lavorix must have twitched or done something the soldier didn't like and he combined the actions of shooting it in the chest and delivering a vicious kick to the creature's head. Satisfied, he advanced to the end door, clearly expecting to find more aliens coming his way.

If Vance was disappointed to find the next room

empty, he didn't say, and the squad advanced once more, this time into a space they'd passed across on the way to the security station. Recker spotted half a dozen Lavorix sprawled on the floor, each with multiple bullet wounds from where they had stumbled into the five soldiers left to guard the room earlier. The alien nearest to the exit had spilled so much blood that the frosted gore made the footing treacherous.

"This way leads to the storage area," said Vance. He blew out between gritted teeth but didn't say anything more.

"If the enemy are there, we'll kill them, Sergeant."

The ten minutes for Gateway activation didn't offer much leeway for the return trip to the *Axiom*, though Recker was more concerned about what the crew of the Galactar were planning. The Lavorix warship had arrived near Excon-1 and then entered lightspeed only a short time later, meaning it had the same propulsion modes as the *Vengeance* and the smaller Lavorix warships which the *Axiom* and *Aktrivisar* had faced earlier.

The important question was how long the Galactar crew would stay at 48 million kilometres and then whether they could immediately re-enter lightspeed for the return journey. The *Vengeance* had a cooldown period of several minutes between its Mode 3 activations and Recker had no way of knowing if the Lavorix technology was equivalent. Thinking about it wasn't helping, though his brain wouldn't stop.

Vance opened the door to the storage area. "Vacuum, for all the difference it'll make to us," he said. "If we run straight through, we'll get ripped to pieces if the enemy catch us by surprise."

Recker squeezed to the front and looked inside. To his right, along the aisle, he could see piles of dented and smashed crates, where the Railer slugs had torn through the warehouse. The place had a scent of something acrid and the air had a peculiar thickness to it, which made Recker think some chemical containers had been ruptured.

The warehouse slowed their progress and he ground his teeth at the reduced pace. The storage area was large enough that it would require a full minute to cross at a sprint and the safe way to progress wasn't half as fast. After the storage area came the docking bay and an eight hundred metre dash to the *Axiom*'s forward boarding ramp, in a full loadout.

It was time for risks and Recker pushed Vance and Shadar to move faster. Neither officer complained – they knew what was at stake. By the halfway point, no Lavorix had appeared. Their main attack had come from a different direction to the storage bay and Recker hoped the bulk of the enemy forces was now behind rather than ahead.

"Look at that," said Private Raimi, when the squad's progress brought them a clearer view of the Railer damage.

Most of the soldiers – Recker included – simply glanced at the massive hole through the metre-thick side wall and at the toppled crates and said nothing more.

Eagerness to escape carried Recker near to the front of the pack. The squad crossed the bay successfully and without further gunfire. Soon, they were inside the loading airlock tunnel that connected the storage area with the main docking bay.

Recker opened the connecting door, confident the *Axiom*'s weaponry would comprehensively slaughter any Lavorix who ventured into sight. After a second or two spent checking for motion – just to be sure - Recker set off in a flat-out sprint for the *Axiom*, the soldiers with him.

"Five minutes," he said.

The image enhancers in Recker's helmet outlined the warship in green and the heavy cruiser appeared incomprehensively vast to his eyes, yet still dwarfed by the enormity of the bay. A scarcely seen shape told him the forward ramp was halfway down and he wondered if Aston had spotted something which gave her concern for the warship's security.

He got his answer. Streams of flickering light jumped out from two of the warship's starboard flank Railers, aimed at the opposite wall of the docking bay. The lack of atmosphere meant the attack was conducted in merciful silence, yet Recker was sure he could sense the savage force of the projectiles like an imagined pressure against him as he ran.

"Keep going," he yelled.

Recker's heart rate climbed and his breathing deepened. The forward boarding ramp was near and he could feel the warship's engine vibration through the solid floor. Aston was ready to depart the moment the soldiers were onboard.

The Railer fusillade continued for a long time and Recker didn't even try to determine the effects it was having on the enemy. A streak of propellant emerged from a different doorway on the other side of the bay and a Lavorix rocket detonated against the *Axiom*'s nose, the payload so pathetically small the Railers didn't even target the missile. One of the turrets directed a short stream of projectiles into the doorway and then went still.

"Stupid bastards," said Vance, his breathing laboured.

Recker couldn't think of a more apt description of the Lavorix effort to take out a heavy cruiser using a shoulder launcher. He was third to the ramp and charged up the steps, ignoring his complaining muscles. The pain in his arm had returned – worse now – and it would need attention once he returned to the bridge.

With ninety seconds left on the timer, Recker dashed across the airlock, past Private Drawl and Corporal Givens who'd arrived before him. On the comms, he ordered Corporal Hendrix to follow him to the bridge and he set off that way, his elbows scraping against the walls as he ran.

"How does this Gateway work, sir?" asked Aston on the comms.

"The control hardware targeted our two ships by name," Recker panted. "I believe it creates the gateway around each ship."

"And off we go to Kemis-5, wherever the hell that is."

Recker had been keeping Aston updated and relying on her to handle Captain Jir-Lazan. She had questions but knew now wasn't the best time to ask them.

"It's not here and that's all that matters, Commander."

"That's the last soldier inside and I'm lifting off," said Aston.

The floor shook underfoot but Recker hardly noticed.

Only another short corridor separated him from the bridge. He turned the final corner, hurtled up the steps, through the blast door and jumped into his seat while checking the sensor feeds. The view on the screens told him the *Axiom* was reversing rapidly through the half-open bay doors.

"Twenty seconds," he said.

"I've got this, sir," said Aston, piloting the ship using the backup control bars.

A figure appeared next to Recker's seat – it was Corporal Hendrix and Recker asked her to stay back.

"Ten seconds," he said. "Does Jir-Lazan know he has to be close?"

"Yes, sir."

The *Axiom* exited the bay, accelerating so rapidly that the bay doors dwindled and the outer edges of Excon-1 became visible. The *Aktrivisar* appeared on one of the portside feeds, the desolator facing the opposite direction to the *Axiom* and accelerating alongside it. Seeing the Daklan heavy cruiser gave Recker a feeling of relief that at one time would have seemed impossible to imagine.

"Five seconds."

The Galactar appeared on the starboard feed, no more than ten thousand kilometres from the *Axiom*. When Recker saw it from so close, he understood at once how the warship had turned the tide of the Lavorix's war with the Meklon.

"Ah crap," said Burner.

The Gateway opened, or rather, it appeared as an expanding sphere of utter darkness, engulfing both the *Aktrivisar* and the *Axiom*. The last thing Recker saw before the sensors went offline was a mesh deflector appear around the Excon-1 station, to defend it from the Galactar's depletion burst.

Then, the sensors went dead and Recker felt an unpleasant wrenching, like his body was forcibly dislocated from reality. The sensation intensified and he clenched his jaw to stop himself from swearing. Behind him, one of the crew – he didn't know who it was – shouted in pain.

The feeling passed, vanishing like a memory of painful, invasive surgery and Recker knew they'd arrived. With an effort, he lifted his head, trying to ignore the renewed throbbing in his arm.

"Commander Aston, I've got the controls," he said, pushing the control bars forward. "I want status reports."

The engines responded, though with a notable lack of urgency. Recker scanned the instrumentation, but the needles hadn't settled. "Something's wrong," he said. "We're way down on power."

"The monitoring tools have gone crazy, sir," said Eastwood. He blew out as if he were recovering from the same sprint across the Excon-1 docking bay floor. "A few ambers have come up, but they're the same ones from our engagement with the Lavorix warships."

"Something is still not right, Lieutenant."

"I know, sir. I'll find the problem."

Eastwood knew this was critical and Recker didn't remind him of the fact. The *Axiom* accelerated sluggishly and, when he banked left, he discovered it was lacking its usual agility.

"Sensors calibrating," said Burner, the words thick like he was recovering from a three-day drinking session.

"Weapons online and available," said Aston. "Waiting on tactical data."

The sensors came up all at once. Most of the screens showed darkness and then one array auto-locked on the *Aktrivisar*. The desolator was also accelerating, keeping pace with the *Axiom*.

"The Daklan made it," said Burner. He cleared his throat. "Near scan clear."

"I'm attempting contact with the desolator, sir," said Larson.

Recker detected an increasing lumpiness to the propulsion that didn't sound anything like normal. "Lieutenant Eastwood?"

"Working on it, sir."

"Work fast." Recker felt a gnawing worry about what damage the Gateway might have caused to his spaceship. He put it to one side. "Lieutenant Burner, keep a watch for that Galactar."

"Can it follow us through the Gateway?" asked Burner.

"Instinct tells me it can't, Lieutenant. My instinct has been wrong before."

"I haven't yet located the cause of our engine problem, sir," said Eastwood. "We're at seventy percent of maximum power."

"I need better than that, Lieutenant." Recker focused his hearing on the propulsion note. If anything, it sounded worse than it had a few moments ago.

"I know, sir. I told you I'd find the cause and I will."

"The *Aktrivisar* also reports engine problems," said Larson.

"Get me Captain Jir-Lazan," snapped Recker.

"Captain Recker," said the Daklan. "We have much to discuss when the time is right. My warship's engines are failing."

"Failing?" said Recker sharply. He turned in his seat to look at Eastwood.

"Down to sixty-five percent," said Eastwood. He looked stressed and angry. "I don't know what's happening."

"You'd better find out quickly!" Recker directed his next words at the Daklan. "Have your technical officers found the cause?"

"Not yet, human."

Recker wanted to swear and he wanted to punch something. He did neither, remembering the warning on Excon-1. *Aktrivisar and Axiom lack mesh deflector protection.* Whatever was happening here must be related to that, he felt sure of it.

We had no choice other than to activate the Gateway, he told himself. Knowing it didn't make him feel any better.

"Travelling through the Gateway has degraded our engines," he said. "The station warnings weren't precise about what would happen if we didn't have a mesh deflector."

"We did what we had to do, Captain Recker. Now we are here and we must deal with the consequences."

"I've located a planet, sir," said Burner. "Two million klicks from our current position."

"Captain Jir-Lazan, did you hear that?"

"Yes, we have just located the same planet. We should set a course for it while we investigate the problems affecting our warships."

A green route line appeared on Recker's tactical and he banked the *Axiom* to follow it. "I agree," he said, cutting the channel so he could focus.

The *Axiom* responded more like a shipyard lifter shuttle and it took far longer than usual to come about. The moment Recker had the warship on course, he directed his gaze towards the yellowy grey planet which Burner had put up on the bulkhead screen.

"Sand," he said.

"That's right, sir. Most of the surface is eroded and the particles are being carried by atmospheric winds."

"There's something down there," said Recker. "Else why make this a Gateway destination?"

"Could be another space station," said Aston.

"There's nothing on the comms, sir. No open receptors."

"Damnit, find me something!" said Recker.

"Propulsion output at sixty percent," said Lieutenant Eastwood. "I think this is terminal, sir."

Recker had already braced himself for the news, but that didn't make it any easier to take. He'd brought his warship and its crew to a place from which they might never return. Even worse - the *Axiom*'s critical systems tapped into the engines for power and once that power source dried up, the life support systems amongst others would no longer function. If the spaceship crashed into Kemis-5, the hull would survive the impact, but without the life support, everyone onboard would be reduced to paste.

Recker knew that if he couldn't figure something out soon, everyone was going to die here in this unknown part of the universe.

CHAPTER SEVENTEEN

"SURFACE SCANS INCONCLUSIVE, SIR," said Burner. "Too much sand. The storms don't cover the entire planet and I'm catching glimpses of the surface, just not enough to conclude with certainty if there's a Meklon installation on the visible side."

The zoomed sensor feed wasn't bad – sharp enough for Recker to see the swirling patterns of wind-blown sand and grit, whilst hiding much of what lay beneath. Kemis-5 was mountainous and some of the largest summits protruded above the sandstorms, like islands in a dull yellow sea.

"I've found no sign of satellites or anything similar," said Larson. "And I don't think the Galactar is coming anytime soon."

"There's a Meklon facility here," Recker said again. "I know it."

"What if it's blindside?" said Aston. "Or destroyed long ago by the Lavorix?"

"Excon-1 offered Kemis-5 as the default destination, Commander. Why would it do that if the place was captured by the enemy?"

Aston's expression was pained. "I don't know."

"Fifty-five percent on the engines, sir," said Eastwood. "The fall is roughly linear."

"Are you any closer to discovering the cause?"

"Lieutenant Fraser and I believe that our ternium modules are decaying."

"What? How? A ternium engine doesn't run out of juice."

"You've seen how the Lavorix power their depletion bursts, sir. They suck the potential out of ternium ore and use it to generate a short-duration spike of energy. I think something similar happened to the *Axiom* and *Aktrivisar*, only it's happening over a longer period. Our engine modules were affected by the transit through the Gateway and now they're failing."

"And you don't have any theories as to how we can reverse this?" Recker asked. "I don't care how far-fetched. Can we put the engines into overstress to see if that changes anything?"

"If we overstress the engines, it'll hasten the process of decay, sir," said Lieutenant Fraser. "As it stands, you should be able to control the *Axiom* long enough to set us down on Kemis-5 if that's where you decide we're going."

"If you don't set us down in time, we're going to drift until everyone dies," said Eastwood. "I can't make the outcome sound any sweeter than that."

"There's got to be something," Recker said again, like the repetition would make it happen.

"Sir, I've spoken to one of the Daklan sensor operators," said Burner. "He's detected an area of interest on Kamis-5."

"What exactly has he found?"

"Nothing specific – anomalous data that might indicate the presence of something."

"The Daklan know what they're doing - concentrate on that part of the surface."

"Yes, sir. It's right on the north-east cusp."

Burner added a circular overlay to the sensor feed to show the area in question and Recker squinted at it. A storm was moving across that area of Kemis-5, making a huge spiral pattern and blocking anything below from sight.

"Either find something or eliminate it as a place of interest."

Recker's patience with the situation was wearing thin and he took a deep breath to calm himself. With each passing moment, the *Axiom* drew nearer to Kemis-5, which he told himself would make it easier for the warship's sensors to pierce the storm. If the Meklon had an installation there, Recker knew he had little choice other than to attempt a landing. Everything after that was unknown.

"Engine output at fifty percent," said Eastwood.

The *Axiom* was travelling in excess of a thousand kilometres per second and fifty percent output wasn't nearly enough to make it go higher. Recker kept his hands on the control bars, dropped the engines to idle and allowed the vessel to coast.

"There!" yelled Burner.

"What?" said Recker, closing his eyes for a moment in thanks for his competent crew. Burner always came up with the goods.

"I've located a ground installation, sir. A big one. I've detected a flat area of metal, with perimeter buildings."

"A landing strip," said Recker.

"I'm sure of it."

"Then that's where we're heading," said Recker, adjusting course. "Lieutenants Burner and Larson, your next priority is to search for signs of a Lavorix presence. I don't know why Excon-1 would have sent us here if this base has been captured, but the Meklon have lost their war and we don't know what effect that's had on their comms."

"I'll soon be able to tell you if the facility has been turned to ruins, sir," said Burner. "Finding out in advance if the Lavorix captured it is going to be a lot harder."

"Captured or destroyed," said Eastwood. "Let's hope it's neither."

"We're due some good luck," said Burner.

Recker didn't like to invoke luck, so he didn't say anything. The words *captured or destroyed* kept jumping into his head, eroding his confidence that Kemis-5 was untouched by the Lavorix.

He considered the two. A destroyed base would almost certainly be abandoned, but was unlikely to have any functioning hardware, while a captured base presented a big list of other problems along with opportunities for anyone willing – or desperate enough – to take a risk.

I hope the base is operational. If it's dead, then so is this mission.

"Forty-five percent on the engines, sir. Once the output drops below twenty percent the *Axiom*'s going to be as responsive as an ocean-going super tanker. At five percent, the ternium drive can't support the weight of the hull."

"Which is why we're heading right for the target, Lieutenant."

"That might not be the best choice, sir," said Larson, her voice raised. "I've detected a spaceship in the sky above the Meklon base. It lifted above the storm for approximately five seconds and then dropped out of sensor sight. Whatever it was, it was bigger than the *Aktrivisar*."

"How long before we can see through the storm?"

"I don't know, sir. Once we're within a couple of hundred thousand klicks I'm sure we'll have a much better idea. The trouble is, I think the enemy ship was putting its head up for a look around. By the time we're near enough for our sensors to penetrate the storm, we'll be vulnerable to detection ourselves."

Recker thought hard. "With operational propulsion and the *Aktrivisar* alongside us, I'd chance a frontal attack on that warship. Right now, our options are limited – if it runs into the storm, we could run out of power with the enemy still active."

"What do you suggest, sir?" said Aston.

"We fly in low and blow the crap out of that spaceship before it sees us coming."

"I can tell you straightaway that if we deviate from our

existing course, we're going to be metaphorically running on fumes by the time we reach that Meklon facility, sir," said Eastwood.

"And we can't guarantee that warship is alone," said Larson.

"What choice do we have?" growled Recker. "If the enemy commander sees us coming and decides to play it cagey, we'll lose." He thumped his fist hard on the arm of his chair. "Get me a channel to Captain Jir-Lazan."

"Yes, sir," said Burner. "Channel open."

The Daklan didn't wait for Recker.

"Captain Recker, we should drop low into the storm far from the Meklon facility in order to take our opponent by surprise."

"That's it settled then," said Recker.

"You thought the same?"

"I did."

"It is good that our approach to battle is so in tune. Our chance of victory is increased because of it."

A few moments later, the details were settled. Recker ordered the channel to be closed and he changed the *Axiom*'s heading, aiming to enter the Kemis-5 atmosphere a full half of the planet's circumference away from the Meklon installation. The delayed response from the controls was obvious and it was only going to get worse.

"We've improved our chances of evading detection, but not eliminated them, sir," said Burner.

"Not much we can do about that, Lieutenant. If we take a longer approach path, there'll be no power to activate our weapons systems when we arrive."

"Two hundred thousand klicks and we'll be in the upper atmosphere," said Larson.

"We're in launch range for both our Hellburners and Ilstroms, sir," Aston said.

"I know, Commander. If that enemy warship is equipped with countermeasures similar to those we saw near Excon-1, we'll waste our opening shot. If we lose our surprise, we lose the engagement."

"Yes, sir."

"Forty percent on the engines," said Eastwood. "This is going to be tight."

"The *Aktrivisar* has a little more in the tank than we do, sir," said Burner. "They're on forty-four percent."

"Let's hope this is done without us needing that extra four percent, Lieutenant."

"Another sighting of the warship, sir," said Larson. "I'd estimate its mass at fifty percent greater than the *Aktrivisar*. Hull characteristics are consistent with those of the Lavorix warships we encountered at Excon-1. It's gone back into the storm."

"No indication it saw us," said Burner.

Despite the chill of the bridge air, Recker felt the sweat beading on his scalp and forehead, while his palms felt clammy. He tightened his grip on the controls and willed the universe to allow him a fair chance at the coming engagement.

The pain in his arm returned in a sudden wave and he gritted his teeth. Turning, he met Corporal Hendrix's eyes. She leaned against the weapons cabinet on the left-hand wall, where her presence wouldn't be a distraction.

"I might need a shot of something, Corporal," said Recker. "For the pain."

Hendrix approached, pulling a selection of injectors from her leg pocket. She chose one and stepped closer, her expression concerned.

"Frenziol?" asked Recker with a smile.

"No, sir, I know you don't like the boosters. This is a painkiller and nothing more."

With an apologetic expression, she jabbed the needle through the material over his thigh and the injector squirted ice-cold drugs into his veins. Hendrix selected a second injector and stuck Recker with it before he could say anything.

"That one helps fight infection," she said. "You should let me look at that injury, sir. When you can."

"I can't see it happening soon, Corporal."

She nodded once and smiled. "If I think your life is endangered, I might have to order you to the bay. Sir."

Recker laughed. "In fifteen minutes, there'll be no power to turn the lights on."

With the treatment done, Hendrix retreated to her position next to the cabinet and Recker turned once again to his console. He could feel the painkillers working already and the throbbing receded.

The *Axiom* came steadily closer to Kemis-5 and the Meklon installation vanished around the cusp, preventing Burner and Larson from scanning it further, while also reducing the likelihood of the unknown warship detecting the approach. Still Recker couldn't relax and he took controlled breaths, while checking the sensors and the tactical to ensure his spaceship was on course.

Soon, the *Axiom* and *Aktrivisar* entered the planet's upper atmosphere and Recker reduced speed to prevent the warship burning up. The storms over this part of Kemis-5 were far less ferocious than elsewhere, allowing him an excellent view of a surface which was harshly illuminated by the unnamed, faraway star. A boulder-strewn plain rose into a range of irregular mountains and everything was the same shade of yellow - dreariness turned stark by the sun's light.

"Another wonder of the universe," said Eastwood. "Thirty percent on the engines."

At the agreed altitude of fifty kilometres, Recker levelled the *Axiom*. On the portside feed, he saw the *Aktrivisar* keeping pace, cleaving through the airborne dust and leaving a trail of heated sand in its wake.

"In a month's time, we might find ourselves in combat with that desolator," said Aston. "Right now, I'm damned glad they're with us."

"Me too, Commander."

For three thousand kilometres, the two warships flew across Kemis-5. Here and there, they entered short-lived pockets of thicker sand which the sensors couldn't penetrate, but visibility was mostly good. Then, Recker saw an immense, roiling wall a few hundred kilometres ahead on the gentle curve of the horizon.

At the same moment as the *Axiom* crossed from the planet's day into night, it plunged into the wall of sand. Burner cursed once or twice as he worked on the sensor adjustments, while Larson kept her cool and said nothing.

No storm could fully defy the sensors of a modern warship and the feed improved markedly, though not so much that Recker could see more than a couple of hundred kilometres. He remembered the engagement on Pinvos after the Interrogator came down. The dust then had been thicker yet and Recker felt the experience had honed his skills in low-visibility combat. If the Lavorix ship was as powerful as he feared, he was going to need every advantage.

Minutes passed and the propulsion output continued falling, which meant Recker had to think much further ahead than normal. No longer could he rely on the *Axiom*'s usual agility and by the time the engines were down to twenty-five percent, it seemed like every response on the controls was delayed by two or three seconds.

Eventually, the time came.

"Range to target: two thousand kilometres," said Burner. "From here, there's a chance the enemy warship will see us from its highest detected altitude."

"Understood."

As the distance to target decreased, Recker felt his tension fade. Battle loomed and he was determined to come out on top, come what may. The rewards of victory were uncertain, but for the moment, he didn't spare a thought for anything beyond the nearing fight.

CHAPTER EIGHTEEN

"NO SIGN OF THE ENEMY, SIR," said Burner. "Another few hundred kilometres and I should definitely have a sensor lock."

"The sooner the better, Lieutenant," said Recker. "Commander Aston, fire at the earliest opportunity."

"Yes, sir. Everything we've got, to knock them out of the sky."

"Range to target: eight hundred kilometres."

"Engines at twenty percent, sir."

Recker's eyes darted between the sensor feeds, the tactical and his instrumentation. The fireworks would start soon and he didn't think it was going to be an extended display.

"Any sign of the surface facility yet?"

"Negative, sir. The storm's no thicker than it has been, but it's still too much."

"There's the enemy, sir!" said Larson.

A red dot flashed up on the tactical, at a greater altitude than the *Axiom* and directly over the Meklon base. The dot vanished and Larson cursed.

"Sensor lock failed," she said.

"Any time now," said Aston under her breath.

The red dot appeared for a second time and this time it remained visible for longer. From his periphery, Recker saw Aston's hands poised over the weapons launch panel. The dot disappeared again and Aston withdrew her hand.

"Nearly," she said. "Didn't want to risk it."

Everything happened at once. A sudden thinning of the storm allowed Recker a much clearer view of the Meklon base. It wasn't as extensive as he'd imagined, comprising a twenty-kilometre square alloy landing strip and a collection of low buildings in the north-west corner. From the roof of what was easily the largest building, four large antennae columns jutted several hundred metres into the sky.

Recker wasn't so much interested in the buildings or the Meklon comms station, as he was in the group of five spaceships parked on the landing strip. It only required a glance for him to recognize that three of the spaceships – parked in a neat row in the centre - were Lavorix in origin, each one somewhere between the *Axiom* and *Aktrivisar* in length. The final two were stationary on the western side of the facility. Judging from their design, they were Meklon, but far bigger than the *Vengeance*. Neither looked in a good way.

"Four against two," said Aston.

The largest, airborne Lavorix ship reappeared on the tactical and this time it didn't vanish. When Recker saw that the enemy craft was stationary, his heart jumped.

"They haven't seen us. Give them hell, Commander! We've got to take them out quickly, before they disable us with a core override."

Recker prepared himself for the assault on his senses.

"Upper Ilstrom clusters one through four launched. Forward clusters one through four launched."

The rumble of the missiles came distantly to the bridge and pinpoints of light raced off into the storm.

"Disruptor drones away," said Aston. "Forward Hellburner tubes one and two locked and launched. Railers targeting airborne ship. Full auto activated."

The Hellburners produced a much louder sound as their engines kicked in, and they streaked through the sandstorm, leaving thick orange trails behind them.

"Whoa crap, the *Aktrivisar* just unloaded," said Burner, getting the words out a split second before the Railers started up, filling the bridge with a roaring sound that battered Recker's senses and filled him with the exhilaration of warfare. Lines of white created by the passage of countless hardened alloy projectiles cut through the sand and crashed into the Lavorix warship far overhead.

In the briefest moment Recker allowed himself to look at the portside feed, he witnessed the *Aktrivisar* at its finest. The quantity of missiles ejecting in staggered waves from the desolator's upper tubes drove home what colossal firepower the Daklan had packed into the warship's hull. So close was the vessel that Recker saw the twin barrels of the forward two Terrus cannons kick back with the enormous recoil of their discharge. Graler fire raked the sky and pre-emptive shock-pulse bombs flashed randomly in every direction.

The enemy ship accelerated, heading directly for the *Axiom* and *Aktrivisar*. Burner locked one of the upper sensor arrays on the incoming vessel, though much of its hull was hidden amongst the overlapping Ilstrom detonations. A pair of much larger flashes made Recker squint and then came another series of explosions against the enemy warship's armour.

Any ship in the Daklan or HPA fleets would have succumbed to the onslaught. Incredibly, the Lavorix ship kept on coming and Recker saw from the tactical overlay that it was almost six thousand metres in length and bulky with it.

Hoping to unleash the *Axiom*'s unspent missile clusters, Recker banked the warship, cursing its lack of responsiveness. The closest edge of the Meklon landing field wasn't far ahead and he doubted the three enemy warships would remain quiet for much longer.

"Enemy missiles launched," said Aston. "Disruptor drones out."

The Lavorix warship was fitted with plenty of missile clusters and the warheads rained down into the storm of ballistic, explosive and guidance-scrambling countermeasures.

"Rear Ilstrom tubes one through four launched," said Aston. "Waiting on front and upper reloads."

Great swathes of the inbound missiles were wiped out by the countermeasures. Recker witnessed enemy warheads exploding fruitlessly against disruptor drones, while others were reduced to useless debris. The *Axiom* took several hits on its upper plating and multiple flashes on the *Aktrivisar* indicated the Daklan hadn't escaped unharmed.

"Get me a damage report," ordered Recker, ignoring the rolling shockwave of vibration which swept through the bridge. Lights went red on his console and suddenly, he was so swept up in the engagement that he didn't care. The *Axiom* would hold together, either through an exertion of his will and determination or because the shipyard built it to take everything that was thrown at it and keep on firing.

"Our topside outer plating is ruptured over the rear and portside sections, sir. No breach through the inner plating."

The Terrus cannons thundered again and Aston fired the *Axiom*'s reloaded forward clusters. All the while, the Railers fired at whatever their targeting system could lock onto.

"I'm detecting an energy surge from one of those parked ships," warned Lieutenant Fraser. "The middle one is about to lift off!"

If it was ready to lift off, then it was ready to fire and Recker prepared for a new opponent to enter the fight.

"Parked warship targeted. Underside Ilstrom tubes fired," said Aston. Her words were spoken calmly, but her eyes were unblinking and her movements quick, like the adrenaline was in control.

When Recker diverted his attention to the underside feed, he saw a pair of Terrus slugs crash into the middle parked ship. Each projectile crumpled the enemy armour and left a huge, burning hot indentation. Missiles ejected from the Lavorix craft's topside launchers, passing the Ilstroms and Feilars heading the other way.

The *Axiom*'s portside flank and underside Railers acquired their targets in an instant and sprayed the inbound missile waves. A moment later, the *Aktrivisar* deployed dozens of shock-pulse bombs, which went off all around, concealing the Meklon base in flashes of light which threatened to overload the sensors.

"Forward Hellburners reloaded. Firing."

"Four missile strikes on our underside plating!" said Eastwood.

A new light went red on Recker's console and he braced for the sound of the blasts, which came with the destructive vibrancy of a technological god. With the hairs on his body standing on end, he did what he could with the *Axiom*, banking and making it twist clumsily through the air.

Another half dozen shock-pulse bombs went off, their light bursts fading in moments. The enemy ship laboured into the air, its upper plating ablaze. The Hellburners struck it where the fires burned hottest and the Lavorix ship was at its weakest. Twin explosions sent a half-billion tons of debris upwards and outwards like a fountain, which crashed against the two flanking warships.

One of the adjacent Lavorix warships launched missiles just as a vast sheet of wrecked plating flew overhead. Ten or more of the vessel's own warheads detonated early and the blasts engulfed most its top section, leaving only the nose and stern visible.

"This is what it means to fight, human!" roared Jir-Lazan on a comms channel to the bridge speakers which

Recker didn't even know was open. "These Lavorix will quake at our presence and shit in their boots when we come for their planets!"

"Propulsion at fifteen percent!" yelled Eastwood. "I repeat: propulsion at fifteen percent!"

The largest of the Lavorix ships wasn't done, though Recker couldn't comprehend how it was holding together - it was little more than a fireball on one of the upper sensor feeds. It descended fast while launching missiles in sporadic waves. Aston responded in kind and the *Aktrivisar*'s weapons officers pursued the kill eagerly, bombarding the inbound warship with the desolator's immense arsenal.

"Ah shit," said Recker when he saw what the Lavorix commanding officer intended. "They're coming straight for us."

He banked again, hoping to throw off the inbound warship. The *Axiom* had nothing more to give and it changed course reluctantly, heading over the western edge of the landing strip. Directly below, the two Meklon battleships were quiet and still, and Recker wished it were otherwise.

Sixty billion tons of Lavorix warship plummeted through the sandstorm, trailing flames behind and firing missiles as it went. Ignoring the ground ships, Aston concentrated on the much larger vessel overhead. Such was the intensity of the blaze that Recker couldn't distinguish any details that might offer hope the Lavorix craft was about to break up.

"It's slowing," he said, hauling the *Axiom*'s controls

towards him. The propulsion didn't so much howl as it gave a spluttering, erratic rumble.

A renewed flash from multiple warhead strikes made Recker squint. He briefly saw a hint of darkness within the explosion and then the Lavorix battleship crunched into the *Axiom*'s rear section.

Alarms went off and the life support sucked precious energy from the failing propulsion in order to keep the interior stable. Even so, Recker felt the entire ship lurch from the collision and the jumping instrumentation indicated the warship was spinning around all three axes. From the corner of his eye, he saw the sensors alternate between total darkness and sun-bright light from the Lavorix craft.

The impact reverberation came and it felt like an earthquake, making the hardware fixings squeal with the strain and producing a groan from the floor and walls which made Recker wonder if the damage was terminal.

Somehow in the chaos, Aston locked and launched the portside Ilstroms. New bursts of light covered the sensors, either from missiles or shock-pulse bombs, Recker didn't know which. He fought the controls and the controls fought back. Having stabilised the roll, he felt another collision, with what, he wasn't sure. A distant booming hinted at the detonation of other missiles on the *Axiom*'s armour plating and red lights sprinkled his console in ever-greater numbers.

Then, it all fell into place. Recker's mind identified a pattern in the *Axiom*'s seemingly uncontrolled spin and his hands instinctively moved to correct it. The heavy cruiser was an unwilling subject, but Recker would not accept failure. Compensating for the reduced engine output, he steadied the ship, just as he noticed how quickly it was losing altitude. He tried to correct the descent, unsure if he was too late.

"Going to crash," said Burner.

A grey object filled the underside sensor feed – one of the smaller Lavorix warships was directly beneath the *Axiom*. The enemy spaceship was off the ground, though not by much, and it accelerated sideways. Pinpoints of light indicated the launch of missiles. The range was short – incredibly, stupidly short – and the detonations ripped into the *Axiom*'s underside plating. Once more, the sensors were made useless by the light and the plasma fires.

Instead of fighting the descent, Recker went with it and dumped the *Axiom* straight on top of the Lavorix warship. The renewed impact made everything shudder and this time Recker was prepared for it. Using the mass and the last vestiges of the *Axiom*'s propulsion output, he drove the enemy craft onto the landing strip. A second booming through the heavy cruiser's structure indicated a collision with the ground.

The topside sensors cleared just as a flame-wreathed section of incomprehensibly massive debris fell from the sky. It was too late to avoid the incoming fireball and it struck the nose section of the *Axiom*, crushing it and then sliding onto the Lavorix warship beneath.

"Prepare for total engine failure!" shouted Eastwood. "We've taken too much damage – they're shutting down!"

"Got you another target, sir," said Burner.

Recker didn't have time to curse. A red dot flew across

the tactical, low and near. Lieutenant Burner locked a functioning sensor array on the enemy craft – it was one of those from the landing strip and had somehow made it into the air. Plasma burned in places on its hull, though not enough to bring it down.

"Sensor lock on the *Aktrivisar*," said Larson.

The desolator was on the brink of failure and it didn't require experience to see it. Pieces of debris dropped towards the ground like embers from a dying flame.

"Help them out, Commander," said Recker. He pulled the controls towards him, hoping the *Axiom* might shrug off the weight and rise from the ground one final time. The engines were dead and the warship didn't respond at all.

"We've lost our upper missile clusters, sir," said Aston. "Wait, got two active tubes out of forty-eight. Locked and launched."

Recker didn't know if the *Axiom*'s missiles helped. In front of his eyes, the Lavorix warship crumpled in a way which only multiple Terrus impacts could accomplish. The front two hundred metres of its nose section were completely sheared off and the vessel immediately began falling towards the surface, its flank covered in circular heat patches from the Terrus slugs.

"Captain Recker, our engines have failed," said Jir-Lazan. "We will land in your vicinity." The familiar laugh came. "The Lavorix believed they had us! An eight-Terrus broadside proved them wrong!"

"Sir, the trajectory of the spaceship overhead suggests it will also land in our vicinity."

Other pieces of wreckage – Recker had lost track, but he guessed they were from one of the mid-sized Lavorix warships – also dropped from the sky. One of the larger sections struck the *Aktrivisar*, glancing off before tumbling onto the landing strip.

"Get ready to leave," said Recker, unable to take his eyes away from the continuing destruction.

He picked his helmet from the floor and put it over his head, while keeping watch on the sensor feeds. Many of the arrays had failed completely and others were effectively blinded by plasma fires. One of the portside arrays displayed an image of technological hell – twisted, billion-ton lumps of alloy littered the ground, and the much larger shell of a still-burning Lavorix cruiser lay half-atop a second. Much further away, a two-thousand-metre piece of another warship had landed in the centre of the built-up area of the Meklon base, crushing the comms station and many of the other structures.

The *Aktrivisar* landed nearby, Captain Jir-Lazan somehow eking enough from the desolator's engines to dump it heavily on the ground instead of on top of the *Axiom*. The incoming Lavorix cruiser wasn't so sympathetic and it plummeted, spinning slowly. Its nose caught the *Axiom*'s flank, while the rest – the heaviest part – of the warship thudded onto the spaceship underneath and then slid onto the landing strip. The sound of it happening would have been deafening and Recker was glad he was wearing his suit helmet to block out the worst of it.

For many moments, a series of grating, shrieking and groaning sounds made it seem as if the *Axiom* was being slowly compressed by the weight of debris. Eventually, the noise lessened and Recker immediately noticed the complete absence of a propulsion note. He checked the gauge and it was at zero percent, along with almost every other status monitoring tool.

"We're running on emergency power," said Recker. "Lieutenant Eastwood, find us a way to get outside. Lieutenant Burner, make sure Sergeant Vance and Sergeant Shadar are aware of our chosen exit."

"Yes, sir."

"Lieutenant Larson, speak to somebody on the *Aktrivisar*. Find out their status."

"On it, sir."

"You should issue a deletion command for our data arrays, sir," said Aston.

It was a job Recker couldn't put off any longer. "You're right, Commander." He tapped in a code, waited for the confirmation request and then entered a second code. "Done. There's no going back from here."

"The *Axiom* won't ever fly again, sir."

"I know it, Commander. I'm going to miss this warship."

"Me too."

"Sensors shutting down," said Burner. "I can tap into the backup power for a low-resolution feed if required."

Recker took one last look at the feeds and realised he was never going to make sense of the exterior. Everything was broken and bent. Fires burned and the shimmering air hid whatever details might have been valuable in building a picture of the destruction.

"Don't bother with the sensors, Lieutenant."

"The crew of the *Aktrivisar* are abandoning ship, sir. Captain Jir-Lazan recommends we steal one of the Meklon battleships."

Recker couldn't help but smile. "I thought he might say that. Tell him we like the plan and will assist – once we get the hell off this warship."

He left his seat, opened the weapons locker and selected a gauss rifle and spare magazines. Slinging the gun, he quickly chose others for the rest of his crew and laid them nearby for easy collection. Corporal Hendrix watched him silently, her eyes wide.

"Did you think a warship crew spent all its time sipping fine wines and discussing the weather, Corporal?"

"No, sir, I did not think that."

A combination of adrenaline and powerful painkillers hit him in a rush and he grinned at her. "Now we're going to steal an alien battleship!"

Hendrix grinned back. "I can't wait."

"Sir, our upper shuttle bay is inaccessible, but I've located a possible green light on one of our Puncher tanks in the underside bay," said Eastwood.

"A *possible* green light?"

"It's the best I can offer you, sir."

Recker performed a quick headcount. The *Axiom* was carrying more than thirty humans and Daklan, of whom about fifteen would fit inside the tank, assuming nobody was fussy about close body contact. Punchers had a gravity drive which allowed them to fall any distance without sustaining damage, but that wasn't much use to whichever soldiers were left behind.

"What about the second tank and the deployment craft?"

"Red lights on their docking clamps. I know we can

blow them out, but I'm getting error codes I don't recognize – like something's completely screwed up."

"We're going for the bay," said Recker. "Whatever the problem with the clamps, we'll figure a way round it."

He waited with Hendrix at the exit door while Larson passed on the order to the soldiers, and the rest of his crew picked up rifles. A few seconds later, they exited the bridge and hurried through the interior, where the lighting had turned red and a siren came from wall speakers.

Recker didn't look behind as he ran and, for some reason, he couldn't keep the smile from his face. The mission wasn't nearly over – in fact, the worst may yet be to come - but the incredible carnage had made him feel more alive than he could remember, like some of Jir-Lazan's battle lust had rubbed off on him.

Or maybe I'm part-Daklan.

He laughed, wondering if he was on the verge of insanity or if Hendrix's painkillers possessed mood-enhancing side-effects. The bay wasn't far and he continued his sprint.

CHAPTER NINETEEN

THE *AXIOM'S* underside bay was full of soldiers and the air temperature was in excess of a hundred degrees and climbing. Three members of Vance's squad milled near the open hatch leading to the portside tank – the one with the green light – while several others, including Sergeant Vance, investigated the starboard tank. Elsewhere, Corporal Givens was halfway into the access hatch leading to the deployment vessel and the Daklan stood to one side, keeping out of the way.

"Sergeant Vance, can we free any of this hardware?" said Recker, striding to meet him.

Vance straightened. "I don't know, sir. We've already blown three of the starboard clamps, but the others aren't responding. If we had the time, I'd cut out the floor and try to access the clamps directly."

The bay floor was thick and even with an industrial laser cutter from the ship's stores it would take an age to cut through. "We don't have time, Sergeant."

"That's what I thought, sir."

"What about the deployment vessel?"

"We've blown half of those clamps. Private Raimi's inside with a portable laser cutter. I've ordered him to cut holes in the hull so we can access the clamp control modules."

Recker opened his mouth to speak but the words were drowned out by an abrasive scraping noise coming from beneath the floor. Everything lurched and he struggled for balance. The scraping ended and Recker steadied himself.

"No life support."

A figure appeared at his side. "Sir, you're the only one who can access the Meklon battleships," said Commander Aston. "I recommend you leave the *Axiom* immediately using the available tank. From there, you'll have an outside view of how these soldiers can escape."

Recker didn't like it and his expression showed his feelings.

"This is one of those times when the right decision is the hardest to make, sir," said Aston.

Wise beyond her years.

"Commander Aston is right, sir," said Vance. "You should take the *Axiom*'s crew and leave at once."

"That's six of us," said Recker. "Sergeant Shadar," he said, waving the Daklan closer.

"You must leave," said the Daklan, without being asked.

"I've got six places already filled, Sergeant Shadar. This is a joint mission and I've got enough leftover space for six Daklan in the hull of that tank."

"Negative, Captain Recker. My squad stays with the

others. I have used your warship's comms network to speak to Captain Jir-Lazan. He will not think you have betrayed us." Shadar wasn't finished. "This is war, human. Sacrifices are required."

"We're about to attempt capture of a Meklon battleship," said Recker. "On a base that was previously occupied by the Lavorix. If we encounter resistance, I would prefer to have as many soldiers with me as possible."

Shadar looked as if he wanted to object and Recker guessed that pride or some other Daklan trait was making it difficult for him.

"I want Zivor and Ipanvir," said Recker, picking the Daklan soldiers with the heaviest weaponry. "Sergeant Vance, who knows the Punchers best from your squad?"

Vance avoided mentioning himself. "Private Montero." He took a deep breath and looked somehow defeated. "I'll order Hendrix, Gantry and Private Raimi to go with you as well, sir."

"And Private Haley. I'd rather have the data cube with me in the tank."

"Yes, sir."

Recker nodded once, turned and indicated to his crew that they should enter the tank. He followed them, still feeling shitty that he was abandoning his own warship and leaving these others behind.

Climbing down the shaft, he entered the tank's low-lit, cramped passenger bay, which had a five-foot ceiling, four opposing hard-polymer seats and twin, three-feet-square exit tunnels leading to the left and right flank exits. A flush cabinet on one wall would usually hold guns, magazines and some medical supplies.

Five officers had preceded him and already the interior was crowded.

"The cockpit's mine," Recker growled.

He kept his tank training updated as a habit from his old days and he pushed through the narrow door leading to a tiny room into which the designers had somehow squeezed two bucket seats, a two-operator console and several screens. Everything was powered up and Recker climbed into the right-hand seat. Green light from the screens added a deathly pallor to the material of his suit and he began a series of checks on the hardware.

Montero arrived shortly after and was required to stand on Recker's thigh to access her seat.

"Sorry, sir."

"Don't worry about it, soldier. The comms are online – your job is to stay in touch with Captain Jir-Lazan and the soldiers we're leaving in the bay."

"Yes, sir."

The nominated soldiers were soon inside, with Raimi being last man owing to his longer trip out from the deployment vessel. Recker twisted uncomfortably to ensure everything was in order behind him. As expected, the passenger bay had little spare room and Private Raimi was already grumbling about his face being too close to Ipanvir's armpit.

"Be thankful you are not closer to my anus, human," said the Daklan. "The food from your replicators does not agree with my stomach."

"Small mercies, huh?"

Recker tuned it out. The entry hatch was sealed and everything was ready to go. He gripped the two stubby joysticks which protruded from the front edge of the console in front of him.

"If these clamps don't blow or the underside of the hatch is blocked, this might be the shortest tank mission ever, Private."

"Only one way to find out, sir."

A push of the clamp release button produced a grating thump in the Puncher tank's hull. The sound was different to normal and Recker checked for a failure light. He saw green on the panel and then felt the sensation of movement as the tank was ejected down its launch chute.

The short ride was bumpier than usual and everything shook. With an echoing bang, the tank emerged into a semidarkness filled with shapes and lines, none of which seemed connected. Here and there, alloy glowed red and orange from the heat of recent combat without offering nearly enough illumination to dispel the darkness.

The tank's gravity engine roared in high-stress state as it slowed the vehicle's descent. A Puncher couldn't fly, but it could drift and Recker was reduced to guessing at the best place to aim it.

"Working on a sensor enhancement, sir," said Montero.

Recker had seen her in action before and she didn't require guidance. The engines howled in a crescendo and then he felt the vehicle settle onto a solid surface, which the instrumentation told him was canted at a sharp angle. The tank drifted sideways and he corrected it with instinctive movements of the joysticks. The correction caused the barrel of the main armament to strike another solid object and the tank juddered.

"Hot outside," he said. "The plating beneath us is six hundred degrees."

"Sensor enhancement complete," said Montero.

At first, Recker struggled to comprehend the feeds on the viewscreens, such was the quantity of information. Quickly his brain assembled it into a picture. The *Axiom* had landed on top of a Lavorix warship – this much he knew – and then slid partway onto the landing strip. In the collision, many of the landing legs had buckled and others snapped, and it was one of these which the tank's gauss barrel had collided with.

To the left, through a hundred million tons of scrap, sullen light glowed from the retained heat of plasma detonations, and right, the story was similar, though the illumination was fainter. Recker guided the tank away from the broken landing leg and turned it, intending to obtain a better view of the landing strip. While he steered, Montero did what she could to aim the sensors where they were most needed.

"Here's what the underside of the *Axiom* looks like, sir. Two hundred metres straight overhead."

The quantity of mangled alloy had turned the familiar into something not recognizable, and Recker understood what a miracle it had been that the tank ejection hatch wasn't blocked. Elsewhere, the heavy cruiser's armour was crushed and torn, leaving huge openings through which heat and fading ternium particles escaped. The warship originally had two layers of armour and Recker guessed he was looking at the inner plating, with the outer being completely gone.

"The Sergeant's going to need some ropes," said

Montero. Her voice betrayed the truth – if Vance and Shadar couldn't free the second tank or the deployment vessel, they were stuck in the *Axiom*.

"We can't think about it now," snapped Recker, more angrily than he intended. "Check in with Captain Jir-Lazan – we're heading for the ground."

He pushed the joysticks forward and the tank surged along the slope of uneven alloy. The edge loomed and Recker didn't hesitate – he drove the tank straight over the side, allowing its auto-stabilisation to keep it level as it began a three-hundred-metre controlled descent towards an angled slab of detached plating, which was orange with heat and badly buckled.

The *Axiom* lay at a diagonal overhead and occasional pieces of debris snapped free, falling heavily to the ground.

"Best hope none of that lands on us," said Montero. "I don't think they built the Punchers to carry a million tons."

The tank landed on the angled plate and temperature alerts went off. Recker wasn't too concerned since he wasn't planning to stick around and he pushed the engines to maximum. The vehicle accelerated and Recker concentrated on figuring out a route that would take the tank and its occupants somewhere safer than this.

"Over there, sir," said Montero. "To the right."

Recker saw the place – where the *Axiom* had landed crossways on top of the Lavorix cruiser, a large, triangular opening was created. Further debris – a mere billion tons or so – had crashed down nearby, creating a huge indentation in the alloy landing strip and partially blocking the way out. A gap remained and Recker steered for it.

"Captain Jir-Lazan has almost completed his evacuation, sir," said Montero. "He sounds impatient."

"It's been a whole five minutes since he blew something up, Private."

The tank raced off the edge of the immense armour plate and dropped the final fifty metres to the ground. As the Puncher descended, Recker noted how the multiple surface impacts had turned this part of the landing field into a cavernous, irregular bowl. Not that the tank was affected – it hit ground level with a roar of engine compensation and accelerated once more, unaffected by the heat and the sloped surface.

"Reports of hostiles," Montero continued. "Numbers and capabilities unknown."

The presence of Lavorix was unwelcome but not surprising, and Recker hoped the quantity of opposition had been badly depleted by the recent devastation.

"If they've reinforced the interior of those battleships, we've got an uphill task in front of us, Private."

"I know it, sir."

Debris continued to fall and Recker realised the engine reverberation was likely dislodging some of the most precariously attached pieces. He slowed – fractionally – and guided the tank towards the opening, now about three hundred metres away. The topside sensor feed was of endless broken alloy, providing another reminder Recker didn't need of how insignificant humanity was in the face of its own creations.

One of the *Axiom*'s landing legs snapped with a

screech and fell towards the tank. On the sensor, it seemed like darkness moving through darkness and Recker steered the tank left. With a mighty crash, the huge piece of alloy landed end-first, twenty metres from the Puncher, and started toppling.

With his teeth bared in angry defiance against the universe and the vagaries of luck, Recker changed course again. With a tremendous, crunching thud, the landing leg came down parallel to the tank, crushing several pieces of smaller debris, but hardly making a mark on the heavily reinforced landing strip.

"Screw you!" said Montero with feeling, offering her middle finger to several million tons of uncaring metal.

Still travelling at near-maximum velocity, the tank approached the triangular opening which Recker felt sure would lead to comparative safety. He heard another scraping sound, this time so powerful that he felt the vibration through his seat and the joysticks. A glance at the right-hand sensor feed showed Recker what happened to those who didn't give luck its proper respect.

Slowly and with increasing pace, the wrecked *Axiom* slid across the hull of the Lavorix warship. More debris came down and the sound which accompanied the movement of the heavy cruiser almost triggered the primeval flight instinct in Recker. He held it together and focused on the opening.

For a few seconds, the scraping, grinding of the sliding warship became everything, and Recker wondered if he'd lost his mind – perhaps the injury to his arm had made him delirious and this was all part of his imagination.

He knew the idea was false and refused to accept the

distraction. Steering the tank around the final obstacle – an unidentifiable, three-metre cube of grey – Recker guided the tank through the opening.

Suddenly, the upper sensor feed was of swirling sand and grit. An enormous, billion-ton mass of debris glowed dark orange ahead, creating a halo in the storm. Recker steered left in front of it and kept one eye on the rear feed, knowing he wasn't yet in the clear. The *Axiom*'s sideways motion was briefly halted by a stack of broken plating piled up against the Lavorix ship. Hardly had the slide been arrested when the enormous weight of the heavy cruiser crushed the resistance and it started again.

The tank sped on and ten seconds later it was out of the danger area, leaving the *Axiom* perched at a peculiar angle, half supported by wreckage and half held in place by the hull of the Lavorix cruiser.

Unwilling to stop, Recker kept the Puncher going for a few seconds longer and then he reduced speed to half in order that he could take stock. The exhilaration from earlier was gone, reducing his appreciation of the chaos and leaving him with a feeling that this mission wasn't nearly over.

He was right.

CHAPTER TWENTY

THE SANDSTORM BLEW AND RECEDED, blew and receded, sometimes offering a clear view of the landing strip before sweeping in and reducing everything to dim shapes. One thing was certain - the Meklon base was effectively no more.

In the approximate centre of the landing strip lay a total of six ultra-powerful warships in varying states of destruction. The *Axiom* was on top of a Lavorix cruiser, while half – maybe more, maybe less – of something else lay on top of that. On the far side of the heap, a nose and midsection of another enemy ship jutted high into the air, pointing at a diagonal that made Recker wonder if that, too, would soon come crashing down.

To the right, a thousand metres of desolator was visible on the far side of the wreckage and it seemed to Recker as if Captain Jir-Lazan hadn't been able to land it quite as straight as he'd wanted, since the hull was leaning sideways. Elsewhere, a three-thousand-metre section of the largest enemy warship had come down about three kilometres away, landing directly between Recker and the Meklon battleships.

Much of the debris glowed from heat and though most of the fires had dwindled and died, a few remained here and there. The light wasn't much, and Recker was glad Montero displayed so much expertise with the sensors.

Recker mentally added up the tally. "A hundred billion tons of scrap," he said bitterly. "And then some."

"At least we climbed out of it," said Montero.

Her response made Recker forget his anger. "Damn right we did, soldier. We live to fight another day and that's something to celebrate."

"Here's where you tell me those celebrations will have to wait until we've captured an alien battleship and flown it home, sir."

Recker laughed. "High command would call that a display of *morale-sapping cynicism*, Private Montero."

"And what do you call it, sir?" Montero's eyes gleamed with humour and it made Recker glad to see.

"I always used to call it *frontline realism,* soldier. Truth learned the hard way by the men and women holding the guns."

When she heard the words, Montero stared at Recker. Really stared at him, like she was just beginning to understand something. Then, she offered him a smile like a sunrise on a summer's day.

"Now that the *Axiom* is shot to pieces, do I have permission to call it the *Gabriel Solan*, sir?" she asked, her expression full of mischief.

"Hell, no, Corporal. The *Axiom*'s a hero fallen in battle – you'll treat it like one."

An inbound comm broke the moment and Montero turned away with one hand pressed to her earpiece.

"Captain Jir-Lazan has completed his evacuation, sir. Only two of the *Aktrivisar*'s shuttles would launch, and they managed to deploy a single armoured ground vehicle. He reports potentially organized resistance." Montero put an overlay on the tank's tactical screen and reinforced it by pointing towards the desolator. "The Daklan are that way."

"Let's join up with them," said Recker. "Ask Jir-Lazan how many troops he commands."

"Forty-eight, sir."

Under Recker's control, the tank accelerated to its maximum speed and raced across the landing strip. Smaller pieces of debris lay everywhere and he guided the vehicle around them. Even these fragments of armour, engines and broken technology were larger than the Puncher, and some had made their own small indentations in the landing strip when they crashed down.

"I've got our comms system speaking to the Daklan comms system, sir," said Montero. "There's a data delay, but it's better than nothing."

The Daklan shuttles and ground vehicle appeared on the tactical, near the desolator and not moving.

"That's much better than nothing, Private," said Recker.

"And I've spoken to Sergeant Vance – the deployment vessel isn't going anywhere, so he's ordered the squad to cut a hole through the bay floor to the second Puncher. Private Enfield is going to blow the stuck clamps."

"What's wrong with the deployment vessel?"

"The underside sensor indicates the launch chute is bent out of shape."

"Damn."

Recker didn't bother wondering how long it would take to cut open the floor around the second tank, since he'd asked himself the question earlier and come up with an answer he didn't like.

"Sergeant Vance won't want to miss the party," said Montero, evidently thinking similar thoughts.

"I'm certain Sergeant Shadar feels the same."

"Those Daklan like to fight, sir."

Recker steered the tank around a two-hundred-metre piece of debris which appeared to be part of a missile launch cluster. "You think?"

"Don't you, sir?" asked Montero, blinking in surprise.

"Do you like fighting, Private?"

Montero had a spark of something – a mind that was wasted on shuttle and tank comms. She opened her mouth and then closed it again without saying anything.

"Not far to go," said Recker.

"I'll check in with the Daklan again, sir. Find out what the plan is." Montero saw Recker's broad smile and her expression became one of confusion. "What's wrong?"

"Ask him."

Montero got on the comms, though not for long.

"I asked Captain Jir-Lazan what the plan is, sir."

"What did he tell you?"

"We're going to rip out the gizzards of those four-armed bastards and take the battleships from them. Most of that was a word-for-word quotation."

"You were expecting something more?"

"The straightforward plans are the best plans, sir, that's what I was always taught."

"And right after that you were told the devil is in the detail?"

"Yes, sir."

"Often the detail slows you down, Private. I've seen engagements lost because an officer took too long working out a clever way to do something that was already easy."

"Assholes like that never realise real people are dying when they screw up."

"That officer was me, Private."

Montero turned and Recker was pleased that she didn't apologise, since it wasn't needed. "I'm glad you learned, sir."

He smiled. "That I did."

The journey's progress carried the tank past the 3000-metre chunk of wreckage and gradually, more of the closest Meklon battleship was revealed. During the heat of the recent combat, Recker hadn't been able to focus his attention on the two identical vessels, but he remembered they were each 4500 metres in length, with sleek mid- and rear sections, and wedge noses.

His first impression also made him think these battle-ships were far older than the *Vengeance* and he wondered if they were left here on Kemis-5 because they were obsolete, or, given the extensive cratering on their armour plates, too badly damaged to fly. His primary concern was bringing the data cube back to the HPA and for that he required a lightspeed-capable warship. Whatever their limitations or how many repairs they needed, the Meklon craft were the only chance at getting home.

If they have a high enough lightspeed multiplier and assuming the Gateway didn't take us across half the universe.

"The Daklan report we've got incoming, sir," said Montero suddenly. "A Lavorix shuttle from the northwest."

"Damnit," said Recker. He checked the tactical, which showed only friendlies. "I can't see it."

"It must have gone out of the Daklan sensor sight."

"Which means it's coming straight over that big section of warship," he said.

Montero quickly adjusted the sensors, just in time to see the enemy shuttle race low over the top of the debris. Recker sized it up quickly and guessed from the vessel's dimensions and the aggressive approach that it was fitted with some potent weaponry.

"Big bastard," Montero observed. "Could fit a couple of hundred troops in that one, easy."

"Bandits online," said Recker, confirming that the tank's twin shoulder chain gun countermeasures were operational.

The guns suddenly fired, with a pulsing clank that made normal-volume conversation impossible.

"Missiles!" said Montero. "Two out of two down!"

The Bandits cut out as quickly as they'd started. Recker pointed the tank towards a buckled section of armour plating ahead and to the left, while adjusting the aim on the gauss turret by using a touchpad on top of the left joystick.

"Firing main armament," he said.

The coils within the upper turret whined and then discharged in a deep bass expulsion of energy that momentarily increased the air pressure in the cockpit before it dissipated. A massive ball of alloy was ejected from the barrel and it hurtled towards the shuttle. The Lavorix pilot was aware of the danger and he threw his craft to one side, causing the gauss slug to skim wide.

"Shit, missed," said Recker.

His words were drowned out by renewed fire from the Bandit chain guns. This time, Recker saw the orange streaks of twin incoming missiles. The Bandits did their job, smashing the Lavorix warheads to pieces.

A drumming started up on the hull, like a thousand hammers striking the external plating. The tank was designed to take a beating, but from the volume of the incoming fire, Recker knew the shuttle's nose gun was too much for the Puncher's armour to withstand for long.

"Main armament reloaded," he yelled, readying himself for a second shot.

The debris he planned to use for cover came between the tank and the shuttle, causing Recker to hold fire. He pulled back on the joysticks and the tank slowed to a crawl, while remaining out of sight. A check of the tactical told him the Daklan weren't being passive and their shuttles were moving into a better position to target the enemy vessel.

"Captain Jir-Lazan reports an increase in enemy activity, sir," said Montero. "They're going for the furthest battleship."

"Any visible way to access those ships?"

"Forward boarding ramp on the target ship, sir, and that's where they're heading. The nearer one is locked up tight."

"If I can reach one of the access panels, I should be able to get onboard," said Recker. He grimaced. "That's if my security tier is high enough."

"The Daklan shuttles have engaged with the enemy, sir," said Montero.

"Let's take a look."

Recker pushed the joysticks forward and the tank leapt into motion. The moment it was clear of the protective debris, Recker slowed it again and hunted for the target. A thickening of the sand over the landing field obscured his view of the Lavorix shuttle, though the sensors detected flickering gauss tracers.

Orange trails of missile propulsion appeared in the storm's gloom, travelling at incredible speed. Recker threw the tank into reverse and the Bandits fired once more.

Too late.

The fleeting thought called it wrong. One of the missiles was knocked out by the tank's chain guns and the second detonated in a blinding flash against the edge of the protective debris. From the size of the blast, Recker wasn't sure the Puncher could withstand even a single direct hit.

He pushed the joysticks forward again, gambling on the shuttle having a long reload on its missiles. Again, the tank thundered out of cover and Recker stared intently at the sensor feed, seeking the tell-tale shape of the Lavorix vessel.

"There!" yelled Montero.

Recker saw it too. Through a stroke of luck, the main armament required almost no adjustment and he squeezed the activation trigger hard. Pressurized bass caught him in the chest and the gun fired just as the airborne sand thinned enough to reveal the target.

The military didn't call these Puncher tanks without good reason and the projectile smashed into the Lavorix shuttle with tremendous force. The spaceship's entire nose section crumpled and a huge, heat-rimmed hole appeared. Whatever was in the cockpit was killed instantly and the transport tilted in the air, while the Daklan shuttles continued bombarding it with slugs from their nose guns.

"Yes!" said Montero.

"Down it comes," said Recker with great satisfaction.

He gave the engine full power again and the tank accelerated towards the Daklan positions. As soon as the main armament reloaded, he treated the stricken Lavorix shuttle to a second direct hit and the vessel's weakened hull plummeted towards the ground.

Not sparing the broken enemy craft any more of his attention, Recker focused on guiding the tank safely to its destination. The journey didn't take long, though during it, he learned that Sergeant Vance had – using a combination of high explosives and two laser cutters – almost freed the second Puncher tank.

As a counter to the good news, he also learned via Private Montero that the Lavorix were piling their troops into the further battleship and had landed another shuttle on top of the closest, with the likely intention of entering and securing that one also.

"Sometimes, I wish things would be just a little easier," Recker said.

"Life would be no fun if everything fell in our laps, sir."

Recker glanced at Montero and shook his head in mock despair. She responded by asking a question he'd been putting off asking himself.

"If the Lavorix got some of the Excon-1 weaponry active, won't they be able to do the same with those battleships, sir?"

"I don't know, Private." He took a deep breath and nodded. "Given time, they'll manage it. How much time, I don't know."

His eyes went to the tank's velocity gauge and suddenly it didn't seem like the vehicle was travelling nearly fast enough.

CHAPTER TWENTY-ONE

HAVING BEEN TAKEN unawares by a savage and uncompromising assault from the *Axiom* and *Aktrivisar*, the surviving Lavorix were recovering quickly.

Under guidance from Jir-Lazan, Recker brought the Puncher alongside the shortest edge of the huge section of spaceship which had crashed onto the landing strip. The wreckage towered overhead, emitting heat and other particulate crap which Recker would have preferred to stay away from.

From here, he was granted a limited view of the new battlefield, though he wasn't eager to poke his nose too far out just yet. Straight ahead, the front thousand metres of the nearest battleship was visible approximately 1200 metres away. The second was parked parallel and Recker couldn't see much of that one – only glimpses of its landing legs.

By this time, he'd learned that the enemy possessed at least two more shuttles and a handful of armoured ground vehicles, these latter being fast-moving, low-profile gravity-engined octagons with deflective sides and chain guns.

The Lavorix forces had either been permanently stationed in the built-up – and now mostly flattened - north-west of the facility, or they'd been in the process of searching it, and it was from here they emerged, seemingly more concerned to reach the battleships than to kill the Daklan.

Recker guessed the enemy had more than one reason for acting in this way. Firstly, they'd seen their air support destroyed and were likely unsure if they faced any other warships. Under those circumstances, the interior of a Meklon battleship was the safest place to be.

Secondly, and most worrying, the Lavorix may well be able to activate the Meklon weapons. Once that happened, all bets were off, unless Recker could beat them to it.

In typical Daklan style, Jir-Lazan had begun extensive harassment of the Lavorix. Using his two shuttles – one of which he piloted himself - he sprayed the enemy ground vehicles with generous quantities of projectiles. In response, the Lavorix shuttles launched missiles, which the Daklan countered by using their single ground vehicle, which was equipped with an advanced track-and-destroy anti-missile turret.

It was a dangerous game and one in which both sides had everything to lose.

"The Daklan cock-gun is the only thing keeping us in this," said Montero, using the nontechnical description. "It's taking out the Lavorix shuttle missiles as quickly as they can fire them."

Recker had never learned the Daklan name for these particular vehicles and in this instance, he was glad to have the *cock-gun* on his side. He'd encountered them before – they comprised a solid gravity engine base, upon which sat a turret housing a mini Graler. This multi-barrelled gun could track numerous targets and knock them out of the sky with incredibly accurate bursts of explosive-accelerated gauss slugs. For ground troops, it was immensely frustrating to see not only air-launched missiles being smashed to pieces, but also those fired from shoulder launchers.

"Shame we were out of its defensive arc when that shuttle came for us," said Recker.

"We weren't. The Daklan only got it working a few minutes ago. Besides, we shouldn't rely on the cock-gun, sir. They aren't infallible."

"Nothing is."

Far away, beneath the shelter of the *Aktrivisar*'s hull, the miniaturised Graler fired, its barrels turning and spitting out fifty-metre jets of flame. Overhead, Captain Jir-Lazan's shuttle flew sideways at high velocity, its gunfire raking into one of the octagonal vehicles which darted amongst the landing legs of the closest battleship. Unable to withstand the punishment, the Lavorix vehicle broke into pieces.

At Recker's request, Jir-Lazan now had an open channel to the speakers in the Puncher's cockpit.

"The enemy are numerous and persistent," said the Daklan. "For every one of their vehicles we destroy, two more emerge from the distant buildings. I cannot kill them all while evading the attacks from their shuttles."

"I've got a second tank preparing to deploy," said

Recker, having heard only moments ago that Sergeant Vance had freed the other Puncher.

"A welcome addition, but perhaps not enough, Captain Recker. We must find a way to access the nearest battleship – a way that does not result in your death."

"The battleships have no open receptors, so I can't even talk to their control computers, let alone transmit my biometric data."

"Every warship can be accessed from above," said Jir-Lazan. "I will find the way, human, and I will fly you to it."

While he talked, Recker had an eye on the tactical. Three red dots appeared, coming fast from the north-west corner of the base. Acting at once, Recker guided the tank away from the cover of the debris, whereupon he was granted a view of the entire length of the Meklon battleship, though the rear section was badly obscured by the storm.

Montero didn't require prompting and she added a filter overlay which improved the distance focus of the lens. Narrowing his eyes, Recker spotted three grey smears amongst the clouds of sand. He fired the main armament at eight thousand metres and, a split-second later, one of the octagons was overkilled by the Puncher's gun. Immediately, the other two split, heading erratically left and right.

"Sergeant Vance is inbound, sir!" said Montero. "He somehow got everyone inside the second Puncher."

"We'll need one of those laser cutters to get them out."

"Definitely. The tank's comms antenna and one of their Bandits was destroyed by...*explosives*...so I can't add them to the local battle network. It's suit comms or nothing."

"Suit comms are better than no comms."

A warning chimed from the tank's console and two shuttle-launched Lavorix missiles streaked between the landing legs of the nearest battleship, heading for the Puncher. At the same moment, a previously unseen enemy soldier fired a shoulder launcher from behind a different landing leg. Recker spotted the shuttle rising to take cover behind the battleship's hull and didn't even attempt to re-aim.

The Bandits clanked and the Daklan mini Graler fired from three kilometres away, while Recker tried desperately to get his tank back into cover. No missiles hit the Puncher. Recker didn't care which of the countermeasures did the job and he drove the tank forward again, chose his target and fired with a tiny lead. Another of the approaching ground vehicles was taken out.

The Lavorix shuttle didn't reappear, but the ground soldier fired a second rocket. This time, Recker was prepared and he took the Puncher straight out of sight and the enemy rocket detonated against the wall of debris.

"Private Raimi, poke your head out of the topside hatch," Recker ordered on the comms. Ipanvir was the better shot, but he wasn't close enough to the exit hatch to get there in a hurry. "There's a tube soldier hiding fifth outer leg from the battleship's nose. Give him something to think about."

"On it, sir."

The hull seal warning flashed a few moments later, allowing heat and ternium particles to flood the interior.

"Ready, sir. I can't see the fifth leg."

"You will."

Recker drove the tank out of cover again. He left Raimi to do his thing and concentrated on the final inbound vehicle. He spotted it at seven thousand metres, cutting left to gain some protection from the battleship's landing legs. Recker breathed deeply, refusing to be distracted by the launch howl of Raimi's shoulder tube coming through the passenger bay behind him. A squeeze of the trigger made the Puncher's gun thunder and the final enemy vehicle was destroyed by a direct hit. Elsewhere, the blast from Raimi's launcher landed dead on target. The kill was unconfirmed, but no more rockets came from that direction.

"Want me to stay up here, sir?" said Raimi. "I don't think the main armament is powerful enough."

"Yes, stay where you are, Private."

Movement on the tactical told Recker that two of the enemy transports had risen simultaneously from behind the battleship. They fired missiles, both aiming for the second of the Daklan shuttles. From down on the ground, Recker couldn't see the enemy to get off a shot. The Graler fired, the Daklan fired and the Puncher's Bandit guns targeted and fired.

"We don't have time for peekaboo," Recker growled.

He chose a destination, which was the place where Raimi had landed his rocket. He pushed the tank's engines to maximum and it surged out of cover. Movement on the right sensor feed caught his eye and a flaming chunk of mangled alloy came hurtling down from above. It smashed with finality into the landing strip five hundred metres away.

"We have lost a shuttle, Captain Recker," said Jir-

Lazan, calmly as if it was no setback at all. "I see you hope to surprise our enemy."

"Damn right I do."

Soon, the tank hit top speed and Recker offered it some blunt, verbal encouragement to travel faster. The shelter of the battleship seemed a long way distant and he willed the Puncher across the intervening space. A menacing shape dropped into sight, through the forest of landing legs.

"Sir!" called Montero urgently.

"I see it," said Recker, steering the tank left and putting a column of alloy between the tank and the shuttle.

"If we can't see them, they can't see us," said Montero.

The enemy flew into sight, hunting a missile lock. Raimi was fast and he got off the first shot, sending a perfectly placed rocket through the landing legs.

"Yee-ha!" he yelled.

The blast engulfed the shuttle's nose, but the enemy fired in return, sending two missiles of their own at the Puncher, and a cascade of Lavorix chain gun fire smashed into the tank's front plating. Swearing loudly, Recker steered right, seeking cover. The Bandit guns fired, destroying one missile, while the other evaded the chain gun slugs.

That one's got our names on it.

To Recker's astonishment, the inbound missile disintegrated right in front of him on the feed, no more than fifty metres from the tank, and the pieces were whisked away amongst a blurred wave of movement.

"I'll never call them cock-guns again," said Montero.

The tank's velocity took it near enough to the landing leg that the enemy's firing angle was eliminated and the drumming against the hull stopped at once.

"No kill," said Recker. He raised his voice. "Private Raimi?"

"I'm not dead, sir. Damn near broke my ankle coming down that shaft so fast."

"Get back up there and close that hatch."

"Yes, sir."

Like the worst bad smell, the Lavorix shuttle didn't go away and it hovered out of sight, its burning nose creating a puddle of flickering illumination which was all Recker had to pinpoint its location.

"They're waiting on missile reload," he said.

"We're going to reach that landing leg first."

"Yes we are."

Recker held course and the battleship's immense form blotted out half of the sky. Smaller shapes darted across the spaces between the landing legs, and the tank's approach brought one of the octagonal vehicles into sight, midway across the warship's beam. The vehicle accelerated, spraying the Puncher with its chain gun.

"Have this," said Recker, firing a gauss slug into the armoured car. The impact flipped the enemy vehicle over and sent the wreckage skittering a hundred metres across the landing field.

A shoulder launched rocket streaked into view from somewhere to the right, coming for the tank, and a faint clattering of small arms fire sounded against the hull. As quick as Recker was on the controls, the tank wasn't agile enough to escape the rocket, which detonated on the

Puncher's front-right quarter. The blast was huge and obscured every sensor feed, but Recker put his faith in HPA engineering and held tightly until the screens cleared.

"Moderate damage, sir," said Montero. "Right side Bandit showing an amber."

The inbound fire stopped the moment Recker tucked the Puncher in against the landing leg. He knew the respite would be short lived and considered his options. Overhead, Jir-Lazan was trading fire with the second Lavorix shuttle, and, even though no more of the octagonal vehicles approached from the north-west, the enemy already had the upper hand in that they'd established themselves at the far battleship.

"We've got to force a result," said Recker. "If Jir-Lazan loses his shuttle, we'll never get into this battleship."

Nobody wanted to try storming the other vessel. Even if it were possible, the casualties would be unthinkable.

A second rocket shrieked across the feed, crashing against the edge of the landing leg covering the Puncher. Recker got the message – the enemy hadn't forgotten about him. He slammed the joysticks left and the tank emerged from cover, with its gun pointing directly at the place he hoped to find the shuttle. The enemy vessel appeared, flying sideways from its hiding place. Recker took a shot, only to find he'd been lured into a mistake by the Lavorix pilot when the shuttle disappeared back into cover without fully revealing itself.

Knowing what was coming, Recker threw the tank back towards the landing leg just as the enemy craft reappeared.

"Too slow," said Montero. Her middle finger was getting a workout today and she raised it at the enemy.

The sensors picked up the sound of a howling gravity engine, as the Lavorix shuttle accelerated across the battleship's underside, the pilot gambling he could beat the Puncher's reload and deliver two point blank missiles into the tank.

"Screw you," said Recker.

He didn't slow the tank and kept it going sideways. As soon as he was past the right edge of the landing leg, he drove it forward, rotating the turret as he did so. The rocket soldier took the opportunity to fire again and Recker ignored the incoming rocket as he hunted for the shuttle. A booming explosion against the rear plating made the console buzz against its mountings.

He found the fast-moving, heat-glowing enemy vessel, still rotating and still expecting to find the tank on the far side of the landing leg. The Lavorix pilot's race against the Puncher reload failed badly and Recker put a slug through the shuttle's plating, creating a huge, visible hole all the way through.

"You go one way and I go the other!" said Montero in excitement. "Oldest trick in the book!"

Recker was certain the shuttle was out of action, but he didn't wait around in case it somehow managed to launch missiles at the tank. He guided the vehicle towards cover again, only to witness a second massive impact against the enemy vessel, this one coming from a different direction and resulting in unmistakeably terminal damage.

"Sergeant Vance apologises for being late, sir," said Montero.

"Tell him he'll have to shoot twice as many Lavorix to make up for it," said Recker with a smile.

Even as he spoke, Recker didn't lose focus on the battle. The rocket soldier was becoming a nuisance and the final Lavorix shuttle was still operational. Not only that, small arms fire continued inexplicably to drum against the Puncher, as if the enemy thought the slugs from their gauss rifles were going to take out a tank. He shrugged mentally – if it kept them occupied, that was fine by him.

Replicating the out-in feint of the shuttle, Recker drew the rocket soldier into sending another of his shots into the same landing leg.

"Let's take care of this bastard and his friends," he said.

With the attacking shuttle out of the way, Recker switched the Bandits to their secondary mode which the software programmers had appropriately named *massacre*. The right-hand chain gun was damaged and locked into a limited firing arc, but the other was fully operational. Both started firing at once and Recker steered the tank at high speed between the landing legs. The Lavorix foot soldiers became aware of the danger far too late to escape, and high-calibre gauss projectiles reduced dozens of them to bloody paste.

Two more shoulder-launched rockets flew towards the tank, this time fired from places beneath the far battleship. One of the rockets crashed into a landing leg and the other hit the damaged Bandit, putting it out of action. The second gun continued firing, changing aim with terrifying speed. Recker did what he could to make the Puncher elusive, by driving it erratically and steering in and out of cover.

"We've got Sergeant Vance with us," said Montero.

Vance wasn't a man prone to hesitation or timidity and he piloted the second Puncher beneath the battleship, three hundred metres south of Recker's position. The other tank had taken a rocket hit but wasn't slowed and Recker was grateful to have another soak for the enemy fire.

"You must destroy the remaining shuttle, Captain Recker," said Jir-Lazan on the comms. "The Churner is almost out of ammunition and my vessel has suffered substantial damage."

Recker acknowledged and altered the tank's course, aiming it directly for the opposite side of the battleship. The Bandit gun roared and the engines did likewise. In a cloud of kicked-up sand and grit, the Puncher raced from beneath the warship's hull. A rocket came from the near edge of the second battleship, too fast to avoid. It exploded on the front plating and the interior cockpit light turned deep red.

Ignoring the alarm, Recker searched for the second shuttle. It was currently out of sensor sight and therefore didn't show on the tactical, yet he knew it was hiding between the Meklon battleships, waiting for its missile tubes to reload.

"There!" said Montero.

Recker got the shuttle – four hundred metres up and a similar distance north - in his sights. It was turning in the tank's direction, but too slowly to launch its missiles. Recker fired. A whump of discharge followed his pressure on the trigger and a gauss projectile thudded into the shuttle, striking it towards the rear, rather than on the side of the cockpit where he'd intended.

The force of the shot exaggerated the enemy craft's rotation, bringing its missile tubes to bear a fraction of a second quicker. Recker tried to escape, knowing it was too late. He saw his death coming and snarled in defiance.

Sergeant Vance came to his aid when everything seemed lost. The slug from the second Puncher struck the shuttle exactly where Recker had wanted his own to land. A hole appeared in the vessel's armour and the surrounding metal shrank inwards from the force of the impact.

Out of control, the Lavorix craft continued rotating, losing altitude as its engines shut down. Having seen enough and with several of his tank's onboard systems flashing red lights in his vision, Recker turned the vehicle and gave it full speed towards the far side of the huge section of wreckage, intending to rendezvous with Jir-Lazan.

As he drove the failing tank onwards, Recker did his best not to think about what he'd seen beneath the second battleship. The Lavorix had two of the boarding ramps open and a dozen or more of the octagonal vehicles were parked in the vicinity. He doubted any assault on the second battleship would succeed, leaving only one way to victory.

"A *Churner*, huh?" said Montero, bring him out of his reverie.

"That's what the Daklan said."

"I'd best spread the word," she said, sounding slightly disappointed.

Recker smiled and shook his head. A short time later, he arrived on the far side of the debris wall and waited for Jir-Lazan to set the shuttle down. When the vessel landed, Recker was shocked at the damage it had taken and the fact that it was still flying was testament to how tough the Daklan built their transports.

No sooner had he brought the tank to a halt than its engines shuddered and cut out. With a bone-jarring thud it dropped to the ground and Recker had no hesitation in ordering the evacuation.

Not long after, he clambered from the upper exit hatch and jumped quickly from the hull to escape the intense heat spilling from its armour. Only once on his sprint to the shuttle did Recker turn. He caught sight of Sergeant Vance's tank coming through the sandstorm.

What really caught his eye was the tank he'd just vacated. The Puncher was a mess of half-melted alloy and heavily pocked from gauss impacts. The only undamaged part was the main armament.

He smiled inwardly. Mostly the gun was all you needed.

With the wind buffeting him and heavy particles of sand cascading against his combat armour, Recker climbed into the Daklan shuttle.

CHAPTER TWENTY-TWO

A SQUAD of Daklan soldiers stood watchfully in the passenger bay. This was the first time Recker had been onboard one of their transports and he wasn't surprised by the sight of bare walls, hard-looking seats and racks of weapons. In the rear of the bay, replacement combat suits and other spare parts had been dumped in a heap.

"Move!" he yelled, turning and waving his crew and the rest of the tank's passengers inside.

Intending to speak directly to Captain Jir-Lazan, Recker hurried towards the open cockpit door. Unexpectedly, sand blew through into the passenger bay and a sense of alarm gripped him.

The cockpit hardware was as predictable as the contents of the bay and Recker didn't spare the pilot's console more than a glance. A jagged tear had been created in the forward bulkhead and it was through this opening that the sand blew. Two of the four sensor screens were twisted and broken, while the other two feeds were fixed on the debris pile a short distance away.

To Recker's left, the backup pilot was dead, his body turned into a pulp by whatever projectiles had breached the shuttle's armour, and his blood coated almost every surface, the smell of it sharp and unwanted. A second Daklan lay nearby, also dead.

Captain Jir-Lazan was big and heavyset like the others of his species. He was sitting in the closest seat, his broad-knuckled combat gloves wrapped around the control sticks. The Daklan half-turned painfully and Recker stared into the deep green eyes of his opposite number.

"I am dying," said Jir-Lazan, indicating the enormous patch of blood on his chest.

Recker couldn't spot the source of the injury and didn't waste time looking. "Corporal Hendrix, get in here!" he yelled.

"You can fly, Captain Recker," said Jir-Lazan, making a weak gesture towards the other seat.

Without hesitation, Recker heaved the co-pilot's body onto the floor. Even with half of its blood and innards missing, it required an effort and when the corpse thumped down, Recker took its place, his hands and arms covered in gore.

"Upon your return, you will treat my species fairly," said Jir-Lazan.

Recker understood the meaning. "The mission spoils will be shared equally," he promised.

Corporal Hendrix appeared, dropped her med-box on the floor and sized up the situation. "Have you taken one of these?" she said, thrusting an injector into Jir-Lazan's line of vision.

"We Daklan do not take..."

Jir-Lazan didn't finish the sentence before Hendrix jabbed the needle into his chest. The Daklan didn't complain and allowed her to attach sensors from the medbox to his chest.

"Captain Recker, you are taking too long," said the alien.

"It's in hand," said Recker.

He gripped the backup controls. HPA shuttles were usually basic and the Daklan equivalent seemed no different. Already, he'd identified the function of several control panels. Once you knew how to fly, it wasn't hard to pick up on similar methods to achieve the same goal.

"Commander Aston," Recker shouted. "We're taking off. Make sure Sergeant Vance knows we're coming back for him." He turned to Jir-Lazan. "How big is the crew in the Churner?"

"No crew, human. I set it to automatic."

Recker had another thought. "What about your bridge team?"

"Here and here," said Jir-Lazan, indicating the dead bodies nearby. The others were on the second of the *Aktrivisar*'s shuttles."

"Damnit!" With all surviving personnel so close, Recker temporarily aborted his plan for lift-off. "Abandon the other tank. I want everyone on the shuttle," he said.

Vance and the other soldiers knew how to move, but Recker found it hard to remain patient during their evacuation of the second Puncher. As each precious minute passed, the Lavorix were more likely to bring the battleship into an operational state.

"How's Captain Jir-Lazan?" asked Recker.

Hendrix didn't lift her head. She'd cut open part of the Daklan's combat suit and was using one of the med-box tools to cauterise the wound. Jir-Lazan's grip on the controls was loose now and his head nodded, like he was falling asleep.

"He's not going to make it, sir," said Hendrix. "The injury I can deal with, but I can't replace the blood loss – not without proper med-bay facilities."

Jir-Lazan wasn't dead yet. "You must destroy the *Aktrivisar*, human. And your own ship with it," he said, his voice faint. "If you do not, the Lavorix will find us. We are not ready to face them."

"I sent a deletion command to the *Axiom*'s memory arrays before I left the ship."

"As did I for the *Aktrivisar*, human. Still, what price certainty?"

The med-box gave two short bleeps and one longer note. It was a combination which Recker had heard too many times before.

"Can you bring him back?" he asked.

"If I do, he'll only die again, sir. He won't enjoy the experience."

Commander Aston stood in the cockpit doorway. "That's everyone onboard, sir." She saw the bodies. "Captain Jir-Lazan?"

Recker nodded.

"Damn," she said. "Want me to let the other Daklan know about it?"

It was a job Recker would have normally taken on. Right now, he had too much on his plate. "I'd appreciate that, Commander." He pulled on the control sticks, testing their weight and responsiveness. Finding nothing he couldn't deal with, Recker brought the shuttle vertically from the ground and held it level at twenty metres.

"Should I try and move the body, sir?" asked Hendrix.

"Please – I need someone on backup." Recker knew just the person. "Private Montero, get in here."

"You liked Captain Jir-Lazan," said Hendrix. It wasn't a question.

"I did. I've seen nothing about any of these Daklan that makes me want to pick up a gun and shoot them."

"Me either, sir. Maybe we'll get back home and find things have changed."

"Maybe."

In truth, Recker thought any thawing of HPA-Daklan relations hinged on the outcome of this mission. If it came back a success, then the next steps would happen. He hoped it would happen anyway – Admiral Telar had a gift and Recker suspected the man juggled a hundred plans. Perhaps he'd pull something off, regardless of whether the personnel on this mission returned.

Private Montero entered the cockpit and helped Corporal Hendrix tip Jir-Lazan unceremoniously onto the floor.

"The dead don't care," said Montero firmly, like the words were a shield.

"No they don't," said Recker. "They leave that job to the living."

Montero dropped into the second seat. "What about your crew, sir?" she asked.

"They can sit this one out," said Recker. "If I had any doubts about your ability, rest assured you'd be out back chewing the fat with those squads of Daklan."

"This hardware's the same as ours," said Montero after a few seconds spent staring at the panel in front. "Or near enough the same."

"We're going straight up and over," said Recker. "The only threat is ground-launched missiles and I don't think this shuttle is going to withstand a direct hit." He turned his gaze to the hull breach. A rocket strike anywhere nearby would fill the cockpit with plasma heat, incinerating everyone inside.

"Corporal Hendrix, get out," he said.

Once she was gone, Recker flicked the switch to close the cockpit door. At least if he and Montero died, someone in the passenger bay might live to take his place.

"I think I've got the hang of the sensors," said Montero.

"Good, because we're not waiting any longer."

Recker fed power into the engines and the shuttle climbed strongly enough to reassure him that the propulsion was fully operational. The sheer cliff of debris sped by on the forward sensor feed and then the transport rose above its highest edge. From here, Recker had a much better vantage of the battlefield.

Ahead and in the distance, the immense Meklon battleships filled the visible horizon, their front and rear sections lost in a sudden thickening of the storm. The top section of the nearest was a pattern of angled plating, here and there burned and cratered, yet with no sign of a breach.

"Scan those battleships," he said, guiding the shuttle slowly over the top of the wreckage.

"I can only see a limited area with any certainty, sir."

"Do what you can," said Recker, not taking his eyes from the feeds as Montero adjusted and enhanced them. He saw no sign of movement on the target battleship, but it was the further one which had him worried.

Having allowed Montero a few seconds, Recker flew them past the debris. The shuttle's sensors detected no movement on the ground directly below, and he was sure any Lavorix troops in the vicinity had been cut down by the two Puncher tanks.

The distance from the wrecked warship to the battleship was only 1200 metres and the shuttle covered it in a few seconds. Montero talked nonstop under her breath as she scanned for anything hostile.

"Midsection clear, left thousand, clear, right thousand, clear. Limited view of the second battleship."

Recker listened and he watched. If the Lavorix had somehow got themselves topside, they weren't showing their faces. The shuttle crossed over the edge of the first battleship and the underside feed reminded Recker of a dark sea, frozen in time. He shook off the thought and concentrated on locating a way in.

"Where's the most likely place for a hatch, sir?" asked Montero. "Otherwise this is going to be a real needle-haystack kind of search."

Recker's only experience with Meklon warships was the *Vengeance*, which was enough to make him sure the operational area of the battleship would be confined to a tiny section of the interior, somewhere between the middle and the nose.

He flew the shuttle slowly across the hull about fifty metres over the plating and heading for the starboard side. He breathed slowly and deeply and watched for incoming attacks.

"Any hatch would have a light on it, right?" asked Montero.

"More than likely. Unless the warship is completely out of power." Recker judged they were near the midpoint of the beam and it felt like approaching an invisible line over which he was reluctant to cross. The further battleship was still obscured and for all he knew, the Lavorix might have a dozen rocket troops up there, waiting for the shuttle to appear in their sights.

"There's a light over there, sir. About two hundred metres closer to the nose."

The words were enormously welcome and Recker banked the shuttle immediately.

Montero focused the forward sensor on a tiny section of the battleship, a little way ahead and Recker spotted a glum orange light, a static pinpoint amongst the moving sands.

"Nice work, Private," he said, guiding the shuttle closer.

Recker set the shuttle down on what was the highest point of the battleship. He'd given the soldiers in the passenger bay advance warning and they acted immediately by opening the transport's side door.

Dim shapes appeared on the portside sensor feed and one of them crouched over the hatch.

"This is a way in, sir," said Vance. "Want me to see if I can open it?"

"Don't bother, Sergeant. I'm on my way."

Recker climbed rapidly from his seat and headed for the exit. He experienced a momentary sadness when he passed the body of Jir-Lazan, since the Daklan had fought so well and had done so much to bring the mission this far.

Leaving the body behind, Recker made his way through the passenger bay, in which the soldiers waited for their next order. The expressions on the human faces gave away little, though Recker could sense the mood – uncertainty vied with an eagerness to get on with things and to get away from this shuttle before it was struck by something explosive launched from the darkness.

The open side door allowed the wind to blow directly inside and the floor was slippery with loose sand. Grabbing the support handle at the doorway, Recker jumped onto the hard surface of the battleship.

Up here, the wind was stronger than at ground level and it tugged angrily at him, while his feet slithered on the sand. All around was darkness, with nothing to betray that the soldiers were several hundred metres above the surface.

Vance and Shadar were at the hatch, along with a couple of others and they shuffled back at Recker's approach.

"All yours, sir."

"The moment of truth," said Recker.

The hatch was about two metres square, its seam

almost invisible. An access panel was embedded in the surface nearby. It was fitted with a stiff, hinged lid to keep it protected and that lid was currently open.

"Did the Lavorix get in this way, sir?" asked Vance. "I was told they had a shuttle up here."

Recker had been wondering the same thing, but text on the panel readout gave him reassurance.

"Negative, Sergeant – the last activation of this access panel happened several weeks ago and there have been no failed attempts to open it since then."

"But the protective cover is open," said Vance.

"So it is."

The wind couldn't have blown it open and, since the Lavorix hadn't tried the access panel – maybe hadn't even seen it - Recker could only think that one of the Meklon technicians must have forgotten to cover the panel during the warship's last maintenance check.

Every time I curse my bad luck, I'll remember this access panel and remind myself it all balances out, he thought, knowing he was lying to himself.

"Does this mean there are no Lavorix inside?" asked Private Gantry.

"Don't get your hopes up, soldier."

The access panel's amber light turned green when Recker touched it. Then, the hatch sank eight metres into the hull and the alloy rungs of a ladder emerged from the wall. At the bottom of the shaft, a crawlspace led to a place unseen. Everything was dark and, though Recker both felt and listened for an indication the propulsion was online, the wind made it difficult for him to be sure of anything.

"Can we get into the main part of the ship from here,

sir?" asked Vance, peering doubtfully through the opening.

"There'll be a way, Sergeant. The Meklon built the maintenance access in such a way that it didn't weaken the armour too much – in case a bunch of missiles landed near the hatch. I'm sure we'll have to pass through several more hatches to reach the control areas."

"That passage looks tight."

Recker nodded. "I'll have to go first. With any luck there'll be an interface panel somewhere in the maintenance passages. From there, I might be able to do something useful like give everyone access to the doors."

He leaned forward, grabbed the top rung and swung himself into the shaft. Descending rapidly, he came to the bottom and dropped onto his knees. The image enhancers in his helmet visor turned up the green and added a few bonus patches of darkness. It was enough for Recker to be sure the way was open.

"Everyone off the shuttle," he said. "We've got a battleship to capture."

With the order given, Recker crawled into the tunnel, hoping fervently that the entirety of the Lavorix forces were on the other battleship rather than this one. Inside, he knew it wasn't to be, no matter how often he reminded himself about the open access panel lid.

On he went, into the Meklon warship.

CHAPTER TWENTY-THREE

THE CRAWLSPACE WENT on for sixty metres before Recker came to a two-metre-square space where he could just about stand. A panel on the wall made him think this was a second lift, heading deeper into the armour, and he stood adjacent to it while other soldiers climbed out of the passage.

"There's no way we're all fitting on here," said Recker, calling a halt with eight of the soldiers, including Sergeant Shadar, standing upright. "The rest of you stay back."

He activated the panel and, sure enough, the lift went down, this time stopping after twenty metres. A passage led off, not quite a crawlspace, but with a ceiling too low for even a short human to stand upright.

The rungs of another retractable ladder emerged from the walls, allowing the soldiers to descend. Recker crouch-crawled into the exit tunnel, waving the other eight to follow in order to make room for the rest.

Two more lift descents later and Recker was

impressed by the thickness of the battleship's armour, even though it was slowing him down considerably. Not many of the soldiers liked being so confined and several of them grumbled until they were ordered to stop.

The fifth lift shaft from the outer hatch was longer than all the others and Recker was certain this frustrating part of the mission was almost over. No doubt the danger level would rise significantly once they entered the battleship's personnel areas, but at least the human and Daklan squads knew how to storm an enemy position in difficult circumstances.

Best of all, Recker could now hear the distant rumbling of active propulsion, which increased his optimism tenfold that he wasn't wasting his time on a warship that was either completely offline or in a state of failure.

A passage led from the bottom of the shaft and this time it emerged into a much larger space – not enough to hold even half of the squad, but enough to allow the first few inside the comfort of moving their arms freely. Two exit passages led away and he aimed his helmet flashlight along both, finding no clues as to which was the best option.

"This is a technician's monitoring station," said Recker, pointing at a row of three wall-mounted screens. "The shipyard would have run final checks from here, and the maintenance teams might have visited to track down some of the more elusive hardware problems."

He touched one of the screens and it came to life, showing a menu of options.

"Can you do anything that gives the rest of us control

over the doors, sir?" asked Vance. "You shouldn't be leading from the front."

Recker searched quickly through the menu functions and found no way to access the warship's security.

"Not from here, Sergeant. We'll have to move on."

"Which exit, sir?"

"That one," said Recker, choosing randomly. "We're close to the operational part of the interior - I'm sure of it."

The chosen passage turned left after a short distance and ended a little way further at another door with an access panel. Recker halted in front of it.

"This is the place," he said, having travelled on enough spaceships to get a feel for them.

"We are ready," said Sergeant Shadar, who'd positioned himself second in the line.

"Where're Raimi and Ipanvir?" asked Recker. "There's nothing like a shoulder-launched rocket to clear out hostiles from a place you don't want them."

Raimi wasn't far back, but the Daklan was towards the rear. Fortunately, Zivor, with his high-powered repeater, was amongst the first group and that was a reassurance.

"Let's do this," said Recker.

He touched the panel and the five-feet-high door slid quietly into a side recess. The space outside was in darkness, but Recker's night vision allowed him to see that he was on the threshold of a much larger passage, which went left and right in front of him. His sense of direction told him that left would take him towards the battleship's nose and it was that way he expected to find the bridge.

Listening carefully, he detected no indication of a nearby enemy presence, though the floor was so dense the

Lavorix would have to be really trying hard to produce footsteps audible over the propulsion.

"We must watch for internal defences," said Shadar.

"Any such defences would target the Lavorix as well as us," said Recker.

"Not you, Captain Recker. You will be safe."

"I can't take this battleship alone, Sergeant. Either way, the internal defences will be switched off."

Recker leaned into the corridor and checked in both directions. Proving his point, a ceiling-mounted minigun was visible twenty metres away. It should have turned to track his movement, but it remained still and silent. He informed the squad and then spent a few moments on tactics.

"What if the internal doors are closed?" asked Vance. "That will make it impossible for you to stay in the centre of the pack, sir."

"I'm hoping they're open, Sergeant. Assuming the Meklon thought they were safe on this facility, it's unlikely anything was locked down."

In truth, Recker didn't know one way or the other and his only point of reference was the methods employed by the HPA military, which he wasn't stupid enough to believe were universal and observed by every other species.

"Whatever we find, we can't piss about," he concluded. "This is balanced on a knife edge."

"Those Lavorix on the second battleship aren't going to blow this one to pieces if they know their buddies are onboard, are they?" asked Drawl.

"I'm not taking bets on anything, Private. It's best we don't give them the chance to show us."

While Recker didn't have an answer, the question nevertheless got him thinking. At no point since the *Axiom* crashed had he seen an indication that the Lavorix were making a concerted effort to access this battleship. That got him worried – it meant the enemy either had enough soldiers onboard for them to close the access ramps, or they already knew this spaceship was out of action.

Only one way to find out.

Recker stepped out into the larger passage and stood to one side while the soldiers emerged. A total of forty had come with him into the battleship. Most went left, towards the bridge, while Corporal Givens and four others turned right with instructions to explore and report.

With seven soldiers in front of him, Recker went left, and Lieutenant Burner followed directly behind.

"Still holding up, Lieutenant?"

Burner's face didn't even hold a flicker of humour. "Yes, sir."

With no way for the Lavorix to know about Recker's ability to access the Meklon hardware, he felt this attack had a good chance of surprising the enemy. Once that surprise was lost, the real test would come.

"Intersection ahead," said Sergeant Shadar.

A moment later, shots came with a crack-crack in the battleship's sub-zero air. Recker heard a thud and Shadar grunted on the comms. More shots came and one of the soldiers in front swore.

"Clear," said Shadar, with unmistakeable satisfaction.

More shots sounded and Recker felt his squad's moments of surprise were already ebbing away. Any organised enemy would have comms and once word got out about this attack, the Lavorix would either hunker down or swarm the area with overwhelming numbers, depending on their confidence.

"Move!" yelled Recker, wishing he knew the distance to the bridge. He was certain the battleship's interior would occupy only a small fraction of the hull's 4500 metre length, but that still didn't mean it was close.

He turned right at the intersection, following Private Gantry. A dead Lavorix almost tripped him and he called out a warning to those coming after. Just ahead, a few more corpses lay on the floor, two of which were Lavorix and three being Meklon. Splattered blood on the walls already glistened with ice crystals.

The pace increased and Recker found himself watching his feet as much as anything else, in case he fell over other dead bodies. It already seemed likely the Meklon crew had succumbed to the same bloodless attack which had allowed the Lavorix to take over the Excon-1 station.

The next turning brought him into an expansive room with rows of bolted-down tables and benches and a single offset exit in each wall. Two flat-fronted machines were embedded in the right-hand wall, which Recker imagined were food replicators, and twin minigun auto-defences hung uselessly from the ceiling. Several Meklon were slumped face-down in trays of whatever food they'd been eating before they were killed, and others were on the floor.

A nearby corpse gave Recker his clearest view yet of the Meklon features – this one had larger eyes than a human, with pale irises. Its nose was less prominent and its part-open mouth revealed square, proportional teeth. On top of its head, grey hair was only a little darker than its grey skin.

"Hostiles," said Shadar, over by the exit in the left wall. The Daklan poked his head into the corridor and withdrew it rapidly. "Five total, forty metres. Safe shot available."

Gunfire started, coming from the Lavorix in the corridor. Recker turned and ordered the soldiers in the passage to hold.

"Raimi!" he barked.

"On it."

The soldier was midway towards the passage already. He lifted his rocket tube into firing position and positioned himself to one side of the opening.

"Get down," he ordered.

Shadar and a couple of other soldiers near the door moved quickly away. A half-step to the side and Raimi fired into the passage. It intentionally wasn't a precision shot and didn't need to be. Sergeant Shadar had called it safe, which meant the blast had somewhere at the far end to channel, ensuring the explosion wouldn't all come back into this mess room.

The passage filled with light and even though Recker had turned his head and closed his eyes, the intensity was painful. A split-second after the light, the explosion rumbled and heat came with the noise.

Hardly waiting a moment, Sergeant Shadar dashed back to the corridor and put his head around the corner.

"Clear," he said, not that the deaths of the Lavorix had been in doubt.

"Hostiles!" shouted Private Gantry. He dropped his MG-12 to the floor, kicking out the tripod as it fell. Within five seconds he had it aimed through the gaps between the chairs and tables into the opposite passage. The weapon roared and Gantry held the trigger down for a long time. Then, he scrambled aside dragging the heavy weapon after him.

"Shit, turret!" he yelled.

Recker heard it then, a whine of gravity motors. The soldiers in the mess room hurled themselves away from the corridor, rolling across tables and clambering over benches in their haste. A spray of inbound slugs tore through the air, pulverising the furniture. Recker saw a spray of blood from a Daklan soldier who'd been too slow to escape.

Raimi fired again and his second rocket left a trail of blazing propellant as it accelerated into the tunnel. He dropped low and checked the reload timer.

"Direct hit," he said coolly.

"The enemy have mobilised their turrets quickly," said Shadar. "This is not a positive development."

Recker heard a second gravity engine, this time coming from the left where Raimi had launched his first rocket. "Where's Ipanvir?"

The huge Daklan erupted from the tunnel where Recker had ordered the soldiers to wait, his launcher in position to fire. More gunfire came and this time it was from the right-hand exit. The human and Daklan soldiers fired in response and Drawl side-armed in a grenade.

"Lavorix from three directions," said Recker bitterly.

"No hostiles this way," said Unvak from along the entrance passage.

The whump of a rocket firing brought Recker's attention back to the room. Faced with the lightning and murderous reactions of a Lavorix automated turret, Ipanvir hadn't risked showing too much of himself and had launched the missile at an angle. The explosion boomed and a wave of superheated air struck Recker like a physical force as he crouched behind the scant cover of a table.

Gunfire cracked and fizzed. Projectiles thudded into the solid walls and then a torrent of slugs poured into the room from the third exit. Drawl threw in a second grenade and then a third. At the same moment, Private Gantry shouted a warning about an attack from the opposite passage.

"Raimi!" yelled Recker.

"Yes, sir."

The soldier's rocket disappeared into one of the passages, producing another explosion. Ipanvir fired as well, into the right-hand passage. The lull didn't last more than a few seconds – only long enough for the soldiers to find better positions that covered the entrances. Gunfire resumed, inbound from three directions. The Lavorix were keeping themselves out of sight and Recker guessed their intention was to keep the attackers pinned while they brought up another turret or something explosive. So far, Raimi and Ipanvir's launchers had made the difference, but their ammunition was limited.

A fist-sized object arced into the room and clinked against the floor ten metres from Recker. Reacting quickly, he threw himself flat in the opposite direction, while the other soldiers nearby did likewise. The grenade went off in a blinding flash. Recker heard a truncated scream and a heavy object fell on top of him. Heat alarms went off in his earpiece. He grunted and rolled, pushing the weight off him, trying to ignore the sweet smell of burning meat and the greasy astringency of suit polymers.

As Recker scrambled to his feet, he discovered what the object was – perhaps he'd known it all along – and he stared at the upper half of a human soldier. Private Bonnie Stevens was dead, with her legs torn off in the blast and the terrible wound cauterised by the heat. A wave of guilt crashed into Recker because she'd taken the worst of the blast and likely saved him from death.

And then he was away, jumping over a mess of twisted tables and benches until he reached one of the side walls, out of the Lavorix firing arcs.

Another grenade went off, missing the soldiers but scattering loose metal. Ipanvir and Raimi both fired, each into a different passage, the immense rocket explosions buying time, but not enough of it. A few Lavorix burst from the third passage, running on two legs and two overlong arms, their spines curved unnaturally to keep their torsos upright.

Recker shot the first and then Gantry's MG-12 started up, cutting the Lavorix down at their waists, as if in belated justice for Private Stevens and Private Redman back on Excon-1. A grenade detonated in the hand of one enemy and the blast sent pieces of blackened flesh and wet entrails in every direction. In the distance, Recker heard the whining of a gravity-engined turret and knew that time was running out.

"Retreat!" he shouted, waving the soldiers towards the passage through which they'd first entered the mess room.

With the Lavorix pressing, escape was not easy and one of the Daklan died when an enemy soldier dashed into the room at full pelt while firing a chain gun. Recker took it down, but the damage was already done.

Recker and his soldiers exited the mess room under heavy fire that would have produced more casualties had Ipanvir not spent his last rocket to provide some cover. The engagement had been bloody and – in terms of the mission objective – fruitless. On the other hand, it had taught Recker several valuable and painful lessons about his opponents. The Lavorix were organized and they would sacrifice their own lives in order to win. If they located any more HPA worlds – assuming they hadn't already done so – the fighting would be brutal.

Snarling with anger, Recker sprinted deeper into the ship, the actions of his enemy forcing him ever further from the bridge.

CHAPTER TWENTY-FOUR

THE LAVORIX DIDN'T IMMEDIATELY FOLLOW the fleeing soldiers, either because they needed to regroup, or because they were content to hold in one area of the battleship. Recker headed back for the maintenance entrance. He remembered the place where two passages led from one of the rooms and he intended to explore the second exit to find out if it would bring him and his soldiers to a more advantageous position, ideally forward of the enemy.

"Where's Corporal Givens," he asked, wondering why the man hadn't re-joined the squad like he'd been ordered.

"He was off comms when we were in the mess room, sir," said Vance. "Too much intervening metal for a signal to get through."

"We're closer now," said Recker, suddenly worried he might have lost five soldiers. The flickering green connection lights on the open comms channel told him otherwise. "Corporal Givens, where are you?"

Givens' voice was faint and he sounded surprised when he answered. "We're holding a room about a hundred metres from the entry point, sir. It's quiet, except for the squealing noise coming from all this alien shit."

Recker almost missed his stride. "What sort of *alien shit*?"

"Consoles and stuff, sir. I don't know what any of it's for."

"I asked you to report what you found, Corporal."

"The comms link dropped, sir. We thought you'd send someone back to get us."

"Those weren't the orders."

"It's just warship tech, sir," Givens repeated, in the tones of a man who suspected he might be trouble. "*Tech* - that's what the squad calls it when we don't know."

It was difficult not to shout at the man and Recker took a deep breath. He reminded himself that he'd expected to locate all the important kit on the bridge and maybe he hadn't made it clear enough to the soldiers that he wanted to know about everything they found, no matter how unimportant they thought it was.

"Never mind," he growled. "I'm coming your way."

Raising his voice, Recker snapped out a couple of orders, telling Sergeant Shadar to choose five soldiers and head for Givens' position. Sergeant Vance he told to secure the route to the maintenance passages in case the Lavorix appeared.

"This is not a good place to hold, sir," said Vance. "If we're forced to retreat into the maintenance area, you'll be cut off from the rest of us."

"It'll take me less than two minutes to reach Corporal Givens and find out if he's discovered something useful."

"Yes, sir."

The first soldiers to make it to the maintenance passage didn't really have anywhere to go and they pressed themselves against the side wall to allow Recker, Shadar and the other chosen soldiers to run past. After that, Vance's bellowed orders imposed a greater degree of purpose on them and Recker noticed that the Daklan were responding without complaint to commands from a human superior officer. It was a significant development, though something to think about later.

With Sergeant Shadar in front and four others behind, Recker dashed along the passage, turned left and continued towards the centre of the battleship. At an intersection, Shadar paused to check he was heading the right way. Along the straight ahead, Recker detected the orange of movement and a shape came around the far corner. For a split-second he thought it was Givens or one of the soldiers with him. The sight of extra limbs and the strangeness of the gait were enough to convince Recker this was no human.

"Incoming," he said calmly.

A spasm of movement from the Lavorix indicated it had become aware of the danger and its limbs flailed as it sought to escape into cover. Recker's first shot took the creature in the head and was certainly fatal. He didn't leave anything to chance and put another two slugs into its body as it fell.

"Corporal Givens is this way," said Sergeant Shadar, indicating the branch from the main passage.

Recker was torn. The appearance of the Lavorix here might just be the start of an attack that would separate him from the rest of his soldiers. On the other hand, if he could access a console that was linked to the battleship's critical onboard systems, he might be able to pull off a few tricks, like sealing the internal doors. He glanced at the two-foot barrels of the stubby minigun directly over his head.

Or activate the defences.

He pointed at one of the accompanying Daklan, a soldier called Lumis. "Stay out of sight and watch this main passage," Recker ordered.

Lumis returned an unnervingly wide smile, providing an excellent view of short, upturned fangs and the rest of his more humanlike teeth. He tapped the side of his helmet in a manner which Recker understood to be the Daklan equivalent of an affirmative.

"Sir," came the voice of Sergeant Vance. "The Lavorix are not holding their positions. We have sighted them close by and I anticipate an attack as soon as they can organise."

"Damnit, hold the corridor, Sergeant, and we'll make a run into the maintenance area if we need to. We've encountered one of the bastards this way as well – they're likely hoping to encircle our position."

"Yes, sir."

Vance was the kind of soldier who had the experience to recognize a mountain of shit when he was standing in the foothills, but who would nevertheless accept his orders without complaint unless he had a better suggestion for dealing with a situation. Recker was grateful to have the man with him.

Twenty metres along the new passage, Corporal Givens appeared out of a doorway and gestured for the approaching soldiers to follow him inside. Moments later, Recker entered a ten-metre-square room in which four human soldiers crouched behind a central console and kept their guns trained on the single doorway.

Seeing the console made Recker's heart jump in anticipation. The hardware was unlit, but like Givens had said, it was squealing. Rather than finding the noise an irritation, Recker was invigorated because it meant the console was online.

"Should it be making that noise, sir?" asked Givens. "And what's all this stuff for?"

Had Givens apologised for screwing up, maybe Recker would have had a bit more tolerance for the banality. The man had also been lacking during the assault on the Interrogator's inner cube and it was hard not to immediately relieve him of his rank and give the job to someone more capable. As it was, he resisted the urge to discipline Givens during an ongoing mission and put the task aside for now.

"I'd suggest you remain quiet, Corporal," snapped Recker as he approached the console.

The device lacked seats, but the operator panels were the right height for easy use. Flicking a blue switch brought the console out of sleep and the screens illuminated shortly after. Drumming his fingers, Recker waited for the input prompt.

During the brief delay, Lumis came onto the comms to advise he'd sighted and shot a second Lavorix.

"Private Carrington, Reklin, go help him out," Recker

ordered. The prompt appeared on the screen. "Here we go," he said, entering the command to access the software.

A new menu appeared instantly.

"Is it what you seek?" asked Sergeant Shadar with interest.

"Yes," said Recker. "This room must be the place where the technicians can run maintenance checks without interfering with whatever's happening on the bridge."

"What advantage will this offer us, Captain Recker?"

"See this menu?"

"Automatic defences," said Shadar with a note of approval.

"All I've got to do is set target exclusions," said Recker. "If you notice, the onboard security has already scanned every living organism inside and categorised it."

"Daklan. Human," said Shadar, leaning closer to read the small text on the screen. "How does the security system know that is how we call ourselves?"

"That's a question I wish you hadn't asked, Sergeant," said Recker, understanding the ramifications at once. "It's something to think about later." He tapped at the console keys. "For the moment, I'm adding every human and Daklan to the excluded list."

"Will it take long?"

Recker shook his head. "Not long at all." He poised his finger over the *Activate?* option on the screen. "Ready for the fun and games, Sergeant Shadar?"

Shadar unleashed a grin that was even wider than the one Lumis had shown earlier. "Yes, I am ready."

A gentle touch on the screen was greeted by a confirmatory message from the security system. At once, a faraway, pulsing noise came to Recker's ears. It sounded exactly like what it was - a multi-barrelled automated gun punching a few thousand rounds into a bunch of four-armed alien scumbags.

"Sergeant Vance has your burden been lifted?" said Recker on the comms. While he spoke, he added every human and Daklan to the security group *personnel*, which would allow them to operate doors and perform other tasks normally required on a warship.

"Yes sir, and just when the weight was becoming too much."

"Casualties?"

"No additional injuries to report."

"We're heading back your way. Our next target is the bridge."

"Sounds good."

Recker got moving, bringing the other soldiers with him. The pulsing of the miniguns had stopped, though a heat shimmer rose from the one at the intersection.

"Dead Lavorix," grunted Lumis, gesturing along the passage towards the starboard flank of the battleship.

"You'd better watch your feet from here, soldier – there're going to be a whole lot more of them where we're going."

Leading the way, Recker arrived at the entry point where he found that Sergeant Vance had already organised advance parties to check the way ahead.

"There'll be no blind spots in the auto defences, Sergeant."

"What about the bridge, sir?"

Recker nodded reluctantly. "Maybe the bridge."

The squads headed once more towards the mess area, since Recker felt sure the forward exit from the room would lead most efficiently to the bridge. Almost every step of the journey required him to avoid bloody pieces of Lavorix and the floor was slick and crispy with crystallized blood. Recker didn't try counting the enemy casualties, but the quantity of gore made it clear they'd begun a forceful effort to flush out the human and Daklan squads. The miniguns overhead steamed in the blood-moist air and they tracked the passage of the soldiers.

"Shit man, that makes me nervous," said Drawl, his tones reverent rather than fearful.

Arriving at the mess area, Recker was confronted by a much greater scene of carnage. A hundred or more Lavorix must have been on their way through when the ceiling guns fired upon them. The enemy had brought two more gravity repeaters, both of which had been smashed to pieces by the ferocity of the battleship's miniguns.

Vance and Shadar were in front and they crunched their way across the floor, swatting aside loose pieces of bullet-holed furniture as they went.

"That way," said Recker, indicating the forward exit.

The passage was a scene from hell and Recker couldn't recall ever seeing such concentrated butchery. Here, the Lavorix had been incinerated by repeat rocket detonations and others had been pulverised, leaving knee-high piles of innards, bones and everything else required to make a biological organism function. A few of the soldiers cursed softly but mostly, they stayed quiet.

Around the next corner the passage was nearly empty, suggesting the Lavorix had sent most of their forces to the mess room. With few obstacles underfoot, the pace increased and Recker felt his eagerness return. He checked in with his crew, who were alive and further back in the line. They weren't exactly in good spirits owing to the blood-soaked passages they were journeying through, but Recker knew they'd do what was necessary once they arrived at the bridge.

For some reason Recker had never understood, every bridge entrance was at the top of steps, and the same was true here. Vance held the squads a short distance away and peered around the corner with one foot resting on a headless Lavorix torso.

"The blast door is closed, sir," he said. "Are members of the *personnel* security group able to operate the access panel?"

"I doubt it, Sergeant," said Recker, suddenly wishing he'd spent a few additional seconds at the security station and given every soldier full *crew* access.

"We could return to the security station, sir. It's the safest way."

"I don't want to waste any more time, Sergeant. We've taken too long as it is."

Vance didn't like it but his expression was one of resigned acceptance. "Let's make the best of it."

Following a short discussion on how to capture the bridge, Recker played his part by creeping up the steps, accompanied by a hand-picked group of soldiers, to a three-metre-square landing at the top. Feeling like a coward, he activated the panel and then sprinted for the stairs. He heard the blast door motors and detected a barely noticeable change of pressure.

Gunfire started before Recker was two steps down. He didn't slow and jumped to the passage floor below, before darting left. Vance and Shadar called out orders. The gauss fire continued for a few seconds longer and then it was over.

"Clear," said Shadar.

Without hesitation, Recker charged back up the stairs and entered the bridge of the Meklon battleship.

CHAPTER TWENTY-FIVE

THE BRIDGE WAS A SLIGHTLY LARGER version of the equivalent on the *Vengeance*, with two more stations and older-looking hardware. It was cold, but well-enough lit, and the hardware was online.

Recker felt instantly at home and dashed along the central aisle to the command console. Bodies – both unmarked Meklon and bloodied Lavorix – were strewn liberally on the floor and on top of the hardware.

A Lavorix with a bullet hole in the side of its head lay across the captain's chair and Recker dragged it onto the floor. Nearby, a metal-shrouded processing box was connected by wires to one of the interface ports and he disconnected it immediately.

"Sergeant Vance, remove these corpses!" Recker shouted. "If you find any more of these encryption breakers, let me know about it immediately."

"Yes, sir."

Recker turned to find his crew entering the bridge.

Apart from Commander Aston, they seemed dazed by the recent combination of events.

"Snap out of it!" Recker yelled. "Find your seats – we don't have long."

The crew got moving, choosing their seats and checking the status monitors. Neither Lieutenant Fraser nor Lieutenant Larson were familiar with the Meklon technology and Recker hoped they were fast learners.

"The sensors are coming up!" said Burner.

"Propulsion modules active," said Eastwood. "A few amber warnings that I'll have to look into. Otherwise, the control system is just waiting for your command to bring everything into a full operational state, sir."

Recker acknowledged the update and continued his own series of checks. The control software was almost identical to that found on the *Vengeance* – a slightly older version, he noticed - and for that he was grateful, since it meant he didn't have to waste time finding out how everything worked.

"The Meklon called this spaceship *Fulcrum*," he said. "The logs show it stopped here on Kemis-5 for resupply."

"What about a refit?" asked Eastwood. "The plating has taken a beating."

"We'll have to live with it," said Recker. "The critical hardware appears to be functioning. Engine modes 1, 2 and 3," he said.

"I've got missiles, countermeasures – including a mesh deflector and something else that isn't fitted to the *Vengeance* - and an Executor, sir, with enough power to fire it from our unstressed engines," said Aston. "No sign of a Fracture."

"I'll check it out once I get a moment, Commander," said Recker. On the *Vengeance*, the deadliest weapon of all could only be accessed from a sub-menu on the command console.

"We've got sensors!" said Burner.

A double row of screens on the forward bulkhead lit up and Burner allocated the feeds amongst them. The scene outside hadn't noticeably changed – the *Axiom* and *Aktrivisar* were visible on the portside, along with the scrap metal from the Lavorix spaceships. The much nearer three-kilometre wall of debris didn't look so monumental when viewed from the *Fulcrum*.

To starboard, the second battleship was in the same place as before and Recker narrowed his eyes, as if he could divine the progress of the alien crew in bringing it to an operational state.

"Sir, I'm detecting an increased output from the second battleship's hull!" said Eastwood. "They're warming up their propulsion!"

"Commander Aston, give them hell," growled Recker, his hands on the controls.

"I've locked our missiles, sir," said Aston. "The range is too close and the warheads won't arm before impact!"

"Let's gain some distance."

Recker placed his hands on the controls and pulled. Their weighting was identical that on the *Vengeance* and he knew exactly how much movement they needed. The *Fulcrum*'s propulsion increased in volume and the sound of it was incredible. A smaller warship's engines could assail the ears, but the battleship's main drive gripped

Recker's whole body and made his cells vibrate in tune to the movement of the ternium atoms.

"Missile launch detected!" yelled Aston.

The second battleship's launch clusters spat out fifty or more missiles. Red dots appeared on the tactical and then vanished in an instant.

"The enemy warheads failed to detonate," said Aston in clear relief. "Lucky us - the mesh deflector is set to manual. Switching it to auto."

"Let's have our turn with the missiles," said Recker.

He lifted the *Fulcrum* a few metres off the landing strip and flew it sideways, knowing that if he gained too much altitude, he'd expose his warship to the enemy's upper launch tubes. They'd made a mistake in firing too soon and their portside launchers would be reloading.

"Massive pile of debris coming up portside," Burner warned.

Recker knew it but didn't try to avoid the broken midsection of the Lavorix warship. He piloted the *Fulcrum* directly into the wreckage and the collision produced the dullest of thudding sounds against the hull. The debris toppled and the *Fulcrum* pushed it along like it weighed nothing.

"Fire when ready, Commander."

"Waiting on green lights, sir."

"The enemy spaceship is taking off," said Burner.

"Starboard missiles launched. Six clusters of ten."

The moment Aston spoke the words, the enemy battleship became ringed in a complex web of overlapping streaks of bright light. The *Fulcrum*'s missiles struck the mesh deflector and exploded all at once, illuminating a huge area of the sky and the landing field below.

"Incoming gauss fire," said Aston.

A drumming sound from the repeating gauss turrets on the second battleship reached the bridge. The slugs wouldn't do much damage to the *Fulcrum*'s armour and the attack showed either intent or desperation on the part of the Lavorix.

"Waiting on our reload," said Aston. "They've got a few seconds."

Recker mentally counted down the enemy missile reload timer, which he'd learned from watching the *Fulcrum*'s own reload interval.

"I'm giving them our gauss turrets as well," said Aston.

Recker was glad his ears were protected by his suit helmet, since the clinking roar of discharging metal would have damaged his hearing in seconds. He clenched his jaw and focused his attention on coming through this engagement without his warship ending up on the scrap pile below.

The enemy battleship rose strongly into the air and Recker took his own ship up alongside it. A speckling of white dots on the other warship's hull alerted him to their missile launch. The *Fulcrum*'s mesh deflector activated, surrounding the vessel in the familiar labyrinthine swordcut pattern. Plasma explosions enveloped the warship and quickly dispersed.

"Enemy missiles neutralised," said Aston. "The mesh deflector is still available."

"Find out the limitations," said Recker. "I need to

know out how often that enemy ship can activate its own defences."

"On it, sir." Aston found the answer a moment later. "We can hold two charges, each with an independent five-minute cooldown. That gives us one more activation and then we have to wait."

Recker kept his attention on the sensors, watching the movements of the enemy ship. It turned, trying to bring its nose towards the *Fulcrum*, and he knew that's where the Executor was fitted. The mesh deflector seemed to counter pretty much anything, but Recker didn't want to test it any more than necessary. He certainly didn't want to use up his second mesh deflector charge if he could avoid it.

So, he constantly adjusted the *Fulcrum*'s speed and orientation in the hope of outmanoeuvring the enemy vessel. Steadily, the two warships drifted apart and gained altitude, lines of white tracer light connecting them as their gauss cannons fired nonstop.

"*Fulcrum* missiles launched. Portside one through six," said Aston. "Setting gauss guns to track and destroy."

"Something dropped out of the enemy's underside bay, sir," said Burner. "A bomb."

The Lavorix crew had some experience under their belt, or at least knew more about the capabilities of a Meklon battleship than Recker. An advisory flashed on his tactical.

Shock bomb detected.

The sky turned a shade of red that made Recker think of the Lavorix blood he'd seen spilled everywhere inside the *Fulcrum*. Electronic needles on his status panel flickered and then settled, with no obvious harm inflicted. On the sensor feed, only a handful of plasma explosions erupted on the enemy hull, rather than the near sixty he'd hoped for.

"Whatever that was, it knocked out the control units on ninety percent of our missiles, sir," said Aston.

"The tactical computer reported it as a shock bomb," said Recker.

"Yes, sir. Seems like we're carrying some as well."

"Figure out how to deploy them. And they didn't activate their mesh deflector."

"Keeping it in the bag for later."

"That's one mesh deflector down for each of us and their turn to fire next," said Recker. "We blew our advantage."

"From the quantity of ternium particles emerging from their hull, I'd guess the enemy activated engine Mode 2," said Eastwood.

"They'll be no more agile than we are," said Recker, watching carefully. He was reluctant to activate the *Fulcrum*'s overstress mode before Lieutenant Eastwood had completed a thorough status check. He kept his finger near the button, but held off.

He watched the enemy ship rotate rapidly and he gave the *Fulcrum*'s engines extra power to keep it parallel with the other vessel's portside flank. The enemy pilot attempted to fool Recker by quickly rotating back the other way, to bring the *Fulcrum* into the narrow firing arc of its Executor.

Having performed the same trick himself with the Puncher tank earlier and having been almost caught out by the same attempt from the enemy shuttle, Recker was ready. He had no way of completely escaping the firing arc, so he accelerated hard across it, reducing the *Fulcrum*'s exposure time.

The enemy fired its Executor. Recker knew the weapon had a short travel time and he swore when he realized the *Fulcrum* didn't have the velocity required to escape the two-thousand-metre blast radius of the weapon. A flash of infinite darkness appeared five hundred metres from the battleship's stern and the mesh deflector activated immediately, protecting the *Fulcrum* from the Executor's effects.

A quiet chiming came from Aston's console. "Just a friendly warning to let us know we're vulnerable," she said. "Deploying interceptors, deploying shock bomb."

The pre-emptive activation of the interceptors sent hundreds of tiny missiles into the sky and the shock bomb dropped from an underside bay.

"Enemy missiles launched," said Aston. "Holding our launch until the shock bomb explodes."

The gauss turrets clanked and the shock bomb flashed beneath the *Fulcrum*, its energy burst causing many of the inbound warheads to fail. A couple of missiles crashed into the *Fulcrum*'s flank, producing explosions visible on the sensor feeds. Having journeyed through the warship's armour to get here, Recker knew the battleship was built to last and he ignored the blasts.

Twisting the controls first one way and then the other, he fought a battle of skill and anticipation with the enemy captain. The Lavorix was a slippery bastard and wasn't easily lured into a mistake. By this point, the Meklon base was far below and the two warships were in the upper atmosphere of Kemis-5.

"*Fulcrum* starboard clusters one through six launched. Rear lowers one and two locked and fired."

The missiles flew into countless interceptors and gauss fire, though not enough to significantly thin the inbound wave. Recker thought this would be a punishing blow and then an enemy shock bomb went off at the last possible moment, disabling almost all of the warheads. A few exploded successfully, but not enough to cripple or destroy the opposing craft.

The enemy ship's portside missile reload timer was almost up and Recker took a chance by accelerating side-on towards the craft. In moments, the two ships were adjacent, separated by no more than a hundred metres. The Lavorix made the same mistake as earlier and launched their missiles. The warheads crashed into the *Fulcrum* at such a short range that they failed to activate and their debris rained down towards the base below.

Having seen his manoeuvre successful, Recker swung the *Fulcrum*'s nose towards the enemy warship, bringing it into the Executor's firing arc.

"We're too close!" said Aston. "We'll be caught in the blast."

"No we won't," said Recker, hauling back on the controls.

The *Fulcrum* accelerated backwards, away from the other ship and Aston stabbed her finger onto the Executor discharge button. The dull bass that Recker remembered from back on the *Vengeance* swept through him, clubbing his body like a hundred rubber mallets and making him bare his teeth with the pain.

Elsewhere on the bridge, the soldiers who'd been given the task of clearing away the bodies and who'd been keeping their heads down during the combat, swore and cursed loudly.

Through watering eyes, Recker saw the mesh deflector activate on the Lavorix-controlled battleship and it rotated, bringing its rear missile clusters to bear. The *Fulcrum*'s gauss turrets fired on automatic, their control computer targeting the launch hatches on the opposing ship to destroy the missiles as they emerged.

"Interceptor storm fired," said Aston, her voice thick from the aftereffects of the Executor discharge. "Upper forward clusters one through three launched."

"Two minutes on the first mesh deflector recharge!" said Eastwood, his voice too loud, as if he'd been deafened by the sound wave produced by the weapon discharge. "Five minutes on the Executor!"

Missiles detonated against the *Fulcrum* and the opposing battleship. Recker continued his fight for the upper hand, mentally tracking the reload timers and doing his best to position his ship to take advantage.

With neither side having a mesh deflector available, this was going to be a messy victory for whoever came out on top and Recker needed this warship to be operational so it could take everyone back home. If the *Fulcrum* suffered too much damage, this mission might never return with the data taken from the Excon-1 station.

An idea hit him like a thunderbolt.

"I'm going to issue a shutdown order!" he said.

"Interceptors launched," said Aston. She raised her head. "You think the Meklon warship will accept one?"

"I hope so."

Recker banked the warship and brought it in a tight circle, keeping near to the enemy's reloading missile tubes. Taking one hand from the controls, he dived through eight or nine sub levels of the security menu, hunting for something he'd never been asked to use before during his service with the HPA.

He found what he was looking for.

Emergency disable: Captured Meklon fleet warship. Target: Bane?

"Do it," Recker spat, sending the command.

At once, the captured warship – *Bane* – stopped accelerating. Its momentum carried it higher, while its hull rotated slowly. When momentum ran out, it hung in the air for a moment and then it fell, dropping like a mountain towards the ground.

"Their propulsion went to near-zero, sir," said Eastwood.

"Blow them to pieces, Commander Aston," said Recker. "Before they figure out what we've done and find a way to fix it."

"Underside six launched," said Aston. "Sixty missiles on their way."

Recker tilted the *Fulcrum* so that its loaded starboard missile clusters aimed downwards.

"Starboard clusters one through six launched."

"And the portside," said Recker, tilting the *Fulcrum* again.

"Sixty more locked and launched."

As the *Bane* plummeted, it was struck unerringly by three waves of missiles. It was a well-armoured ship and would likely have survived the first sixty explosions. Possibly even the next sixty. The battleship couldn't withstand 180 plasma missile strikes and it was turned into a white-hot ball of flame.

Recker followed it down, warily, though he was certain the enemy was done. Pieces of debris fell away from the light-cloaked wreckage and they trailed in its wake, also burning, like a hundred thousand meteorites.

At the end of its long fall, the *Bane* crashed onto the Meklon base, landing half on top of the *Aktrivisar* and half on top of the other broken ships. Somehow, it seemed like a fitting end.

"What's the recharge time on the Executor, Commander?"

"Less than a minute, sir."

"I promised Captain Jir-Lazan I'd destroy the *Aktrivisar* and *Axiom*, to ensure the Lavorix can't learn anything if they ever recover the hulls."

When Executor finished recharging, Recker – without relish - ordered Aston to fire it at the centre of the debris pile. The thumping discharge was no more pleasant than the last one and it took an enormous effort for Recker to keep his eyes on the sensor feed in order to watch the outcome.

The visible effects of Executor were a cross between an explosion and a disintegration. A sphere of darkness came into being and tore the ruined warships to pieces, hurling riven alloy thousands of metres in every direction. Whatever was caught in the two-thousand-metre centre was reduced to dust and fine particles, which were quickly swept away by the ever-present storm on Kemis-5.

Recker watched for a time, needing to be sure. At last, he accepted that nothing useful could be obtained from the debris which remained.

"Done," he said. "Let's get out of here."

He tightened his grip on the controls and the *Fulcrum* flew upwards.

CHAPTER TWENTY-SIX

RECKER HAD LONG since grown accustomed to the bleakness of the universe – maybe even learned to love it – but his main thought was to escape from Kemis-5. The *Fulcrum* showed no ill-effects from its recent confrontation and it surged above the planet's atmosphere and into space. Believing it best to get away from the planet, Recker chose a direction at random and pushed the spaceship to maximum speed. Kemis-5 dwindled on the rear sensors.

"Sir?"

The question prompted Recker to half-turn in his seat.

"What is it, Sergeant Vance?"

"What did you do to the enemy warship?"

"I sent it a shut down code. Every warship in the HPA fleet is coded to go offline when it receives one, and most senior commanding officers can issue such a code. It's a failsafe in case a warship crew goes rogue. We've just found out that the Meklon have similar protections in place."

Vance nodded his understanding. "Would such a code work against the core override, sir?"

"It's a good question, Sergeant. When the *Expectation* was hit by the Interrogator's core override at Pinvos, the first part of the security system it went for was the shut down control."

"I guess they thought of everything, sir."

Turning away, Vance ordered the soldiers to resume their clean-up of the bridge. Recker let them get on with it and locked his gaze on the sensor feed once more.

"What next, sir?" asked Burner.

"We have to find out where the Gateway sent us and then we're going home."

"I've had a look at the *Fulcrum*'s star charts and I'm having a hard time tallying them up with anything known to the HPA. I think we've come a long way."

"I trust you and Lieutenant Larson will be able to figure something out between you."

"I'm sure we will, sir."

"Oh shit," said Eastwood.

Somehow, Recker knew exactly what was coming and his muscles tensed in anticipation. "A ternium wave," he said.

"Yes, sir."

"The Galactar."

"It's too big to be anything else."

"And it's arriving at the exact place the Gateway dumped us."

"Yes, sir. Two million klicks beyond Kemis-5."

"Shit." Recker exhaled, feeling suddenly tired. "They worked out how to follow us."

Aston realized why Recker sounded so drained. "We can't go home."

"No, Commander, we can't go home. Not unless we want to lead that spaceship directly to an HPA world."

"What are we going to do, sir?" asked Larson.

For a moment, Recker didn't have an answer. He pulled himself together, though it took all his strength.

"I've got no intention of dying out here, Lieutenant," he said. "Time is wasting and soon the Galactar will locate the mess we left on Kemis-5. Then it'll follow us out here and destroy the *Fulcrum*."

"We should leave," said Aston.

Recker nodded. "Lieutenant Eastwood, what's the warmup time on the lightspeed drive?"

"Five minutes, sir. The same as on the *Vengeance*."

"Lieutenant Burner, is there anything on the Meklon star charts that will help us?"

"I don't know, sir. It'll take me a while to study them properly."

"In that case, pick somewhere twenty-four hours lightspeed from here and pass the coordinates to Lieutenant Eastwood."

"Done."

Recker switched the *Fulcrum*'s propulsion into mode 2 and the background note became instilled with serenity, rather than urgency. Several output gauges rocketed, giving hints at the unlocked potential from the overstressed ternium modules.

"Mode 3," said Recker, pressing his thumb onto one of the buttons on the left control bar.

The sensors went blank and the *Fulcrum* surged into a

short duration lightspeed jump, with an accompanying howl from the engines. Recker held the button, wondering how long the battleship could hold this state.

The increased speed didn't last long and the *Fulcrum* emerged from lightspeed at zero velocity and with its propulsion returned to mode 1.

"Lieutenant Eastwood, get us away from here."

"Ternium drive warming up, sir."

The five minutes dragged and Recker's eyes kept jumping to the sensor feeds. He'd seen enough of the Galactar to fear it.

"How can we fight something that turned the tide of a war between two empires?" he said, not expecting an answer.

"We have to run and we have to keep learning, until we find a way to escape the Galactar," said Aston. "And then we take our knowledge back home."

Recker nodded and his eyes drifted to the lightspeed countdown timer. "The final thirty seconds," he said.

I can't let fear rule me. If I do, the battle is already lost.

With his crew and soldiers relying on him, and two data cubes filled with potentially vital information on the Meklon and the Lavorix, Recker knew that this time, more than any other, he couldn't fail.

The timer hit zero and the *Fulcrum* entered lightspeed, its destination a solar system that wasn't on either the HPA or the Daklan charts.

As the warship tore across the ruins of the Meklon empire, Recker's mind recalled a recent conversation with Admiral Telar, in which he'd been described as a fulcrum. And now Recker was in command of a battleship with the same name. Fate and the universe worked in the strangest of ways and he wondered what his future held.

Whatever came, he'd be ready for it.

―――

Sign up to my mailing list here to be the first to find out about new releases, or follow me on Facebook @AnthonyJamesAuthor

OTHER SCIENCE FICTION BOOKS BY ANTHONY JAMES

Survival Wars (Seven Books) – Available in Ebook, Paperback and Audio.

1. Crimson Tempest
2. Bane of Worlds
3. Chains of Duty
4. Fires of Oblivion
5. Terminus Gate
6. Guns of the Valpian
7. Mission: Nemesis

Obsidiar Fleet (Six Books – set after the events in Survival Wars) – Available in Ebook and Paperback.

1. Negation Force
2. Inferno Sphere
3. God Ship
4. Earth's Fury

OTHER SCIENCE FICTION BOOKS BY ANTHONY JAMES

5. Suns of the Aranol
6. Mission: Eradicate

The Transcended (Seven Books – set after the events in Obsidiar Fleet) – Available in Ebook, Paperback and Audio

1. Augmented
2. Fleet Vanguard
3. Far Strike
4. Galaxy Bomb
5. Void Blade
6. Monolith
7. Mission: Destructor

Fire and Rust (Seven Books) – Available in Ebook, Paperback and Audio.

1. Iron Dogs
2. Alien Firestorm
3. Havoc Squad
4. Death Skies
5. Refuge 9
6. Nullifier
7. Scum of the Universe

Anomalies (Two Books) – Available in Ebook and Paperback.

1. Planet Wreckers
2. Assault Amplified

Printed in Great Britain
by Amazon